Aunt Bessie Finds

An Isle of Man Cozy Mystery

Diana Xarissa

To the wonderful people of the Isle of Man who made us so welcome when we lived there.

ACKNOWLEDGMENTS

My beta readers continue to work hard to help make Bessie better. Thanks to Ruth, Charlene, Janice and Margaret for your continued support.

My editor, Denise, continues to put up with my creative spelling, questionable grammar and inconsistent punctuation. Any mistakes that remain are mine.

Thanks, as ever, to Kevin for the wonderful photographs that grace the covers of my books.

And a huge "thank you" has to go to my readers, who continue to follow Bessie along on her adventures. I would love to hear from you. My contact details are in the back of the book.

Author's Note

Welcome to the sixth book in the Aunt Bessie, Isle of Man Cozy Mystery Series. The book titles are in alphabetical order so that you can be sure you are reading the series in the correct sequence. Every book is designed to stand on its own, but I think they're best read in order so you can watch the characters grow and develop.

For those of you who don't already know, Aunt Bessie began her existence in my Isle of Man Romance *Island Inheritance.* She was the source of the inheritance there, so I've set the cozy mystery series about fifteen years before the romance, beginning the series in March 1998. The series moves along slowly, each book being set in the month following the previous book.

There are characters who appear in both series (obviously, they are older in the romance series), so if you read the romances, you'll find out more about some of the characters in Bessie's world. You don't need to read the romances to enjoy Bessie, and each romance is meant to be a stand-alone title, although some characters do appear in more than one book in that series as well.

The romances and the cozies are both set on the Isle of Man. It's an amazing little island in the Irish Sea. While it is a crown dependency (relying on the British Crown for defense and immigration control, among other things), it is an independent country with its own government, stamps and currency. It is approximately thirty-two miles by fourteen miles, which means you are never far from the sea, but each part of the island has its own unique character.

Around eighty-five thousand people are lucky enough to call the island home. Many find employment within the banking and finance sector, but tourism, farming and even the space industry also offer opportunities to residents.

The cover photo shows a section of the sunken gardens on the Douglas Promenade. The photo was taken in 2014, so it isn't exactly how things would have looked in Bessie's time. If I had known when I moved to the island in 1998 that I would one day be writing these books, I would have taken a lot more photos of the scenery for cover art!

This is a work of fiction and all of the characters within it are fictional. Any resemblance between them and any real person, either living or dead, is entirely coincidental. The names of shops and businesses on the island are fictional as well. Manx National Heritage is real, but the employees of MNH in this story are entirely made up. Similarly, the Isle of Man Constabulary is real, but the policemen and women in this book are entirely fictional (and probably don't behave at all like they should).

All of the Bessie books are written using British English, with a smattering of Manx thrown in. Please see the Glossary of Terms and Notes in the back of the book for translations and explanations. As I've been living in the US for the last six years, it is probable that a few Americanisms and American spellings have snuck into the text. I do apologise for that and if you point them out to me, I'll correct them.

I hope you enjoy this little peek into life on a small island. I greatly enjoyed the time I spent living there and I hope to return to the island one day.

DIANA XARISSA

CHAPTER ONE

It was early August and it was already quite warm when Bessie woke up on a sunny Tuesday morning. She glanced at her clock and smiled to herself. It was one minute after six, the perfect time to wake up, at least in her opinion. She stretched and then got out of bed and had a quick shower. After patting on her rose-scented dusting powder and getting dressed, she headed down the stairs to her small kitchen.

It was too warm for toast, she decided, so she fixed herself a bowl of cereal with milk to go with her tea. It was never too warm for tea, of course. Breakfast out of the way, she headed out for her regular morning stroll along the beach. She'd been walking up and down this beach for more years than she wanted to remember, and the addition of a row of holiday cottages a short distance from her home didn't interfere with her routine.

The cottages were full to overflowing this time of year, of course, but as it was still quite early in the morning, Bessie had the beach almost entirely to herself. In a short while, as small children began to wake up, the beach would begin to feel quite crowded. By that time, however, Bessie would be busy with other things.

Back at her own little cottage, Bessie forced herself to focus on a few projects she'd been putting off. She'd given a paper at the Manx Museum in May and she'd never finished editing it for

1

publication. The deadline for submitting it was fast approaching and she knew she couldn't put it off any longer. In the spare bedroom she used as an office, she got down to work.

By eleven she felt like the end was in sight. A couple more hours on another day would finish the job. Now she had to get ready for lunch with a friend, though. Bessie changed into a light cotton dress and added matching low heels. She combed her short grey hair and added just a light dusting of makeup to her face. She frowned at the sticky feeling the lipstick she applied gave her lips. She rarely wore makeup and every time she did wear a bit she remembered why. With one last glance in the mirror, she headed back down the stairs.

Having never learned to drive, Bessie relied on friends, public transport and a small taxi service to get her around the island she called home. She'd booked today's taxi several days earlier and now she waited impatiently for the driver to arrive. Bessie hated being late for anything, even something as casual as lunch with a friend.

She needn't have worried, though, as Dave, her favourite driver, arrived right on time.

"Good morning, Bessie, my dear," he said as he climbed out of the car to hold the passenger door open for her. "My schedule says you're off to Douglas this morning."

"Yes, I'm having lunch with a friend," Bessie told him.

"I do hope you're all recovered from all of the recent unpleasantness," Dave said, looking at her intently. "I'd hate to think my favourite passenger wasn't at her best."

July had been a difficult month for Bessie, on top of several unsettling events in the months that preceded it. Bessie was still recovering emotionally from it all. She was starting to think that a change of scenery might be nice and was thinking seriously about a visit to Derbyshire.

She'd recently met the Markham sisters when they had been holidaying on the island. She and Janet Markham had been corresponding back and forth since the sisters had returned home. Janet was very keen on having Bessie visit them and Bessie was beginning to think that some time away might improve her mood.

Dave didn't need to hear all of those things, though.

Instead, Bessie smiled at the man. "I'm fine," she told him, the words coming slightly more easily off her lips now than they would have even a week earlier.

"That's good to hear," Dave told her. He started the car and pointed it towards Douglas, chatting amiably with Bessie about nothing at all as they went. He dropped her off, as requested, on the Douglas promenade.

"I'll have to ring when I'm finished," she told him. "I have no idea how long I'll be visiting."

"I'm going to stay in Douglas for a while," Dave told her. "I have a few hops around the area to do. Hopefully, I'll still be here when you're done."

"That would be nice," Bessie told him with a smile.

She made her way across the promenade towards a short road that ran behind it. Her friend lived in a small flat in a fairly recently built building just behind one of the hotels that made up the bulk of the properties along the sea front. A moment later, she was pressing the buzzer for her friend's flat on the panel by the front door.

"Hello?" a voice crackled at the intercom next to the door.

"Bahey? It's Bessie."

"Ah, come on up."

A moment later a loud buzz filled the small entryway as Bessie pulled on the glass entry door. The door suddenly unlocked and opened, allowing Bessie to step into the tiny foyer. There was a rather fat man with untidy hair sitting behind a small desk in one corner, and he smiled at Bessie.

"Do you know where you're headed?" he asked.

"Yes, thanks," Bessie replied.

Bahey had given Bessie very specific instructions for finding her, so now Bessie pushed the call button for the lift and waited patiently for it to arrive. She could feel the man at the desk watching her and she had to force herself not to turn around and speak to him. Bahey had warned her that once you started a chat with the building manager, you'd be there for hours, and Bessie didn't want to risk being late for lunch.

The car finally arrived and carried Bessie up to the first floor. Bahey's flat, number eleven, wasn't far from the lift. Bessie lifted her hand to knock on the door, but Bahey pulled it open before she knocked.

"There you are," Bahey exclaimed, putting Bessie into a hug. "I was worried that Nigel had started talking at you. I was afraid I was going to have to come down and rescue you."

Bessie laughed. "I remembered your warning and I completely ignored the poor man," she told her friend.

"Ha, the poor man kept me talking so long one day when I went to get my post that my dinner burned up," Bahey replied.

"Which just meant that I had to take her out for a meal, instead," a rich baritone chimed into the conversation.

Bessie smiled at the man who'd joined Bahey in the doorway.

"Ah, Bessie, you remember Howard, right?" Bahey asked, flushing.

"Of course I do," Bessie said with a smile, as she took the man's outstretched hand.

"Anyway, you should come in," Bahey said, clearly somewhat flustered.

Bessie smiled and followed the others into the flat. The entryway opened into a living space that was larger than Bessie had been expecting. The room was graciously furnished with a mix of antiques and modern pieces that had obviously been carefully selected and arranged.

"This is lovely," Bessie exclaimed.

"Thanks," Bahey blushed. "The Pierces gave me a lot of bits and pieces over the years and I have a few things that were my mother's as well. Joney had the lot until I moved back, but I dare say she was happy to offload some of them to me now I'm settled here. Her house was already full when mum died."

Bessie smiled. "It's amazing how much we accumulate without even trying," she said.

"I moved over here with next to nothing," Howard told her. "My daughter and her husband moved into the house that my wife and I had shared. When I decided to move across here, I figured it would be better to leave the furniture and everything else with them and start fresh."

"How long have you been here?" Bessie asked.

"About six months," Howard replied.

"And is your flat just about full already?" Bessie couldn't help but ask.

Howard laughed. "Absolutely," he said. "I'm running out of places to put things, which is silly, because I don't feel like I've bought much of anything."

"There isn't enough storage in these flats," Bahey said. "I ran out of room ages ago. I keep buying more wardrobes and cabinets to put things in."

Bessie laughed. "I have two spare bedrooms and I haven't enough space for all the things I've acquired over the last, um, many, many years. Although my biggest problem is books."

Bahey shook her head. "I don't read all that much," she said. "Although I've been doing more of it in the last few years than I ever did when I was working. I try to get all my books from the library, though, so that I don't end up keeping them."

Bessie grinned. "I should do more of that," she said.

"Oh, but please have a seat," Bahey said, shaking her head. "I don't know where my manners are today."

Bessie sat down on a comfortable-looking sofa that was angled to take in the view out the large window. From her seat, she had a somewhat obstructed view of the promenade. Mostly what she could see was the back of the hotel and their small car park.

"I know the view isn't much," Bahey said with a sigh. "I can see more of the sea from my bedroom, though, and the location is very convenient. I couldn't have afforded a flat with a real sea view. Those buildings are very expensive."

"Well, I'm glad you're in this building," Howard said with a smile. "Otherwise, we might never have met."

Bahey flushed. "There is that," she said, looking down at the floor.

Bessie smiled at her friend's reaction. She'd known Bahey for many years, as Bahey had grown up in Laxey, where Bessie had lived since the age of eighteen. Bahey was about ten years younger than Bessie, so Bessie rather felt as if she'd watched the other woman grow up. Bahey had spent most of her working years across, as nanny and then housekeeper to the wealthy Pierce family. The family had spent every summer on the island, though, so Bessie had never totally lost touch with her friend.

After some thirty years of service, Bahey had retired a few years ago. She and Bessie were working on renewing their friendship in spite of Bahey's decision to settle in Douglas. As far as Bessie knew, Bahey had never dated when she was younger, and Bessie was enjoying watching her friend working cautiously into something like a relationship with Howard Mayer.

Bahey was around Bessie's height, with grey hair and brown eyes. She tended towards plump, but Bessie was sure that her friend had trimmed a few pounds from her frame recently. Howard was several inches taller than the two women, and mostly bald. His eyes were grey and they sparkled with a real enthusiasm for life that Bessie found attractive. He seemed kind and his old-fashioned manners added to his appeal.

Now he smiled at Bessie. "My flat is right next door," he told her. "So I have a rather similar view. It was the first flat that I saw that was within my budget, and I was thrilled to have even an obstructed view of the sea. Bahey tells me that you have wonderful views from every room in your cottage, though."

Bessie smiled. "I live right on the beach," she replied. "But I bought my cottage so long ago that it was very affordable."

"I'd love to see it some day," Howard told her. "Maybe Bahey and I could pay you a visit one afternoon, or something."

"I'd like that," Bessie said. "You're more than welcome, both of you."

A buzzing noise from the small kitchen interrupted the conversation. The kitchen itself was more like a corner of the large room than a space of its own, and Bahey jumped up quickly.

"That'll be lunch ready," she said, crossing the room in a few steps. She grabbed oven gloves and pulled open the wall oven. Bessie's stomach growled as wonderful smells reached her nose.

Bahey pulled a casserole dish from the oven and then carried it carefully to the small table that took up another corner of the large room. There were four chairs around the table, but only three place settings were laid.

"Come on, then," Bahey called. "Let's not be too formal."

Bessie and Howard joined Bahey at the table. A bowl of salad was in the centre, with a basket full of bread rolls beside it. Bahey placed the steaming casserole next to the rolls and stuck a spoon in it.

"Everyone help yourselves," she invited. "It's just a cottage pie," she said to Bessie. "It was quick and easy."

"And it smells wonderful," Bessie said. Howard waited politely until the ladies had fixed their plates before fixing his own. The trio ate quietly for a few moments.

"Bahey, this is delicious," Bessie said after several bites. "The rolls taste homemade."

"They are," Bahey replied. "But they're nothing special. I used to make all sorts for the Pierces, before Mrs. Pierce decided that they needed a proper chef, that is."

"If you wanted to make things like this for me every day, I would never complain," Bessie told her.

"Me either," Howard said, patting Bahey's hand. "But you know I love your cooking."

Bahey flushed. "Oh, but I've forgotten drinks," she said, jumping up from the table. "Bessie, what would you like?"

"Oh, anything," Bessie replied. "Something cold would be nice, maybe iced tea or something fizzy?"

"I can do iced tea," Bahey assured her. She took a large pitcher from the refrigerator and poured out three glasses full of tea, carefully adding ice cubes to each glass. Howard jumped up and carried two of the glasses across the room for Bahey.

"Oh, thanks," Bahey said as she rejoined the others at the table, carrying her own glass.

The conversation over lunch ranged from the weather to the state of the island's economy. Once lunch was finished and Bahey had served generous helpings of a Victoria sponge, the conversation finally came around to the reason for the luncheon.

"So, Bessie, the thing is," Bahey began. "Well, it's just that some weird things seem to be happening in the building. I know you've done some investigating with the police, what with what happened with Danny Pierce and all the other things that have happened since. I thought maybe you'd have some idea about what's going on."

"If you need something investigating, you should ring Inspector Peter Corkill of the Douglas CID," Bessie said. "He's a professional and a rather nice man, really."

Several months after their first meeting, Bessie and the inspector were slowly beginning to appreciate one another. Now Bessie had no qualms about recommending the man to her friend.

"Oh, no, it isn't anything to worry the police about," Bahey said insistently. "In fact, Howard thinks it's all in my head."

Howard sighed. "That isn't true," he said. "I'm just not as bothered as you are, that's all."

"Well, I'm not sure about any of it," Bahey said, shaking her head. "That's why I want Bessie to investigate."

"Investigate what?" Bessie asked.

"The things that keep happening," Bahey answered. "It's all just stupid little things, but it doesn't make sense, like."

"What sort of things?" Bessie asked.

"There's a mirror in the hallway that keeps moving," Bahey said. "One day it's outside my door and then the next day it's downstairs. It never seems to be in the same place for more than a day or two."

"Have you asked the building manager about it?" Bessie asked.

"I did," Bahey replied. "He said that sometimes it gets moved when the cleaners come through, but they don't come through all that often, leastwise, not as often as that mirror goes walkabout."

"Is that it?" Bessie asked.

"No," Bahey said. "The flat underneath mine is empty and it has been for months, but every once in a while I can hear people talking down there."

"Maybe someone has been showing the flat to prospective purchasers?" Bessie suggested.

"Whenever I ask Nigel about it, he tells me I'm wrong and that no one has been in the flat," Bahey answered. "And it's never at the sort of time that you'd expect them to be showing the flat, either. It's usually in the middle of the night or very early in the morning."

"Could it be someone's television in another flat and the sound just travels strangely through the building?" Bessie asked.

Bahey shrugged. "That makes more sense than Nigel Green's explanation," she said in a frustrated voice. "He told me I must be dreaming."

"So the hallway mirror won't stay in one place and there are sometimes strange noises from an empty flat. What else?" Bessie asked.

"The post takes too long to get here," Bahey said, looking sideways at Howard.

He sighed and shook his head. "I told you the building management has no control over how badly the postman does his job," he said. "I'm going to have a word with that postman the next time I see him."

"Is all your post delayed?" Bessie asked.

"No, just some of it," Bahey shrugged. "It's hard to be sure, of course, but sometimes it takes three days for a letter to get from my sister in Foxdale to here. If I send her a letter, she always gets it the next day."

"There could be a lot of possible explanations for that," Bessie said, thoughtfully.

"Aye, but it's just strange, that's all," Bahey said with a sigh. "I told you before, it's lots of little things that just don't seem quite right. I'm starting to feel like I'm losing my mind or something."

"Is there more?" Bessie asked, patting her friend's hand.

"The woman next door to me died about three months ago," Bahey continued. "But she's still getting post."

"Maybe her family never bothered to tell the post office she's passed away?" Bessie suggested.

Bahey shrugged. "I don't know."

"I told you," Howard interjected, "it was probably just an advertising circular or something that you saw. Those come to everyone."

"What exactly did you see?" Bessie asked.

"We all get our post in boxes off to the side of the foyer," Bahey explained. "They're mostly closed up, like, so we can't really see what everyone else is getting, but there's a little window in each one. Anyway, the flat next door has the box next to mine and one day last month I could see an envelope through the little window. It looked like a proper envelope, too, not advertising. There was another one last week. But why would a dead woman get any post?"

"Are you sure it isn't just piling up because she isn't collecting it?" Bessie asked.

"Whatever was there was gone a few hours later, both times," Bahey said. "Someone must have collected it."

"Do the dead woman's relatives have her keys? Maybe they are still coming and collecting her post," Bessie suggested.

Bahey shook her head. "The flat's been up for sale for over two months. The woman was from across and her family came over, cleared out the flat and then put it on the market."

"And no one has purchased it yet?" Bessie checked.

"No, and I'm starting to worry about how long it's been for sale," Bahey told her.

"I thought the housing market was very competitive right now," Bessie said. "I'd have thought a nice flat in a central location would go quickly."

"It should have done," Bahey agreed. "We don't have that much turnover, but the last couple of flats in the building that have gone up for sale have sold within a few weeks. The one underneath me isn't even on the market, as far as I can tell, which I don't understand either. It's all very strange."

"Or maybe not," Howard said with a chuckle. "Who understands the property market? I certainly don't."

Bahey nodded. "I told you that Howard thinks I'm making something out of nothing," she reminded Bessie.

Bessie smiled. "Each thing is a little thing, but when you add them up, well, it does seem like maybe something strange is going on."

"So you'll investigate?" Bahey asked excitedly.

"I was thinking maybe you should ring the police," Bessie

replied.

"No point in that," Bahey said. "It's all just little things. If I tell them that I have a bad feeling about it all, they'll either laugh or lock me up."

"Inspector Corkill would listen and take your concerns seriously," Bessie told her. "I'm not sure what you want me to do, anyway."

"Well," Bahey flushed and looked down at the table. "I was sort of thinking that maybe you could take a look at the flat next door. Maybe you could pretend that you're thinking of moving down to Douglas, like, and then you could see if there's something wrong with the flat or whatever, so we'll know why it isn't selling. Maybe you could even find out about the flat underneath mine, why it isn't on the market, like."

"I suppose I could do that," Bessie said. "Having a look around an empty flat isn't a big deal, and I am curious, in a way, what it could cost to move to Douglas. Sometimes I think it would be nice to be so centrally located."

"It's brilliant," Bahey told her. "We can walk to all the shops and restaurants and the beach is only a few steps away. I know you have the beach on your doorstep, but you have to admit that shopping is a lot of trouble for you."

Bessie laughed. "I wouldn't say 'a lot of trouble,'" she replied. "But the only shop I can walk to is one that I'd rather not shop at, which is frustrating."

"So you'll take a look at the flat?" Bahey asked.

"I suppose it can't hurt," Bessie answered. "I shall feel bad wasting some estate agent's time, of course, but it shouldn't take long."

"I tried asking to see the place myself," Bahey told Bessie. "I was going to pretend to be someone else, but the estate agent who's handling the sale wanted all sorts of information before he'd make an appointment. I finally gave up. I couldn't persuade Joney to take a look, either. She thinks I'm trying to trick her into moving in here, and she wouldn't listen when I told her about all the weird things going on."

"It would be nice for you both if she was closer, though,"

Bessie said.

"Ha, I think my sister being in Foxdale is just about right," Bahey said stoutly. "She's close enough that we can see each other regularly, but we aren't on top of one another. I definitely wouldn't want her in the same building as me. Maybe I didn't try to persuade her to do the investigating all that hard because I was afraid she might fall in love with the place and move in," Bahey admitted sheepishly.

Bessie laughed. "Well, there's no danger of that for me," she told Bahey. "Even if I love the place, I have no intention of moving away from Laxey. It's been home since I was eighteen, and it will be home until I die."

"But you won't tell Nigel and the estate agent that, right?" Bahey asked.

"I won't tell Nigel or the estate agent that," Bessie agreed with a chuckle. "Now you've made me curious about the place, I'm almost eager to have a look at it."

"It should be almost identical to this," Bahey told her. "All of the flats in the building are meant to be the same. The building was purpose-built, you know, and every flat is the same size with the same layout, except the ones in the back are mirror images to the ones at the front. I gather keeping the layouts the same made it easier for the builders; they just had to keep doing the exact same thing, over and over again."

"Easier, but probably quite boring," Howard said. "I can't imagine how tedious it must have been building and decorating twelve identical flats."

"Of course, the end units have a few extra windows," Bahey said. "And the flats at the front of the building that face the sea are worth a bit more than the ones at the back that face the car park."

"But all of the interiors are the same?" Bessie asked.

"They were meant to be," Bahey told her. "But apparently a few of the original owners who bought off-plan made some modifications. I guess a few of the flats have better quality materials and things like mixer taps and fully tiled walls in their bathrooms, rather than the half-tile I have. I've only ever been in my flat and Howard's, so I'm not sure how true that is, though."

"I've been in a few of the others," Howard said. "And there are minor cosmetic differences, but nothing that seemed important to me."

"Whose flats have you been in, then?" Bahey demanded.

Howard laughed. "When I first moved in, I was invited into nearly all of them," he told her. "At least where the occupants are female. There are a lot of widowed women living in the building."

He addressed the last remark towards Bessie, who nodded. Bahey was frowning.

"So they all invited you around for a cuppa?" she asked, clearly upset.

Howard took her hand. "Most of them invited me around for a cuppa," he said. "You were the only one who didn't. That's why I've been chasing after you ever since."

Bahey blushed. "I never thought to ask you in for tea," she muttered.

"Exactly, and that made me curious about you," Howard told her.

Bessie grinned at the pair. Bahey reminded her of a teenager, working out how relationships work for the first time. "So as far as we know, all the flats are more or less the same, even if a few have slightly nicer details?" Bessie checked.

"Except for Nigel's, of course," Bahey said. "The flats are all meant to have one bedroom, and one bathroom, but Nigel told me that he's built up a few extra walls in his to make a second bedroom, and added an extra bathroom as well. His mother lives with him, you see, and he wanted to give her some privacy."

Bessie looked around the flat. It was spacious, but not enormous. She wasn't sure where someone could fit an extra bedroom and bathroom into the floor plan. "Is it okay if I take a look around?" she asked.

"Oh, sure," Bahey said. "Let me show you the rest."

Bessie stood up and followed Bahey through the room, back towards the entryway to the flat. The kitchen was tucked up in the corner that made a sort of L-shaped room out of the living space. One door opened up next to the kitchen, and Bahey pushed it open to show Bessie the modern bathroom. At a ninety-degree angle from that door was the second door that Bahey now opened.

"Here's the bedroom," she announced, standing back to let Bessie peek inside.

Bessie didn't want to appear too nosy, so she simply glanced quickly into the fairly large and comfortable-looking bedroom. It too was furnished with a mix of modern and antique pieces with a large bed in the centre of the space.

"It's bigger than I expected," she told Bahey. "But I can't see how anyone could divide it into two."

"I guess he moved the kitchen to the opposite wall and then put up a wall there for a bedroom. That bedroom has access to the bathroom that was originally in place. Then he added a tiny bathroom next to the main bedroom. He had to knock a hole in the wall for a door between the bathroom and bedroom, and take away space from his living area, but I guess it works for them," Bahey said.

"You seem to know a lot about our building manager's living arrangements," Howard said.

"He's forever talking to me about something," Bahey replied. "He wanted me to come in and have a look, but I couldn't care less about his flat."

"Maybe he was flirting," Howard suggested. "Is he less friendly now that we're a couple?"

Bahey frowned. "Now that you mention it," she said after a pause. "He has been less friendly lately. I didn't make the connection, though."

Howard shook his head. "You don't make it easy for us men," he told her with a sigh. "There he was, trying to chat you up, and you thought he was just telling you about his flat."

"Well, it isn't like I wanted him to chat me up," Bahey said, indignantly. "He's kinda creepy and strange."

Howard laughed. "I guess I don't have to worry about him, then," he said.

"How old is he?" Bessie asked. "I don't mean to insult anyone, but he looked to be somewhere in his fifties to me."

"By which you mean too young for me," Bahey said, laughing.

Bessie flushed. "I didn't necessarily mean that," she said, although that's what she'd been thinking. "I just wondered at his age."

"He is in his fifties," Bahey confirmed. "And that's probably why I just assumed he was just being friendly. I'm way too old for him."

"I heard he had a little romance with Linda," Howard said.

"Really?" Bahey demanded. "Why didn't I hear about that?"

"You don't really talk to the other residents," Howard replied.

"They don't talk to me, either," Bahey snapped back.

"Yes, well, they do talk to me, sometimes," Howard said. "And one of the ladies told me that Nigel and Linda were dating."

"Linda seemed like such a sensible woman," Bahey tutted. "What on earth did she see in him?"

"I think she was flattered by the attention," Howard told her. "She was very lonely with her children across. Her husband died quite suddenly while they were in the middle of planning their move over here. She told me more than once that she was sorry she went ahead with the move."

"So why did she?" Bahey demanded.

Howard shrugged. "I guess moving over here was always her husband's dream. They'd sold the family home, anyway, so she had to go somewhere. I think things were too far along in the move for her to feel like she could change the plans, but once she got here, she was sorry."

Bahey shook her head. "She should have just gone back," she said. "Why stay here and be unhappy?"

"I gather her children were happier with her here," Howard said, dryly.

"And once more I'm glad I never had any of the little dears," Bahey said with a satisfied smile. "Your daughter seems okay, from what I've heard, but most of them don't seem worth the bother."

"My daughter is lovely and she misses me, which means she appreciates me when I visit. Once the grandbaby gets here, I might be sorry to be a bit further away than I used to be, but I love this island and my little flat as well," Howard said.

"Well, I'm glad you're here," Bahey said. She flushed and then turned and headed back towards the main living space. "Why are we standing around talking? We could be sitting comfortably," she muttered.

Bessie followed her friend across the space and sank down on a sofa across from the chair Bahey had claimed.

"You don't think that Linda's death was suspicious, do you?" she asked the other woman after Howard joined them.

"Oh, good heavens, no," Bahey said. "She was one of the fatalities in that bus crash back in May. The police report reckoned it was just an unfortunate accident."

Bessie nodded. She'd heard all about the crash, of course. Tragic events received a lot of press coverage on the small island. An elderly man, out walking his dog, had rushed into the path of an oncoming Douglas bus when the dog had suddenly slipped off its lead. The driver had slammed on his brakes and slid sideways into a lamp post and a row of parked cars. Two bus passengers were killed, and three others suffered serious injuries. The driver was still recovering, three months later. The man and his dog had both escaped without harm.

"So is there anything else I need to know about this place before I take a look at the flat next door?" Bessie asked her friend.

Bahey shrugged. "I can't think of anything," she replied. "It's probably all just my imagination, anyway. I'll just feel better if I know there isn't anything weird about the flat next door. There've only been a few showings."

Bessie nodded. "I'll ring the estate agent first thing tomorrow and see about getting an appointment to take a look," she promised. "We can talk again once I've done that."

"That sounds like a plan," Howard said.

A sudden crashing noise startled them all.

"What was that?" Bessie asked.

"It sounded like it came from the flat downstairs," Bahey said. "The empty one."

"Let's go check it out," Bessie suggested.

Bahey and Howard exchanged glances as Bessie stood up.

"Come on," she said. "Maybe Nigel can tell us what the noise was."

The trio took the lift down to the ground floor. When they emerged, Nigel was nowhere to be seen.

"How do we get to the flats on this level?" Bessie asked, looking around the small foyer.

"Down the corridor," Bahey said, gesturing towards a door in the wall behind the manager's desk.

Bessie pulled the door open and the trio looked down the hall. Bessie could see three closed doors on either side of the hallway.

"So number five is the one under your flat?" she checked with Bahey as she walked slowly down the hall.

"That's right," Bahey said.

Bessie stopped in front of the door to flat five and knocked. After a moment she knocked again, more loudly. The door to the flat opened slightly under the pressure.

"Maybe I should go first," Howard suggested.

Bessie thought about arguing and decided against it. She stepped to the side and let the man push the door open the rest of the way.

"Hello?" Howard called, his deep voice echoing in the dark space.

"Is there a light switch near the door?" Bessie asked.

Howard nodded. A moment later Bessie heard the click of a switch and a bare bulb came on in the short corridor inside the flat.

"Hello?" Howard called again, taking a hesitant step into the flat.

Bessie fought the urge to push the man, instead following behind him so closely that he quickly took another step. Bahey looked around before joining them. With Bessie impelling him from behind, Howard slowly made his way down the short hall and into the living area of the flat.

"Oh, dear!" he exclaimed.

Bessie gasped. In the centre of the otherwise empty room, lying on the ugliest orange and brown carpet Bessie had ever seen, was a man who looked as if he'd been beaten to death.

CHAPTER TWO

"Ring 999," Howard said, rushing to the man.

"Don't disturb the crime scene," Bessie said, trying to catch his arm.

"I'm not worried about the scene; I'm worried about the man," Howard told her.

Bahey was talking to the emergency operator, giving out the address. Bessie watched Howard as he tried to find the man's pulse.

"He's alive," Howard announced, looking up at the women. "But he needs an ambulance."

Time seemed to stand still for Bessie as they waited for the ambulance, but it was really only a few minutes later that Bahey let the paramedics into the building. They quickly had the man loaded onto a stretcher, checking his vital signs and ignoring the onlookers. There was still no sign of Nigel and it seemed as if no one from the other flats on the floor was at home. If they were home, apparently they weren't curious as to what was happening in flat five.

"What can you tell me about him?" one of the men asked Howard.

"Nothing at all," Howard said. "We just found him here. We have no idea who he is or how he got here. You should speak to the building manager, but I don't know where he is at the moment."

The man shrugged. "I'm more concerned with getting him taken care of than anything else. We'll let the police investigate why he was here, if anyone cares. We're going to take him to Noble's now. He's badly beat up, but I think he'll survive."

They'd only just pushed the stretcher out the front door of the building when Bessie spotted a man with a familiar face getting out of a car in the car park.

"Inspector Corkill, what brings you here?" she asked as the man approached.

"I might ask you the same question," he replied, giving Bessie a thoughtful look. Corkill was in his mid-forties and his hair seemed to have more grey now than the last time she'd seen him. He also appeared to have put on a few extra pounds.

Bessie had met the inspector just after finding a body a few months earlier. At least this time the man she'd found was still breathing. She could only hope he'd stay that way.

"I was having lunch with friends," she told the inspector. "We heard a strange noise from the flat under the one we were in, so we went down to investigate."

"Who owns the flat where the man was found?" he asked.

"As far as we know, it's empty and up for sale," Howard replied. "The building manger, Nigel Green, is who you need to talk to."

Corkill nodded. "And where is Mr. Green?"

Bessie exchanged glances with the others. "We don't know," she said after a pause.

"Is he meant to be working?" Corkill asked.

"He might be taking a lunch break," Bahey suggested. "From what I understand, his arrangement with the owners of the building is somewhat flexible. He's on call all the time, so he doesn't really have to stay at the foyer desk for any set hours. I gather his biggest responsibility is letting the postman in every morning."

"Which flat did you find the man in?"

"Number five," Howard supplied the answer.

"Right, I'll just go and have a look around, then," the inspector told them. "At the moment we don't know if a crime has been committed or not, but it won't hurt for me to have a look around and maybe take a few photos."

"It's just an empty flat," Howard remarked.

"There's a folding sort of bed in the bedroom," Bahey said. She flushed when everyone looked at her. "I was trying to find a quiet corner to talk to the emergency operator," she explained.

"I'll check it all out. From what the paramedics said, they didn't find any identification on him. If there isn't anything in the flat and the manager doesn't know about him, we'll have to wait until he wakes up to find out who he is," Corkill said. "I don't suppose any of you recognised him?"

The trio exchanged glances.

"I certainly didn't," Howard replied after a moment.

"I didn't either," Bahey said.

"Sorry, but he didn't look familiar to me, either," Bessie chimed in. "I didn't get a very good look at him, though," she added.

Corkill nodded. "We'll figure out who he is eventually."

"Do you want formal statements from us?" Bessie asked.

"Not at this point," he replied. "Let's wait and see what happens next."

The foursome walked back into the building. At the lift, Bahey, Bessie and Howard headed back upstairs while the inspector continued to flat five. Back in Bahey's flat, Bessie felt unsettled.

"Well, whatever else is happening here, that was definitely odd," Bessie said to Bahey.

"It certainly was," Bahey agreed emphatically. "Are you still willing to investigate or do you think I should talk to the inspector about my concerns?"

Bessie shook her head. "I don't know," she said after a moment. "Let's see what the mystery man has to say when he wakes up."

"Maybe he's homeless and he saw the empty flat and decided to crash there," Howard suggested.

"How did he get beaten up, then?" Bessie asked.

"Maybe Nigel found him there and they had a fight," Howard said.

"I can't see Nigel successfully fighting anyone," Bahey laughed. "The man looked to be about Nigel's age, but he also looked in much better shape. He'd have flattened Nigel."

An hour later, after talking themselves in pointless circles for the whole time, Bessie finally decided to head for home. She noticed that the inspector's car was already gone from the car park when she walked past. She'd have to ring him in the morning and find out what was happening, she decided, after she'd rung for a taxi.

Dave was still in Douglas and the taxi ride home was uneventful, as was the evening that followed it. Bessie took herself to bed hoping that the mystery man was doing well.

The next morning Bessie was up at six again.

Firmly pushing the injured man and Bahey's concerns from her mind, she enjoyed her beach walk even more than normally as she let her mind play with the idea of a holiday in Derbyshire. She looked at the beach differently, experiencing it as if the change of scenery were actually planned.

As ever, she walked past the row of holiday cottages, glancing in where curtains were open. She never ceased to be amazed at how untidy they all looked.

Small children were already rushing about in several of them and Bessie shook her head as one small boy threw his breakfast cereal bowl at his mother. With the sliding patio door shut, Bessie couldn't make out exactly what was being said inside the cottage, but she was pretty sure she could guess what the mother might be saying. Bessie hurried on towards the mansion that was just visible in the distance.

From the beach, all that could be seen of the Pierce mansion, Thie yn Traie, was the huge wall of windows that faced out towards the sea. Bessie knew that the house itself was much larger than it appeared from where she was standing. It had been empty since March, as several potential buyers had made offers that had fallen through for a variety of reasons. Bessie had heard a rumour that yet another offer had been made and she was hoping this time the sale might actually happen. She was still hoping the new owners might settle there for good, rather than use the enormous house as a summer home the way the Pierces had.

At the base of the wooden stairs that ran up the cliff face to the home, Bessie stopped. She considered going further, but the August morning was already growing warm. With a sigh, she turned and headed for home. She had work to do, anyway. She needed to contact the listing agent for the flat in Bahey's building and make arrangements to see it. The sooner she did that the better, and then she could get on with planning her holiday.

Bessie sat down at her kitchen table to make the phone call. The three estate agencies on the island sent their monthly listing magazines to every house and Bessie was pleased to discover that she hadn't yet thrown the most recent ones away. She flipped through them, looking for the flat in Bahey's building. After going through them all twice, she gave up and rang Bahey.

"Who's listing the flat?" she asked Bahey when her friend answered. "I've been through the listings for all three agencies and I can't find it anywhere."

"It's being sold through 'Island Choice Properties,'" Bahey replied. "And before you ask, I'd never heard of them before, either. As far as I can tell, the flat in my building is their only listing, although I haven't been all over the island looking for others, so they might have more that I don't know about."

"I'm surprised I haven't heard anything about it," Bessie said. "A new estate agency is pretty big news."

"I don't know about that, but I have the phone number here. I wrote it down off their 'For Sale' board that's posted in the foyer here. I told you I rang, but they wanted too much information and I had to give up. I'm sorry I didn't think to give you the number yesterday," Bahey said.

"It's no problem," Bessie assured her. After a few minutes of idle conversation, Bessie hung up and rang the number Bahey had given her. The phone rang many times and Bessie was about to hang up when an answering machine suddenly picked up.

"You've reached Island Choice Properties and IC Mortgage

Services. Please leave a message after the tone and someone will ring you back."

Bessie sighed deeply and then complied.

"My name is Miss Elizabeth Cubbon, and I'm interested in seeing the flat you have listed in Douglas on Seaview Terrace." She left her phone number and hung up feeling annoyed. Surely an estate agency should have office staff available at half nine on a Wednesday morning? And what was IC Mortgage Services?

She did a few little chores around the house, starting a load of laundry and tidying the downstairs. It was more than an hour later when her phone finally rang.

"Mrs. Cubbon? This is Alan Collins from Island Choice Properties, returning your call."

Bessie bristled instantly at the oily salesman's voice that came down the phone to her ear. Even though he'd only introduced himself, Bessie felt an irrational dislike for the man.

"It's Miss Cubbon, actually. I'm interested in the flat on Seaview Terrace in Douglas," Bessie replied. "I'd like to arrange to have a look at it, please."

"Certainly, Mrs. Cubbon. I'd be happy to arrange that for you. Let me get a few details from you before we make that appointment. If I could just get your address, please?"

"Why?"

"I'd like to put a brochure in the post to you with some of the particulars of the building and the flat. I've found, in the past, that some clients discover that they are no longer interested in a given property once they've seen the particulars."

"I have a friend who lives in the building," Bessie told him. "I already have a pretty good idea of what to expect."

"Oh, excellent," the man said with what sounded like fake enthusiasm. "That certainly makes my job a good deal easier. Of course, I'd also like to send you the details for a few other flats in the Douglas area. It's always best to have something to compare a property with, I find. Your address?"

Bessie just barely held back a sigh. The man's argument seemed perfectly logical and it really wasn't his fault she'd already decided that she didn't like him. He was probably a perfectly nice person, simply trying to do his job.

"Treoghe Bwaaue, Laxey," Bessie told him, reciting the postal code slowly.

"And do you rent or own that property?" Alan asked.

"I own it," Bessie said sharply. "If it's any of your business."

The man chuckled annoyingly. "I am sorry," he said, sounding anything but contrite. "I love my job, but it is sometimes frustrating to show multiple properties to people only to discover that they are merely renting their current homes and simply don't have the resources to purchase anything. The property market on the island is getting increasingly challenging for first-time buyers, so I've taken to asking people about their current status in an effort to help me prepare them for the harsh realities of the seller's market we're experiencing."

"I see," Bessie said.

"With that in mind," the man continued, "I hope you'll understand if I ask you for a reference? Just a friend or family member who can verify your existence."

"My existence?" Bessie asked.

Alan chuckled again. "You'd be amazed at how many people think it's quite fun to go around and see dozens of houses or flats with no intention of buying anything. I've wasted many, many hours of my time showing flats to nosy neighbours who just want to see how exactly Mildred rearranged the furniture or what that extension Mark added looks like from the inside. I now ask everyone who rings for a reference and I have to say, I haven't had to deal with time wasters since."

Bessie almost laughed. She was exactly the sort of time waster the man was hoping to guard against. She had no intention of buying anything, but she was quite capable of providing him with a reference.

"You can ring my friend, Doona Moore," Bessie told the man. "The easiest place to reach her is at the Laxey Constabulary." She recited the number that she knew by heart. "That's their non-emergency number. Doona works at the reception desk and she'll happily confirm that I'm a real person who actually owns her own home and is thinking about moving from Laxey into Douglas."

Alan chuckled again, an unpleasant noise that grated on Bessie's nerves. "That's wonderful. Thank you for that. I'll just have a quick chat with your friend and then get back to you to set up that appointment."

He hung up before Bessie could argue. "Oh, bother," she muttered into the phone. She quickly dialed the number she'd just given to the man.

"Laxey Neighbourhood Policing, this is Doona. How can I help?"

"Doona, it's Bessie. I don't want to take up any time with explanations right now, but if an Alan Collins or anyone from Island Choice Properties rings you, please tell them that I exist, that I own my little cottage and that I'm considering a move into Douglas."

"Pardon?" Doona said, the shock in her voice evident.

"I'll explain later," Bessie told her. "Can you come over for dinner tonight?"

"I'm supposed to be having dinner with Spencer Cannon," Doona replied. "But I can ring him and reschedule. We've already had dinner together twice this week and it's only Wednesday."

"I don't want you to change your plans for me," Bessie protested.

"It's fine," Doona assured her. "We're spending too much time together. I need a break, even if he doesn't."

"Maybe we need to talk about that tonight as well," Bessie suggested.

"Maybe," Doona replied.

Bessie hung up and then paced around her small kitchen. She had no idea whether the man would ring Doona right away or if he might wait several days. She felt impatient and annoyed with the man, without knowing if it was deserved or not.

She fixed herself a light lunch and then dug around in the freezer for something to make for dinner for herself and her friend. There was nothing that appealed to her, but she didn't want to walk up to the little shop at the top of the hill in case Alan Collins rang her back.

There were several new books in her sitting room that had arrived from the bookstore in Ramsey that kept her supplied with everything new that they received from her favourite authors. Now she opened a box at random and pulled out the book on top. She opened the front cover and read the short introduction, frowning as it failed to catch her interest. The phone rang just as she was about to try the next book in the box.

"Ah, Mrs. Cubbon, it's Alan Collins. Thank you so much for providing such an, um, interesting reference. Mrs. Moore sounds like quite a fascinating woman. I don't suppose she'll be accompanying you on your tours?"

"I don't suppose she will," Bessie said tartly. "And it's Miss Cubbon."

"Yes, well, ahem, well, anyway, I'm just looking at my diary and I can show you that flat on Monday morning at nine if that suits you."

"Not until Monday?" Bessie asked, making her annoyance evident in her tone.

"Yes, well, I'll put the particulars in the post to you today, along with the details for a few other properties in the area. You should get them tomorrow or Friday, and that will give you the weekend to look them over before we meet."

"I suppose that will have to do," Bessie said grumpily. "If you can't manage anything sooner."

"I'm sorry, but I really can't," the man replied. Bessie wasn't convinced that he was genuinely sorry, but she couldn't argue. At least she had an appointment, even if it wasn't as soon as she'd like.

"By the way," the man continued. "You mentioned having a friend in the building. To whom were you referring?"

"Why does that matter?" Bessie asked.

"We always like to thank people who send business our way," the man replied smoothly. "For instance, if you were to purchase the flat in question, Island Choice Properties would send a gift basket to the person who referred you."

"Oh, well, I know a few of the residents in that building," Bessie said after a moment's thought. "It was Howard Mayer who suggested I look at the flat. I understand he's just down the hall from the available unit."

"I'll just make a note of that," the man said. "I'm afraid I don't know anyone in the building myself, of course."

"I understand, from my conversation with Mr. Mayer, that there's a second unit that's also empty in the building," Bessie said, trying to keep her tone casual. "I'd love to have a look at that unit as well. I understand that that one is on the ground floor, which might suit me better."

"I'm afraid I only have the listing for the one unit for sale," Alan told her. "We're listing flat number ten, but I'll certainly see what I can find out before Monday and if there is a second unit, I'll try to get the information for you."

"I'd appreciate that," Bessie told him. She wasn't sure why she hadn't given him Bahey's name, but it was too late now to change her mind. Since she wouldn't be buying the flat, Bahey wouldn't be missing out on the gift basket, anyway.

With the call out of the way, Bessie could now walk up the hill to the small shop at the top. She hated shopping there, as the shop assistant was rude and rather thick, but it was the only place she had time for today. She was surprised to see Anne Caine behind the till when she arrived.

"Anne? But what are you doing here? I thought you'd given up this sort of work for good," Bessie exclaimed.

Through some very long overdue good fortune, Anne had recently come into enough money that she no longer needed to work. The last Bessie had heard, the forty-something woman was taking a much-deserved rest and thinking about going back to school.

"Oh, I'm just helping out now and then," Anne told Bessie. "I do a few hours on Mondays and Wednesdays in the afternoon while the owner's daughter is in school. Apparently she's finally decided she wants more out of life than a job in her dad's convenience store, so she's taking classes in hairstyling and that sort of thing."

"I hope they teach her some manners as well," Bessie muttered as she scanned the shelves for inspiration.

Anne laughed. "I think that might be a lost cause," she told Bessie.

"Well, anyway, I'm glad I can start shopping here again, at least on Mondays and Wednesdays," Bessie told her friend. "I haven't been buying my lottery tickets lately and I've been having to buy extra loaves of bread on my big weekly shop in Ramsey to freeze some. This way I can get fresh when I need it."

"Always happy to help," Anne laughed. "But if you win the lottery you do have to share your winnings with me."

Bessie laughed. "What would you do with even more money?" she teased.

Anne smiled. "You're right. I do rather feel as if I've already won the lottery after my recent good fortune. More than anything else, I'm just so glad that Andy now has a chance to do what he's always dreamt of doing."

"How is Andy?" Bessie asked, recalling the handsome young man who'd spent a great deal of time in her spare room as a child.

"He's doing very well," Anne assured her. "He's only here for a few more weeks and then he's off to catering college in Leeds. He's ever so excited about it. I just hope it's as wonderful as he's expecting it to be."

"Tell him he must stop and see me before he goes," Bessie told her. "I'll cook dinner for him, and he can bring pudding."

Anne laughed. "I know he'll love that," she told Bessie, promising to pass along the message.

Back at home, Bessie quickly threw together a lasagne for Doona and herself. She'd bought a tub of ice cream at the shop, so that would have to do for a sweet course. She simply couldn't be bothered to make anything. With dinner in the oven, Bessie settled down with a book, but she was interrupted only a few minutes later by a knock on the door.

"Spencer? What brings you here?" she asked the bald and plump fifty-something man who was standing on her doorstep.

The man flushed and looked at the ground. "I was just, well, I brought these for Doona," he said, thrusting a huge bouquet of flowers at Bessie. "She said she was having dinner with you tonight, but I'd already bought them, so I thought I would just leave them with you."

"Oh, right, well, that's fine," Bessie said, feeling unexpectedly flustered. "Would you like to come in for a few minutes? I could make you a cup of tea."

"I'd love to, if you don't mind," Spencer replied. He followed Bessie into the kitchen so closely that Bessie nearly tripped over him.

"Please sit down," she told the man. "I'll just find somewhere to put these," she said. She set the flowers down on the counter and dug around in a cupboard for the vase she knew she had somewhere. It had been a while since she'd used it, but it was exactly where she remembered putting it. She filled it with water and dropped the flowers into it.

"There, now, what about some tea?" she said, mostly to herself.

"Doona said you have something important to discuss with her," Spencer said, his tone anxious. "I hope, I mean, I've really been enjoying spending time with her. I hope she isn't just trying to put me off."

"We do have some rather important things to talk about," Bessie told him after she'd filled the kettle. "And they really can't wait, either, unfortunately. I'm awfully sorry that you had to change your plans for tonight, though."

"It's okay," Spencer said, waving a hand. "We've had dinner together for the last two nights and I'm quite sure Doona is ready for a break from me. I get rather too intense in relationships. I'm trying to learn to be more relaxed, but it doesn't come naturally to me."

"When do you go back across?" Bessie asked, aware that the man was only meant to be on a two-month holiday, which he was spending in the rental cottages down the beach from Bessie.

"Early next month," Spencer replied in a gloomy tone. "I'm not looking forward to it, either. When I was a kid, I thought living across would be wonderful, but now, having done it for fifteen-odd years, I'm ready to come back to the island. It's the one place in the world that truly feels like home."

"I felt that way as well, when I came back," Bessie told him.

"Even though I'd moved to the US when I was only two. When I came back here at seventeen, the island felt like where I wanted to be. Of course, if things had gone differently, I'd have ended up back in the US, but now I can't imagine that."

"I can't imagine you anywhere but here," Spencer said. "You've been a fixture on Laxey beach for as long as I can remember."

"I know you initially moved across on a transfer for your work. Do they still need you over there or is there a chance you could move back?"

Spencer shrugged. "I don't actually work for that company anymore," he told Bessie. "I'm sort of between jobs at the moment. I'd been planning this holiday for the last year and just before I was due to travel, I got made redundant. Since everything was already paid for, I decided to come and have my holiday anyway. As soon as I get back home, of course, I shall have to start sending out my CV to all and sundry."

"Maybe you should be looking for jobs over here," Bessie suggested.

"I've thought about it," Spencer told her. "I guess I'm just dragging my feet and trying not to think about the whole issue. You're right, I should be applying for jobs here. I'd love to move back, but it's easier to play golf and sit on the beach and pretend that I still have a job to go back to in a few weeks."

"Perhaps you should dust off your CV tonight, since your plans with Doona were cancelled," Bessie said. "I can lend you a typewriter if you want to borrow one."

Spencer laughed. "I have my laptop with me," he told her. "I should make a start. Maybe Doona will take me more seriously as a suitor if I'm looking to stay here, rather than leaving soon."

"I'm not sure Doona is looking for a suitor," Bessie said, choosing her words carefully.

"I know, she's been totally upfront with me about everything," Spencer said gloomily. "She's not really looking for anything more than a friend. But she's an attractive and interesting woman and I can't help it. I'm really falling for her."

Bessie sighed and poured the tea. "I wish I could give you

some advice," she told the man. "But I'm the wrong person to ask about romance."

"I don't believe that," Spencer told her. "You must have seen a lot of relationships succeed or fail over the years, and you're Doona's closest friend. I'm sure you could give me great advice. I'm just probably too dumb to take it."

"It seems to me," Bessie began cautiously, "that you're at something of a crossroads in your life right now. I think maybe you should focus on figuring out what you want to do before you worry about getting another person involved."

Spencer nodded. "You're right, of course," he said. He sipped his tea and then bit into a biscuit. After a moment he smiled at Bessie.

"I'm going to go back to my cottage and get to work on finding a job," he said. "I understand the banking industry is growing quickly on the island at the moment. And I don't need a work permit, which might just give me a small advantage."

"I did hear that the work permit committee is quite backed up," Bessie told him. "It's taking months for them to approve permits at the moment, and some companies are getting quite frustrated. Not needing one should be a real plus."

"I'm not sure I can afford to buy a house back here, of course," Spencer said thoughtfully. "I can't imagine I'll make enough from the sale of my little place across to be able to buy anything here. House prices are quite ridiculous as the moment."

"They are quite mad," Bessie agreed. "But there are still bargains around if you're happy to do some renovations."

"That's a thought," Spencer said. He finished his tea and grabbed another biscuit.

"I'll just take this one for the walk back to my cottage, if you don't mind," he told Bessie.

"That's fine," Bessie laughed.

"I'm quite eager to get back there now," he said. "I'm going to start working on my CV and maybe make a few phone calls as well. Maybe I can line up a few interviews before I head back home."

"I'm afraid I don't actually remember what you do," Bessie

said apologetically.

"I work in IT," he told Bessie. "Mostly in systems management."

Bessie laughed. "I'm not sure I know what that is, but let me give you a few names, anyway."

She tore a sheet of paper off the tablet she kept by the phone and copied down the names and phone numbers of three people from her address book.

"I don't know if any of them will be able to help," she told Spencer. "But if they can't, they might know someone else who can."

"I can tell them you gave me their names?"

"Of course," Bessie laughed. "I don't know if that will help or hurt you, but you can certainly tell them that."

"Ah, Aunt Bessie, thank you so much," Spencer said, giving Bessie a hug. "This could be just the break I need."

"Just be sure you're thinking of moving here because it's what you want," Bessie cautioned him. "Don't be thinking you're moving so that you can be with Doona. I don't think that's going to happen."

Spencer frowned. "I wish I could disagree with you, but I think you might be right. I do enjoy her company, though. I hope we can still go out while I'm here and maybe, if I do move here, she'll give me a proper chance."

He looked at Bessie and laughed. "From the look on your face, maybe not," he said with a shrug. "Never mind, I'm definitely wanting to move back for me, so that's okay."

"I'm glad to hear that," Bessie told him.

With Spencer out of the way, Bessie checked on the lasagne, which was bubbling away nicely in the oven. She switched the oven off and left the lasagne in it to stay nice and warm. Doona was due in about half an hour and Bessie wasn't sure what to do with the time.

The book she had been reading didn't really appeal. She looked out the window at the afternoon sun shining on the beach. She headed out the back door and walked to the water's edge, barefoot.

The water was cold, the sea never really got warm, but it felt good as it splashed against her legs. She waded in a short distance and simply stood, eyes closed, and enjoyed the feeling of the warm sun on her face and the cold water at her feet.

Bessie could hear excited children shouting and shrieking as they played on the beach in front of the holiday cottages. In spite of the fact that the entire beach was a public one, for some reason the families in the cottages generally seemed to stay right in front of their temporary homes, rather than spread out towards the stretch of beach behind Bessie's house.

After a few minutes, Bessie sat down on the large rock that was behind her house. Its base was currently partially submerged, as the tide had only just begun going out. She turned to watch the holidaymakers for a short time before turning back to simply watch the sea. So many upsetting and unsettling things had happened in Bessie's life recently. While she used to lose herself in books, she now found more comfort in simply sitting and watching the water. She still read a great many books each month, but the sea calmed her anxious spirit in ways that books did not.

When she heard a car pull into the small parking area beside her cottage, Bessie climbed down off the rock. She smiled when she recognised Doona's sensible sedan. Her friend was just climbing out and she spotted Bessie as she did so.

"I brought an apple pie," she called to Bessie after she'd shut her car door. "I hope that's okay."

Bessie grinned. "It's just about perfect," she replied.

CHAPTER THREE

Bessie opened the door and the two friends made their way into Bessie's kitchen. The whole room smelled of garlic and tomato sauce.

"What did you make that smells so wonderful?" Doona asked as she set the pie on the counter.

"It's just a lasagne," Bessie told her. "It was fairly quick and easy and it sounded good."

"Well, it smells amazing," Doona replied. "Is it ready?"

Bessie laughed. "It should be." She pulled the dish out of the oven and put it down on the counter. She could see through the clear glass of the casserole dish that it was done."

Doona pulled down plates and quickly set the table with flatware. "Your flowers are beautiful," she commented to Bessie as she did so.

"Thanks, but they're your flowers," Bessie told her.

"What do you mean, they're my flowers?" Doona asked.

"Spencer dropped them off for you earlier," Bessie explained. "He'd already bought them for you for tonight and he didn't want them to go to waste."

Doona sighed. "You'll keep them, won't you?"

"But they're lovely," Bessie protested.

"Yeah, so were the ones he gave me last night and the ones he gave me the night before. I understand that he's trying to be romantic, but there is such a thing as too much of a good thing."

Bessie laughed. "If you're sure you don't want them, I'll happily keep them," she told her friend.

"What did you and Spencer talk about, then?" Doona asked as Bessie slid generous squares of lasagne onto plates.

"Lots of things," Bessie said, deliberately vague.

"You're not going to leave it at that, I hope," Doona said with a grin as she carried the plates to the table.

Bessie poured iced tea for them both and then carried the glasses to the table, where she joined Doona. "No, I'm not going to leave it at that," she laughed.

"This is delicious," Doona told Bessie, interrupting the conversation about Spencer. "Why is it so much better than mine?"

Bessie shrugged. "I make my lasagne American-style, with cheese layers instead of béchamel sauce," she told Doona. "That might be why it tastes different."

Doona nodded. "I like it a lot. You'll have to give me the recipe so I can try it at home."

"Remind me," Bessie said.

"I definitely will," Doona replied, forking up another bite.

The pair ate silently for a moment. It was only when plates were empty that Doona restarted the conversation.

"So what did you and Spencer discuss, exactly?" she asked.

"He was telling me how he's between jobs right now," Bessie replied. "I encouraged him to start job hunting here if he thinks he might want to move back. There's no point in waiting until he gets back across and then sending applications over. He'd be better off trying to get interviews before he goes."

"I told him that as well," Doona said. "He didn't seem to be listening to me, though."

"I hope he listens to me," Bessie answered. "I gave him the contact details for a few friends as well. I don't know anyone who's actually hiring at the moment, but at least it gives him a starting point."

Doona sighed. "I'm not sure I want him moving back here," she said, staring down at her empty plate.

"Why not?" Bessie asked.

"He's a really nice man," Doona said.

"But?"

"But he isn't right for me. There just isn't any spark. I've gone out with him nearly every night for the past fortnight, and try as I might, I can't generate anything other than mild affection for him."

"Poor Spencer," Bessie said with a small chuckle. "I hope you've told him that."

"I've told him that, repeatedly. He keeps insisting that I give it more time, and I do enjoy his company, so I keep agreeing. I was actually going to tell him tonight that I thought we should stop seeing each other. He keeps saying he understands how I feel, but I feel like I'm giving him false hope."

Bessie nodded. "I think you should stop seeing him," she told her friend. "He did say that you've been very honest about your feelings, but he does seem to be hoping for more. I think the kindest thing to do is to stop seeing him."

"I'll tell him tomorrow night," Doona told Bessie. "He insisted we reschedule tonight's meal for then."

"I'm still rather hoping he moves back to the island," Bessie said. "It's always nice when good people move back."

"But that's enough about Spencer," Doona said as she served up slices of apple pie with Bessie's ice cream. "What is this about moving into Douglas? You can't be serious."

Bessie laughed. "No, I'm not serious," she assured her friend. "But Bahey is worried about some strange things that have been happening in the building she lives in and I told her I'd poke around a bit."

"Bessie, surely you know better than to get involved in any investigations," Doona said, shaking her head. "What would John say?"

John Rockwell, the CID inspector who ran the Laxey police station, was Doona's boss, and was also Bessie's friend. He valued her insider knowledge of the island and its people, but he hated when she got involved in police investigations.

"It isn't a proper investigation," Bessie protested. "And nothing that's happened would be of any interest to the police, either. There are just lots of slightly odd things happening. Bahey's always been a bit of a worrier anyway, and since everything that happened with the Pierces she's been somewhat worse."

"What's happening exactly?" Doona demanded.

Bessie shook her head. "I forgot all about the strange man in the empty flat," she exclaimed.

"What strange man?" Doona asked.

"We heard noises in the flat underneath Bahey's and when we went down to investigate, there was a man on the floor inside the flat. I was going to ring Inspector Corkill to see what the man had to say when the police talked to him," Bessie explained.

Doona quickly made a call to the station in Douglas, requesting the information.

"They're going to ring me back," she told Bessie after she hung up. "In the meantime, what else is going on?"

Bessie quickly told her friend about the handful of unusual incidents that Bahey had described. "Howard doesn't seem to see anything odd about what's going on," she added. "Really, I'm just indulging Bahey. I think she's mostly worried about her investment. Two empty flats in the building could damage the value of the remaining properties. I think she just wants me to have a look around and reassure her that there's a good reason why the empty flats haven't sold."

"What sort of good reason?"

Bessie shrugged. "Maybe they're both hideously decorated," she offered. "There are a lot of reasons why a flat or house doesn't sell. Bahey only needs one or two to make her feel better. Certainly the flat where we found the unconscious man needed new carpeting."

"Why didn't she just have a look around herself?" Doona asked.

"Ah, that's where Alan Collins comes in," Bessie replied. Doona's mobile rang, interrupting them.

Bessie watched her friend's face as Doona murmured "yes" and "uh huh" and then "thanks," which was nothing but frustrating.

"So, what's happening with the man?" Bessie asked when

Doona had finished.

"No one seems to know," Doona replied. "He was treated at Noble's and then checked himself out without answering a single question."

"So we don't even know his name?" Bessie asked.

"He refused to give his name or to provide an address where he was staying," Doona told her. "The doctor who examined him reckons he was in his fifties somewhere and was reasonably fit, at least until he got into a fight with someone."

"And he wouldn't answer questions about that, either, I suppose."

"Nope," Doona replied. "The best guess at this point is that he's homeless and spotted the empty flat and decided to move in, but it's just a guess."

"What about the fight?"

Doona shrugged. "Life on the street is tough," she told Bessie. "There could be a dozen explanations, really."

"It's strange to think of people being homeless on the island."

"It's an old problem that never seems to go away," Doona told her. "The Douglas Constabulary has a small division to help deal with it, but mostly it's down to various charitable groups to try to help the people."

"Why didn't he just stay in hospital, then? They would have looked after him until he was well again."

"Again, there could be dozens of reasons," Doona said. "But you were going to tell me about Alan Collins," she reminded Bessie.

"Honestly, you'd think the flat was his personally and showing it to me was going to cost him money, the way he went on and on about it. He certainly doesn't make it easy for people to see it, which could be why it's just sitting on the market."

"He seemed rather strange on the phone when he rang me," Doona told her. "He asked a lot of questions and I told him more than once that I didn't think they were things that were any of his business."

"What did he say to that?"

"Oh, he always had a smooth excuse for why he was asking,

but I didn't tell him everything he wanted to know, that's for sure."

"What did he ask, exactly?"

"First he said he just needed to verify that you were a real person, which, of course, I was happy to do. Then he asked about your home. He wanted to know where it was and what I thought it was worth. Of course I told him I have no idea what it's worth. He's an estate agent; surely he should be able to figure that one out."

Bessie laughed. "I've no idea what my cottage is worth, either," she told Doona. "As I have no intention of ever selling it, that's something my heirs are going to have worry about, not me."

Doona nodded. "Anyway, after that he wanted to know about your reasons for moving to Douglas. As we didn't have a chance to discuss that, I just babbled on a bit about the convenience of being able to walk to the shops and whatnot. What should I have said?"

"I don't suppose it much matters," Bessie said. "I said something similar and I also mentioned knowing people in the building. I'll make something up on Monday when I meet him."

"He asked me what your budget was for your new flat. I told him that I had no idea and that he needed to talk about that sort of thing with you, not me."

Bessie shook her head. "I suppose I'll need an answer to that by Monday as well. He did mention that he's going to put the particulars of some other flats in the post to me. I can't wait to see what he sends."

"Don't be surprised if he sends details for some rather expensive properties," Doona told her. "I may have hinted that you were fairly wealthy."

Bessie laughed. "Let's hope he doesn't ring my bank manager," she said. While she was able to live comfortably and didn't have to worry about little extravagances like books, Bessie didn't consider herself wealthy.

"He also asked a bunch of very nosy questions about your family," Doona said.

"My family?"

"He wanted to know how much family you had on the island,

whether you had children here or across, that sort of thing."

"And how did he justify asking those questions?" Bessie demanded.

"Oh, he said he was just trying to figure out how large a flat you might need. You know, you might have grandchildren across that came to stay with you for weeks at a time in the summer holidays. You'd need a guest bedroom in that case, you see."

Bessie nodded. "He certainly has an answer for everything," she said. "What did you tell him?"

"I told him that your family was mostly in America and I wasn't sure how often they visited or where they stayed when they came."

"Fair enough," Bessie said. "Did he ask you anything else?"

"He wanted to know about your health," Doona replied. "He asked how old you were and if your health was good."

"What nerve," Bessie said angrily. "I've half a mind to ring him up and tell him what I think of his nosy questions."

"Again, he justified it by talking about the different types of accommodation that are available. There are buildings of flats for the over fifties or the over sixties, for example. He wondered if you'd be happier in a building like that, or even somewhere with basic medical staff available. I told him your age and your health were your concerns, not mine, and certainly not his."

"Thank you," Bessie said. "I shall tell him much the same thing when I meet him. If I were looking for a place with medical staff, surely I would have mentioned it." She shook her head. "I hope he's better in person than he's been on the phone."

"I wouldn't count on it," Doona said with a laugh. "After he'd finished asking all those rude questions, he actually asked me out."

"He did say that you sounded 'quite interesting,'" Bessie told her. "He asked if you'd be coming on the house hunt with me."

"I could ask John for the morning off, if you want me along," Doona said.

"Don't be silly," Bessie replied. "You go and do your job and I'll deal with Alan Collins. All I want is a sneaky look around an empty flat so that I can set Bahey's mind at ease. It isn't a big deal."

Doona looked as if she might argue, but in the end she opted for a second, somewhat smaller, helping of pie instead. Bessie just had ice cream this time around.

Thursday was uneventful for Bessie, although she found she was appreciating her little cottage and her wonderful views even more than she usually did as she flirted with the notion of a holiday. She even let her mind play with the idea of moving to Douglas. Of course it was just make-believe, but it was interesting to consider.

There had been a brief period of time in her life, many years earlier, when she'd considered moving to Australia, but beyond that she'd never really considered leaving her little cottage. Now she let her mind run with the idea, thinking about what furniture she'd keep and what she wouldn't miss and how she could possibly thin out her enormous book collection. After everything that had happened recently, it proved to be an interesting exercise for her brain.

On Friday she made her usual trip into Ramsey for shopping. Her favourite driver, Dave, from her regular taxi service, picked her up after her morning walk.

"How are you, my dear?" he asked, his usual cheery question seemingly laced with some concern.

"I'm fine, Dave. How are you?" Bessie replied.

"Oh, I'm good. I'm just a little worried since I hear that my favourite customer might be moving to Douglas, that's all."

Bessie sighed deeply. "Really? Should I ask where you heard that from or is it such widespread skeet now that you can't even remember?"

Dave laughed. "My mother-in-law knows a girl who works part-time for Island Choice Properties, so that's where I heard it. But you can bet if my mother-in-law heard about it, the rest of the island has as well."

"It's quite out of line for the girl to be gossiping about customers," Bessie said sharply.

"Oh, aye, but she's young and stupid," Dave told her cheerfully. "It's only a part-time, temporary job anyway, and I hear she isn't fond of the boss. Maybe she's hoping to get fired."

"Well, I'm happy to talk to her boss and recommend just that," Bessie replied. "I'm really unhappy with the idea that people are talking about my moving."

"So you really are thinking about moving?" Dave asked.

"I don't know," Bessie said, her mind racing. "I wasn't really, and then I had lunch with a friend at her flat in Douglas and she mentioned that there was a flat for sale in the building. It seemed like a nice place, and being close to the shops and the museum for my research made it seem even more tempting. Anyway, all I've done is ask to have a look around the flat. I'll probably hate it and that will be the end of that."

"Well, let me know if you do decide to move," Dave told her. "I'll have to get on to the boss and get him to transfer me to Douglas for you."

Bessie laughed. "I'll let you know," she promised.

Dave let her off in front of the large bookstore, agreeing to collect her from ShopFast after she'd had time to do all the shopping she needed to do. Inside the bookstore, she spent a happy half-hour browsing the shelves.

"Ah, Bessie, but you aren't moving to Douglas because they have a better bookstore, are you?" the young assistant asked her when she went to check out with her purchases.

"I don't know that I'm moving to Douglas at all," Bessie told her, trying not to sound as annoyed as she felt. It wasn't the girl's fault that the person at the estate agency had a big mouth. "And if I do move, I shall be sure to keep shopping here regularly. You know this is my favourite bookstore on the island."

"That's good to know," the girl said as she bagged Bessie's books. "Some weeks I think you're the only person keeping us in business."

Bessie wandered through a few charity shops, but didn't find anything to add to her purchases. Staff in two out of the five shops questioned Bessie about her proposed move. The other three were staffed by quite young women who didn't seem to care about much of anything other than chatting on their phones or painting their fingernails.

ShopFast was busy, and Bessie fought back a sigh as she collected a trolley and pushed it into the store. She guessed that she'd have at least a dozen people stop to question her, and she was only off by one by the time she exited the store.

Maggie Shimmin was the first person she saw as she made her way through the fruit and vegetable section.

"Bessie, tell me it's all a vicious lie," she called from the bananas.

Bessie shook her head. "I can't believe how excited everyone is getting over something so simple," she told the fifty-something woman with the long dark hair. "All I did was ask to see a flat, because I was curious what it might be like. Everyone is acting like I've put my cottage on the market and packed my things."

"If you do decide to sell," Maggie told her, "please let us have first refusal. I know Thomas would love to build more holiday cottages."

Maggie and her husband Thomas owned the row of rental cottages that stretched along the beach next to Bessie's cottage.

"I'm not planning on selling," Bessie said, just barely repressing a sigh. "But if I do, you'll be among the first to know."

"The cottages are really hard work," Maggie told her. "But Thomas loves the work and he loves working for himself. He works far more hours than he ever did when he was in banking, but he never complains."

Maggie complained enough for both of them, as far as Bessie was concerned, but she smiled. "Are you shopping for the cottages today?" she asked, glancing at her friend's trolley. It was already nearly full of staples like bread and pasta and jars of sauce. Maggie was adding bunches of bananas to the collection.

"I am, indeed," she told Bessie. "I have to shop for them folks every single day. Thomas insists that we offer grocery delivery on a daily basis, since people are coming and going all the time. He doesn't seem to care that I'm the one who spends all her time running back and forth to Ramsey to fill their orders."

"At least it's already August," Bessie said. "Only a few more months and tourist season will be over."

Maggie sighed. "And then I'll be stuck with Thomas at home

and underfoot until the spring," she said. "Anyway, must dash."

Bessie's reply was lost on the woman's back as she rushed away. Shaking her head, Bessie decided she might as well buy a few bananas since she'd been looking at them for so long. The trip around the grocery store took far longer than it should have. In nearly every aisle Bessie had to reassure friends and acquaintances that she was only just vaguely thinking about moving and that nothing was decided yet.

"I suppose, at your age, being closer to Noble's must be a temptation," one woman mused. Bessie bit her tongue.

"I can't believe you'd give up your views," another remarked. "I'll bet Thomas Shimmin would pay a fortune for your place, though. He'll just tear it down and build more of those ugly little cottages of his, more's the pity."

By the time Bessie was done with her shopping, she was beginning to think that her simple little plan to help Bahey was turning into a huge nightmare. Dave was waiting for her, as planned, and Bessie was happy to get home. Of course, her answering machine was full of messages from concerned and nosy friends and neighbours. She listened to them all and then deleted the lot, only returning a single call.

"Doncan, I'm not seriously planning on moving," she told her advocate when the call was connected. "I'm just taking a little look at a flat in the building where a friend lives. It's more about being nosy than anything else."

Doncan laughed. "Well, that's better than what I heard. Someone told me that you'd already put your cottage on the market. I told them I highly doubted it, but I thought I'd better ring and check on you."

"Make sure I haven't lost my mind, you mean," Bessie replied.

While the pair were chatting, Bessie's post arrived. She smiled excitedly as a large envelope dropped through her letterbox. That had to be the details on the flat from the estate agency.

"Give my best to your lovely wife," Bessie told the man, wrapping up the call. "You'll be one of the first to know if I decide to move."

Hanging up the phone, she picked up the post. The large envelope was printed with an odd-looking logo that she could just about work out as the initials ICP, linked together with all sorts of curlicues and swirls. She couldn't imagine who might have designed such a ridiculous symbol for the company. Her name and address had been printed almost illegibly across the front.

Bessie quickly dealt with her other post, immediately discarding the junk mail and tucking the postcard from a friend on holiday into the frame of a picture on the sitting room wall. It would sit there for a few days or weeks before Bessie added it to the box of such things in her spare bedroom.

She made herself a cup of tea and then sat down with a few biscuits and the packet from Island Choice Properties. The letter had the same horrid logo across the top and it was addressed to "Mrs. Elizabeth Cubbon." Bessie gritted her teeth as she read it quickly.

Dear Mrs. Cubbon,

It was a pleasure speaking with you today about the Douglas flat you are interested in viewing. I look forward to showing it to you on Monday morning, as arranged.

Please find enclosed the details for that flat, as well as the particulars for several other flats in the Douglas area that I though might be of interest.

I shall take the liberty of making viewing appointments for a few of them for Monday, to follow on from our viewing at Seaview Terrace. If that isn't convenient, they can be easily rescheduled.

Thank you for choosing Island Choice Properties. I look forward to meeting you.

Sincerely, Alan Collins

Bessie sighed. She didn't really want to see the Seaview Terrace flat. Now it looked as if she was going to have to go around a few others as well in order to persuade Mr. Collins that she was genuinely interested in moving.

"No more favours for friends," she muttered to herself as she put the letter down and took a look at the brochure for the flat in question.

The price shocked her, but it shouldn't have. She knew

property prices had gone up dramatically in the last year or so. Her own cottage had to be worth at least as much as the flat she now read about.

While the estate agent had done his best to describe the flat in glowing terms, it was obviously just a small flat in a small building. Bessie read through the descriptions of each room, thinking how much they reminded her of Bahey's place.

Putting that paper aside, she flipped through the half-dozen or so other properties that Alan Collins had included. If the price of the first flat had surprised her, she was speechless at some of the others. The listings had been arranged in the envelope in ascending price order and by the time Bessie reached the last sheet, she was laughing to herself. Even if she could afford a million-pound property, there was no way she would ever consider buying one. What on earth had Doona told the man that made him think she might?

The property in question, a penthouse flat in a brand-new building, sounded lovely. It was right on the promenade and there was no doubt it would have amazing views from its "floor to ceiling walls of windows," but Bessie already had amazing views and she certainly didn't need three bedrooms and four bathrooms in downtown Douglas.

She put the paperwork back, giving the letter a dirty look as she slid it into the envelope. Something caught her eye that had her pulling the letter right back out again.

"Interesting," she said out loud as her brain registered what she'd seen. Down the left hand side of the page was a list of "Directors." Bessie read the list again. There were only three names on it. Alan Collins, George Quayle and Grant Robertson.

Grant Robertson she knew more through reputation than anything else. He'd worked for the Manx National Bank for many years and had earned a reputation for being both ruthless and slightly dishonest. He'd retired early and taken several board positions with local companies. He was also well-known for being willing to invest in locals with big ideas and small budgets. Bessie knew of three or four small business owners who owed their success to his assistance, which was often not simply financial.

She'd been told more than once that the man was very willing to get his hands dirty, helping a small business get started.

George Quayle was another matter. He had grown up on the island and then moved across. He'd made his fortune in sales and had recently returned with his wife and their children and grandchildren. He was a loud and boisterous man that Bessie found she could only take in small doses, but she was enjoying a growing friendship with his shy wife, Mary.

But what was he doing acting as a director for Island Choice Properties, Bessie wondered. There was only one way to find out.

"Mary? It's Bessie Cubbon. How are you?" Bessie began when the phone was answered.

"Oh, Bessie, I'm fine, thank you. What can I do for your today?"

"Two things," Bessie replied. "First, can you meet me for tea on Tuesday somewhere lovely?"

"I'd like that," Mary said. Bessie could hear the smile in her voice. "How about that new little tearoom in Ramsey that wasn't open yet when we tried to go last time? I'm sure it's open now, but I haven't managed to get inside yet."

"That's perfect," Bessie said. With their plans made, Bessie moved on to her next question.

"I had lunch with a friend the other day and she is trying to persuade me to move into her building in Douglas. I told her I'd have a look at an empty flat there and it's listed with Island Choice Properties. They've just sent me the details and I see that George is a director there. I'd never even heard of them before."

Bessie stopped there, well aware that she hadn't actually asked any questions but unsure of how to phrase what she wanted to know, which was anything and everything about the company.

"Oh, I'd love it if you'd move to Douglas," Mary told her. "We could get together far more regularly."

Bessie laughed. "I'm really just looking at the flat to humour my friend," she said. "But I suppose it's possible that I'll fall in love with it."

"I do hope so," Mary replied. "But I don't know anything about

George being a director at any estate agency. I don't really keep track of all the things he does. I'll have him ring you back, shall I?"

"That would be great," Bessie forced herself to say, hoping that Mary wouldn't pick up on her lack of enthusiasm.

Bessie looked at the clock and sighed. She'd been so interested in her post that she'd forgotten to have lunch. The tea and biscuits had been a poor substitute, so now she fixed herself a tin of soup and ate it with a slice of bread.

George Quayle rang her back in the afternoon, just when she'd reached the very best part in the book she was reading.

"Hello?" she said, her mind still lost in the pages of the thriller.

"Bessie, my love, it's George. Mary said you wanted to talk to me."

Bessie held the phone away from her ear as his voice boomed down the line at her. Why did he always talk so loudly, she wondered.

"Ah, yes, I was just telling Mary that I saw your name on the letterhead for Island Choice Properties," Bessie replied.

George laughed. "Ah, that's Grant's baby, nothing to do with me, really," he said.

"But you're listed as a director," Bessie said.

"I put up a bunch of the money," George explained. "But I don't have anything to do with the running of the company or anything. Grant brought Alan Collins in from across to handle the day-to-day operations, and I gather he keeps a close on eye on everything Alan does."

"I've only met Mr. Robertson once or twice," Bessie said, almost to herself.

"Oh, you'll have to come to our barbeque the week after next," George said. "Grant will be here, and I'm sure Mary's planning to invite you."

"I'm having tea with Mary on Tuesday," she told him.

"Oh, good, glad you two ladies are keeping up your friendship. Mary rather needs friends."

"Yes, well, she's lovely...." Bessie trailed off. "Hello?" There was no reply. Clearly George had decided that their conversation was finished.

CHAPTER FOUR

The weekend was a relatively quiet one for Bessie. Spencer stopped by on Saturday to thank her again for her help in his job hunt.

"I have three interviews lined up for next week," he told her excitedly.

He didn't mention Doona, so Bessie didn't either. Otherwise, Bessie was on her own, just the way she liked it. She pottered around her cottage, doing some cleaning and tidying when she felt like it. She ate what sounded good at whatever time she felt hungry and she read her way through a dozen books. To Bessie, that was just about a perfect weekend.

On Monday morning Dave picked her up and took her into Douglas. She'd arranged to meet Alan Collins in the foyer of the building on Seaview Terrace.

"Do you know what time you'll need driving home?" Dave asked as he pulled up to the curb.

"I've no idea," Bessie said with a sigh. "Mr. Collins may have arranged for other viewings, so I'll have to ring you."

"Sounds good," Dave told her. He jumped out and held her door for her as she climbed out of the car. "Have fun," he whispered.

"Not likely," Bessie muttered in reply.

She quickly walked up the short pavement to the building's

entrance door. The door had been propped open with a block of wood and Bessie frowned at the compromised security. While the island was a very safe place to live, she didn't think it was wise to invite trouble. If this sort of thing happened regularly, it was less surprising that someone had found his way into the empty flat.

It was quite warm in the small foyer, and Bessie could understand why the building manager, who was once again sitting behind his small desk, had propped open the door. A very light breeze coming in from the sea was the only thing that was moving the air around the stuffy space.

"Good morning," she said politely to him.

He looked up from his newspaper and squinted at her. "Morning," he said in a grumpy voice.

Before Bessie could continue, a man rushed into the foyer.

"For goodness sakes, man, there's a prospective buyer coming through in a minute. What did I tell you about propping open that door?" he shouted towards the building manager.

Bessie studied him as he bent down to move the wooden block. He looked to be in his mid-thirties, with a small amount of dark hair that he'd combed from one side of his head to the other in an effort to disguise the fact that he was mostly bald. He was wearing an ugly brown suit in a chequered pattern that he must have bought when he'd weighed at least a stone more than his current weight. Perhaps he'd been taller in those days as well, Bessie thought, as she noticed that the trousers were considerably longer than they ought to have been.

Now he straightened up, allowing the door to slam shut. He wasn't much taller than Bessie, and he glanced at her through beady little eyes before turning his attention back to Nigel Green.

"I told you we need to make a good first impression," he said angrily. "The flat's been on the market for three months and this woman definitely has the funds to purchase it. Not only that, I got told on Friday that she's friends with George Quayle. Do you know what that means?"

"It probably means you shouldn't be talking about her right in her face," Nigel drawled, glancing at Bessie.

The man flushed and looked from Nigel to Bessie and back

again. "Isn't this your mother?" he hissed at Nigel.

Nigel shook his head and then laughed. "Mum's tucked up having a nap," he told the man. "I reckon this is your prospective purchaser and I also reckon she's none too pleased with you."

The man took a deep breath and then straightened his shoulders and turned to face Bessie. "Mrs. Cubbon?" he asked. "I'm Alan Collins. I'm very pleased to meet you."

Bessie forced herself not to laugh; instead she followed his lead and pretended that she hadn't just witnessed the little scene she'd thoroughly enjoyed. He was sadly mistaken if he thought she wouldn't remember it, though.

"How do you do, Mr. Collins," she said, offering her hand.

"You must call me Alan. And I'm terribly sorry, but I don't shake hands," he told her. "I've a very weak immune system, you see."

Bessie raised an eyebrow. "Perhaps you're in the wrong line of work," she said dryly.

"Oh, but I love my job," he told her. Bessie couldn't detect any enthusiasm in his words. "But shall we have a look at that flat, then?"

"Yes, let's," Bessie agreed, eager to get things over with.

Nigel handed Alan a key ring and then sat back in his chair with a smile on his face. "I hope you like it," he told Bessie politely.

"This is the main entrance foyer, of course," Alan told Bessie, ignoring Nigel completely. "As you can see, it has a security door and a doorman on duty during the day. Each flat has its own intercom that connects to the system, so if someone rings the bell for your flat, you can find out who it is before you unlock the door for them."

"How nice," Bessie murmured.

"The postboxes are all back here," Alan continued, leading Bessie across the small space. Along the far wall the two rows of metal postboxes were arranged at a convenient height next to a small door.

"The door opens into the post room," Alan told her. "Only the postman has a key to the room, so he can go in and distribute the post and nothing can be tampered with. It's very secure."

"Indeed," Bessie replied.

"This would be your postbox," Alan told her, gesturing towards the box labeled "10." He inserted a key from the ring that Nigel had given him and pulled open the box door. The small box was empty, which was to be expected, Bessie supposed. She glanced inside and made what she hoped was an appropriately appreciative noise.

"Right, then, let's head up to the flat, shall we?" Alan said with much more enthusiasm than Bessie felt.

"Certainly," Bessie said to his back as he strode away.

It only took three steps for her to catch up to him at the tiny lift. It took several minutes for the lift to arrive, during which Alan kept up a steady stream of comments about the amenities of Douglas.

"Of course, the island's only hospital is here," he told her.

"There's a hospital in Ramsey," Bessie pointed out.

"There is?"

"Only a small one," Bessie explained. "But it is quite useful for the people who live in the north of the island."

"Well, Douglas has the best shops, of course, being the island's capital. And we have...." Bessie tuned him out as he droned on. She'd lived on the island for more years than he'd been alive. She was well acquainted with everything Douglas had to offer.

The lift, when it finally arrived, smelled peculiar.

"What is that smell?" Bessie asked as Alan punched the single button that made the car travel between the two floors.

"I don't smell anything," he said.

The lift rose slowly before the doors gradually slid open. Alan stepped out quickly, tripping over the two-inch difference between where the lift had stopped and the actual first floor. He nearly fell over, just barely catching himself. Bessie decided to ignore the muffled curse she heard as she carefully followed him out into the corridor.

Number ten was the first flat on the right, and Alan had the door open quickly. "In we go, then," he said, holding the door open so that Bessie could walk through.

The flat appeared to be identical to Bahey's, as Bessie had been expecting. She walked in slowly, studying the main living space with a critical eye.

The walls were that particular shade of cream that builders and estate agents seem to love. The floor was covered with wall-to-wall carpeting that matched the walls exactly. The curtains that covered the windows were the same bland shade and Bessie felt slightly disoriented by the sheer relentless lack of colour.

"It's just been redecorated to a very high standard," Alan told her. "The carpets and drapes are new and the walls were just painted."

"Who buys paint in this non-colour?" Bessie asked, shaking her head.

"It's a lovely neutral shade," Alan replied. "The carpets and walls would complement any furniture you chose to put in here."

Bessie didn't bother to argue. For all she knew, he was right, but it was incredibly boring. She strode to the largest window and pulled back the curtains.

"Of course, the views are excellent," he told Bessie.

She looked out at the back of the hotel on the promenade and sighed.

"You can see the sea," Alan told her. He pointed to the gap between buildings where Seaview Terrace ran. Bessie could see the promenade, and if she worked at, she could just about see the water as well.

"Of course, the tide is out," Alan said. "You'll have a better view when the tide comes in."

Bessie bit her tongue and walked over to the side window to see what she could see from there. Bahey's flat was in the middle of the row of three, so she didn't have a side window. Bessie pushed back the curtains and smiled. Because the building had been built on an angle towards the sea, there was a better view from here.

"This flat has the best views in the building," Alan told her in a confiding tone. "This is the only one on this end of the building to have side windows. The foyer, the lift and the stairs are in the way of the others."

"The flats at the other end of the building won't look out on the sea from their side windows, will they?" Bessie asked. "Perhaps they should have put the lift and the stairs at that end."

Alan shrugged. "Blame the architect," he said. "Anyway, the kitchen is very modern."

Bessie crossed to the small space that was fitted as the kitchen. The lack of cupboard space would have worried her if she were seriously considering moving, but otherwise the area was well laid-out, with all of the most modern equipment.

Alan opened the large "American-style" refrigerator. "Look at all the room you get in here," he said enthusiastically. "I'd love one of these in my place."

"It's very nice," Bessie replied. "As is the entire kitchen."

"Yes, well, the bathroom has every modern touch as well," he told her, leading her towards it. He turned on the light and then gestured for her to step inside.

Bessie noted the pedestal sink with a mixer tap and the large shower cubicle. "There's no tub," she said in surprise.

"People don't waste time with long soaks in the tub anymore," Alan told her. "Showers are quicker and more efficient."

Bessie shook her head. "I quite like a bath now and then," she said, even though she couldn't actually remember the last time she'd bothered to take one.

"It's just as well I've booked us in to see some other flats, then isn't it?" he asked. "Some of the others will have bathtubs in them."

Bessie opened her mouth to reply and then snapped it shut. She'd been stupid enough to get herself into this mess; she'd just have to keep going.

"Do you want to see the bedroom or does the lack of a tub make this flat a definite no?"

"Having come this far, I might as well see the bedroom," Bessie said.

The room was pretty much as expected, what felt like endless acres of unremitting beige.

"Right, well, that's that," Alan said as he led Bessie back to the front door. "Tell me what you thought."

"It's nice," Bessie said, her tone noncommittal. "I don't know that it's nice enough to tempt me away from my little cottage, though."

The man nodded. He followed Bessie out of the flat and then locked it up behind them. They heard the sirens as they were waiting for the lift. After a moment, a fire alarm began to ring and doors began to open all along the corridor.

"What's going on?" Alan demanded of the elderly man who emerged from apartment seven.

"Fire in the lift mechanism," he replied morosely. "Happens all the time. You'll have to take the stairs."

Bessie and Alan followed the man down the stairs and out of the building. A large fire truck was parked outside and Bessie watched as two men emerged from it in full safety gear.

"I'll get the keys back to Nigel later," Alan muttered. "I'm sure he has his hands full at the moment."

"No doubt," Bessie replied. She spotted Howard and Bahey in the small crowd that was gathering in the hotel car park. She nodded a quick greeting, but decided not to try to speak to them.

"Right, then, if you want to just follow me in your car, we'll head down a few blocks to the next place," Alan announced brightly.

"I don't drive," Bessie told him. "I came in a taxi."

"Oh, dear," Alan said. "I suppose you'll have to ride with me, then."

"Or we could just call it a day," Bessie suggested.

"Oh, no, I'm sure you'll find something you like. I've three other flats lined up."

Bessie shook her head and followed him to his car. Fortunately, he had parked just far enough away that the fire truck wasn't blocking him in. Bessie stood by patiently as he cleared huge piles of paper and rubbish from the passenger seat and foot well.

"There you go," he said finally. "I don't usually have passengers, you see."

"Clearly," Bessie muttered as she slid into the car. The floor

55

under her feet was sticky with something and the seatbelt didn't seem to work properly. She gave it a firm tug, and that finally released it enough so that she could fasten it around herself. Alan climbed into the driver's seat and gave her a grim smile.

"Here we go," he said.

"What about the other empty flat in that building?" Bessie asked. "I understand it's on the ground floor, so the lift wouldn't be a concern."

Alan shook his head. "There isn't another empty flat, or rather there isn't any other flat for sale. If someone owns one and chooses not to live in it, well, that's their business and nothing to do with me, or you for that matter."

"Why would someone buy a flat and not live in it?" Bessie asked, trying to keep her tone conversational.

"Perhaps they've bought it as an investment and intend to rent it out at some point. Or maybe they're planning on living in it one day, but aren't ready to move in yet. The possibilities are endless," the man told her.

Bessie nodded, letting her mind race through another dozen possibilities while Alan drove. He drove only a short distance down the promenade, pulling up in front of a large building that had once been a hotel.

"They split this building into flats about three years ago," he told Bessie. "The one that's available is on the penthouse level."

Bessie sighed and followed him out of the car. The lobby area was clean and looked as if it had just been redone. The man sitting behind the desk was wearing a neatly pressed uniform with "Security" embroidered on the front pocket. He'd buzzed them in and then asked Alan for identification before he turned over the keys to the unit.

"There are postboxes in a separate room," Alan told Bessie, gesturing vaguely towards the back of the building. "We don't really need to see them, unless you really want to."

"I suppose, having seen one postbox, I can imagine what all others look like," Bessie told him.

"Right, then, the lifts are through here." He led her across the lobby and into a short corridor. The two lifts were both open and empty.

"The old kitchens are back that way," Alan said, pointing further down the corridor. "There's a chef who comes in five nights a week and prepares meals for the residents who request them."

"Is it a building for pensioners, then?" Bessie asked.

"There aren't any age restrictions, but I believe the vast majority of the residents are retired and enjoy things like grocery delivery and prepared meals."

"Do they have those amenities at Seaview Terrace?" Bessie asked as they rode the lift up to the sixth floor.

"There's grocery delivery and there's a doctor's surgery right next door. I understand the surgery specialises in, um, senior concerns."

Bessie nodded. Bahey had told her as much. Bahey herself didn't choose to use the neighbourhood surgery. Out of a sense of nostalgia, she'd gone back to the doctors in Laxey that she'd used as a child. None of the same staff were there, but they were still in the same building, and she'd told Bessie that it reminded her of her youth.

On the top floor, Bessie followed Alan down a short corridor. He stopped and unlocked the door to the last flat on the left and motioned Bessie inside. The flat was much larger than the one on Seaview Terrace, with a sleek and modern kitchen, three bedrooms and two bathrooms, one of which was en-suite to the spacious master bedroom.

"It's lovely," Bessie told Alan honestly. "But it's far more space than I need and I'm sure it's out of my budget anyway."

Alan told Bessie the price and she laughed. "Definitely out of my budget," she said.

"Well, the next flat on our list is less expensive," Alan told her. "Let's see what you think of it."

Bessie followed the man back down through the building and reluctantly climbed back into his car. "You know, I really need to think about things," she said. "I'm not sure I'm ready to move to Douglas. I've lived in Laxey for a very long time."

"Yes, well, at least this way you'll have a good idea of what's available, should you decide to relocate," Alan replied.

Unable to argue with the logic in that, Bessie sat back and waited to see where they were going next. Alan drove slowly along the promenade and then headed away from the water.

"The next place is in Onchan," he told Bessie. "It's a little further from the sea and downtown, but that makes it much more reasonably priced."

"How reasonably priced?" Bessie asked.

The figure he gave her was about halfway between the two flats she'd already seen.

"It's bigger than Seaview Terrace," Alan continued. "But not as large as the one on the promenade itself."

"I'm not sure about the location," Bessie said doubtfully, as Alan pulled into the building's car park. They were some distance from the Douglas city centre. "I'm not sure this would be terribly convenient for me, as I don't drive."

"This is a senior living development," Alan told her. "They run shuttles into town and to the grocery store every day. They also have grocery delivery and a full medical suite in the administration building at the back."

Bessie looked around at the cluster of buildings. There were three of them, although only two looked like apartment buildings. Those two buildings were each three stories high and had been built on the hillside overlooking the sea. Behind them was a smaller and shorter building that Bessie now assumed was the administration building.

"All of the postboxes for the complex are in the administration building as well," Alan told her. "And there's a hairdressers, a dental surgery and a convenience store."

"I'd never have to leave the site," Bessie mumbled to herself.

"Exactly," Alan said happily. "This place has everything you need, all in one place."

"Oh, goody," Bessie said, this time making sure that Alan didn't hear her.

"If you want to just wait here," he said now, "I'll run over and get the keys."

Bessie thought about arguing, but she had no interest in

seeing the administration building, and it was a lovely day for a short stroll. "You go ahead," she said. "I'll just walk around the front of the buildings and enjoy the view."

The view was spectacular, Bessie admitted to herself as she came around the corner of the apartment block. From this spot, high above the sea, with nothing to interrupt them, the views seemed endless. Bessie watched as an electric train slid into the station below her. For a brief moment she was tempted by the view to think seriously about a move.

"Ah, there you are," Alan said. "I was afraid you'd wandered off."

Bessie swallowed a sigh and turned to follow him into the nearest building.

"The flat that's for sale in on the ground floor. This is it." The man stopped at a door only a few steps inside the building and turned the key. Bessie stepped inside and frowned.

"There's no view," she said.

"Well, no, or rather, this flat has land views rather than sea views."

Bessie laughed out loud. "No offense to the lovely town of Onchan, but I'm not moving out here to be able to look at it all day and night."

She moved through the flat quickly, noting the modern appliances in the kitchen and the boringly neutral décor. There was nothing especially attractive about the place and the views were primarily of the short and squat administration building and the massive housing estate behind it.

"I'm afraid this one is out of the question," Bessie told Alan as she rejoined him near the front door. He'd been flipping through paperwork while she'd taken herself around the flat; now he frowned at her.

"I'm sorry to hear that," he said. "I'm afraid our last showing of the day has had to be cancelled. Apparently, the flat sold on Friday, so I guess that's all I can show you today."

"That's fine," Bessie assured him. "I'll go home and have another look at the particulars you sent me and have a good think. I'll be in touch if I need more information."

"I'll give you a ride home," he told her. "I can have a quick look at your cottage and give you a rough idea of what it's worth, if you'd like."

"That isn't necessary," Bessie replied. "If I decide I want to move, we can worry about it then."

The man smiled tightly. "Let's go, then," he said, leading Bessie back to his car. She fought the seatbelt into position and then gave the man directions to her cottage. It was quickly obvious that he'd never been to Laxey before.

"How long have you been on the island?" she asked.

"Just a few weeks," he said, as he slowed down for a curve. "I'm still learning my way around."

"What brought you here?" Bessie figured he'd asked enough nosy questions about her; it was only fair she asked a few of her own.

"Grant Robertson offered me the job of running his new estate agency. I'd done some work for him in my previous position and he was, well, happy with my performance."

"What made him decide to open an estate agency?" Bessie asked.

"I can only tell you what he told me," he replied. "He said there are a lot of people moving across at the moment and the three agencies already on the island have had a virtual monopoly for years. He wanted a chance to cash in on the sudden rush of new arrivals."

"I suppose that makes sense," Bessie said thoughtfully. "But I'm surprised he didn't hire a local person to run the agency, just to take advantage of local knowledge."

"I'm a quick learner," the man replied, smugly.

Bessie repeated the directions she'd given him as they approached Laxey. He missed the turning for her road and she had to take him around a few back roads until they could join back up with the steep incline that took her home. Alan was looking a bit pale when he pulled into the parking area beside Bessie's cottage.

"That's some hill," he said, sounding anxious. "I'm just glad we didn't meet anyone trying to come up it."

Bessie laughed. "There are passing places," she told him. "You just have to be quite careful."

"Rather."

Bessie climbed out of the car and headed towards her door. Alan was quick to follow.

"Your views are incredible," he said, as he surveyed the quiet beach.

"They are," Bessie agreed. "You can see why I'm reluctant to move."

"I don't suppose I can bother you for a cup of tea?" he asked. "I'd love to see the inside of the cottage and I'm quite parched as well."

"Certainly," Bessie said politely. She wanted to refuse, but couldn't possibly be that deliberately rude.

She opened her door and escorted the man into her small kitchen. "Have a seat," she told him, gesturing towards the small table in the corner.

He crossed to it and sat down while Bessie filled the kettle. After she switched it on, she busied herself putting biscuits on a plate and slowly getting the tea things ready. The kettle boiled while she was still busy filling time. She poured the hot water into her teapot and set it on the table.

Alan waited politely for her sit down and pour tea for them both. Then he gave her a smile.

"So, how serious are you about moving?" he asked. "I mean, I look around this kitchen and I can see why something modern would be tempting, but then I look out at your view and I wonder if I've wasted my morning."

Bessie forced herself to smile back. "Exactly," she said. "There are sound reasons for moving and for staying here. I'm going to take a good look at the details on each place and have a good think. I'll probably chat to a few friends as well, to get their thoughts. I may well surprise us both."

Alan nodded and sipped his tea. "Well, today has been interesting," he said. "To be honest, the only flat I can actually see you being interested in is the one on the promenade. Seaview Terrace was too small and the views were obstructed, and the flat in Onchan was facing the wrong way."

"As I said, I'm going to give all my options very serious thought," Bessie replied noncommittally.

"Before you make any final decisions, there are several other flats that I can show you," he said. "Maybe you'd like to look at a few on Wednesday or Thursday? I can set up a few more places now that we've met and I have a better idea of what you're looking for."

"Thank you, but for now I'd just like to consider what I've already seen," Bessie told him. "I'll be in touch if I need anything."

Alan nodded. "I'll ring you in a few days, then, just to touch base."

Bessie decided not to argue. She rarely answered her phone, preferring to let the machine pick up and letting the caller leave a message that she could return or not as she chose. Chances of her returning calls from Alan Collins were slim.

"Thank you for the tea," he said now, as he stood up to go. Bessie watched as his eyes darted around the room. He was clearly eager to see the rest of the cottage, but she wasn't about to offer to show him. "Are you sure you don't want a quick valuation on this property?" he asked.

"I'm quite sure," Bessie said, meanly smiling to herself as she saw the disappointment in his eyes.

Bessie showed him out and shut the door behind him. She leaned against it, counting slowly to a hundred before pulling it open slowly. His car was gone and Bessie sighed with relief. She hated lying and subterfuge and the morning had been a strain for that reason as much as for the difficulty of spending so much time with a man she disliked.

She sat back down at her table and poured herself another cup of tea. Her mind was racing as she ran back through her morning. The phone took her by surprise and she stared at it while the machine picked up.

"Bessie? It's Bahey. I hate machines. Ring me back, please."

Bahey hung up before Bessie managed to pick up the call. Bessie quickly dialled her friend's number.

"Bahey, sorry, I was just sitting here, lost in thought," she told the other woman.

"I'd love to hear about your morning," Bahey said. "But first I have a question for you."

"Go ahead," Bessie replied.

"Who was the man you were with when you came out of the building after the fire alarm went off?" Bahey asked.

"The man in the ugly brown suit?" Bessie asked. "That was Alan Collins from Island Choice Properties, why?"

"It was just strange, that's all," Bahey said.

"What was strange?" Bessie demanded.

"I guess it's another odd thing about this place," Bahey said after a moment. "The lift keeps having these little mechanical fires," she told Bessie.

"One of your neighbours mentioned that you've been having them fairly regularly," Bessie told her. "It certainly made the flat seem less desirable."

"But that's just it," Bahey exclaimed. "Every time we've had one of these lift fires, that man you were with today has been in the crowd when we've come out of the building."

"But that doesn't make any sense," Bessie said. "He said he doesn't know anyone in the building, so the only reason he would have for being there is if he was showing the empty flat. How many times has the lift had a fire?"

"Maybe six or seven," Bahey said. "I haven't always been home, but Bertie, across the hall, always tells me about them. He watches a lot of daytime telly and he gets quite annoyed when something interrupts it."

"So you weren't there to see Alan Collins every time," Bessie suggested.

"No, but Bertie has been. He told me after the last one that from then on, if ever he saw the man in the brown suit coming in the building, he was going to set up his VCR to record whatever programme he was watching. He was quite pleased with himself today when it worked."

"And the lift has never had any problems when Alan Collins wasn't there?" Bessie asked.

"Oh, it has problems all the time," Bahey told her. "But it only has fires when Alan Collins comes around."

"That doesn't make any sense, although it does go a long way towards explaining why no one has made an offer on the flat," Bessie mused.

"I don't understand," Bahey said.

"I don't either, but it seems to me as if someone is trying to discourage people from buying that flat."

CHAPTER FIVE

Bessie told Bahey about the three flats she'd seen, and they spent a few minutes discussing Alan Collins as well. By the end of the phone call, Bessie didn't feel any closer to understanding what was going on in the building on Seaview Terrace. She fixed herself a quick lunch and then rang Doona.

"Are you free for dinner?" she asked her friend.

"I am, indeed," Doona replied. "Shall I bring a pizza?"

"That sounds good," Bessie said. "I'll make some shortbread, I think."

"Yummy," Doona said with a laugh.

The afternoon passed quickly as Bessie mixed up and baked a batch of shortbread before curling up with a new book. She was quickly lost in the collection of short mystery and detective stories, all written by female writers. After the third story, she stopped to collect paper and a pencil, carefully writing down the names of two of the authors of the stories she had just read. She'd never heard of either of them before, but she'd enjoyed both of their stories and she'd be looking for more by both of them on her next trip into Ramsey.

Doona arrived just as Bessie finished another of the short stories. She sighed as she headed for the door. This book was going to end up costing her a fortune, as she'd liked everything she'd read so far and many of the authors were new to her. She welcomed Doona with a quick hug, reaching around the pizza box to do so.

"I've had a very strange day," Bessie told her friend. "I'm hoping that talking it through with you will help me make sense of it."

Doona laughed. "Maybe we need a bottle of wine as well?" she suggested.

"I think I need to keep a clear head," Bessie replied.

She quickly pulled down plates and the pair sat down with their pizza.

"This is really good," Bessie said after a few bites. "Where did it come from?"

Doona named a small restaurant that Bessie knew well. "They've just started featuring 'American-style' pizza for take-away," Doona told her. "They left a whole bunch of flyers and coupons at the station and the young constables have been raving about it."

"I can see why," Bessie said, grabbing a second slice.

"So, what was Alan Collins like in person?" Doona asked.

Bessie thought about her reply for a moment. "Sort of strange and creepy and also a little sad," she replied.

"Sad?"

"Well, I think he's really trying to do his job," Bessie explained. "But it seems like his efforts are being sabotaged, at least at Seaview Terrace."

"Okay, tell me the whole story," Doona demanded.

Bessie gave her every detail she could remember about her visit to the flat on Seaview Terrace.

"Mr. Collins, who insisted I call him Alan, by the way, got off on the wrong foot by mistaking me for the manager's mother, but beyond that he tried really hard to sell me on all of the flats."

"But with the door propped open and then the fire in the lift, you weren't tempted?" Doona said teasingly.

"I wasn't tempted," Bessie agreed. "Until I talked to Bahey this afternoon."

"What did Bahey say to change your mind?"

"It seems the fires in the lift mechanism always seem to

coincide with Alan Collins being in the building," Bessie told her.

"Sorry, do you think he's setting the lift on fire for some reason?" Doona asked, her expression confused.

"No, I think someone else is trying to discourage prospective buyers from buying that flat," Bessie said.

"But why?" Doona demanded.

"That's a very good question," Bessie replied. "I haven't the foggiest idea."

"You can't be seriously considering moving to Douglas," Doona told her.

"No, not really, but I am tempted to pretend to be," Bessie replied. "It might be quite interesting to see what would happen if I made an offer on that flat."

Doona shook her head. "Maybe you should talk to John," she suggested. "Maybe the police should investigate."

"Investigate what?" Bessie asked. "Besides, John works in Laxey, not Douglas. Douglas is out of his jurisdiction."

"And he's not on the island at the moment, either," Doona said with a sigh.

"He's not?" Bessie asked.

"He's across in Manchester with his wife and kids," Doona told her. "He's taken a fortnight's holiday."

"I suppose he's earned it," Bessie said. "Who's in charge in Laxey, then?"

"Inspector Kelly is covering for him," Doona told her. "And I have to say, I didn't miss the man."

Bessie laughed. Inspector Kelly had been Doona's supervisor for a while, before John Rockwell was assigned to the Laxey station.

"Two weeks isn't that long," Bessie told Doona. "Although somehow the island doesn't feel quite the same without John here."

"You've only known that he's gone for a minute," Doona said with a laugh.

Bessie laughed at herself. "I know; I'm being rather silly. Still, it's nice for him to get away."

"Yes," Doona said slowly.

"And what's behind that?" Bessie asked.

"I don't know. He certainly didn't seem to be looking forward to it and when I asked him what all they were going to be doing during the fortnight, he was vague and didn't want to talk about it."

Bessie frowned. "I hope everything is okay," she said. "I really hate the thought of him moving back across."

"As do I," Doona said with a sigh.

Over tea and generous servings of crumbly shortbread, Bessie told Doona about the other two flats she'd seen in Douglas.

"The one on the promenade sounds temping," Doona told her.

"But too expensive," Bessie replied. "Even if I did want to move to Douglas, I couldn't afford anything that grand."

"But you don't really want to move to Douglas, right?"

Bessie sighed. "I don't really want to move, but I am curious as to what's going on at Seaview Terrace. I guess I'm a little bit worried about Bahey as well. It certainly seems like something odd is going on."

"Maybe you should go and see Pete Corkill," Doona suggested.

"I might," Bessie said. "But first I might try making an offer to just see what happens. On the other hand, I've been thinking about a change of scenery. Maybe a holiday in Douglas, at one of the hotels near Seaside Terrace, would be a good idea."

Bessie was almost as surprised as Doona by the thought. She hadn't realised that she'd been considering Douglas rather than Derbyshire for her holiday, but once she'd made the comment, she could see a lot of merit in the idea. She and Doona talked about that as well as several other things until it was rather later than either had planned.

Doona went home with a large container of shortbread, leaving the last two slices of pizza with Bessie.

"That's more than a fair trade," she insisted.

Bessie put her lunch for the next day into the refrigerator and headed to bed. She had a lot on her mind, but she still fell asleep quickly and slept well.

On Tuesday she did a few chores around the cottage,

vacuuming the rooms upstairs and dusting every room. When she'd first moved into the cottage, she'd stuck to a very specific routine with cleaning and laundry and the like, but after a short while she'd decided that such a routine was too much like work.

Ever since, she'd cleaned when she felt like it, trying to do a little bit each day so the job never got too big. She did laundry when she needed to and the only thing she scheduled regularly was her big weekly grocery shop in Ramsey. Since she had to arrange a taxi for that, it was easier to have a standing appointment.

At half one her taxi arrived to take her into Ramsey for tea with Mary Quayle. Because she hadn't booked in advance, her usual driver wasn't available, but the man who collected her was perfectly adequate. He wasn't chatty on the short drive, which suited Bessie today as she was trying to work out what she wanted to ask Mary.

Mary was already settled at a small table in the corner when Bessie walked into the small café.

"Ah, good afternoon, Bessie," Mary said, giving Bessie a shy smile.

"Hello, Mary. It's good to see you again," Bessie replied, sliding into the seat opposite her friend.

Mary was a tiny woman with grey hair that was nearly always kept in an immaculate bun. She was always expensively dressed but never seemed to be flaunting her wealth. The only jewellery she wore was her thin gold wedding band. She was at least a few years younger than her sixty-something husband, but she looked older and somewhat fragile.

The waiter bustled over and took their order. The restaurant offered "Hot tea, served with a selection of bite-sized cakes and biscuits," and both women agreed that it was exactly what they wanted. Once he was gone, Bessie reached over and patted Mary's hand.

"How are you, my dear?" she asked, feeling slightly concerned by how tired the other woman looked today.

"I'm fine," Mary replied automatically.

Bessie frowned at her. "Of course you are," she said. "But

how are you, really?"

Mary chuckled, although there was no humour in it. "You always read me so well," she replied. "I'm okay, really, just a bit tired."

Bessie didn't want to pry, even though it was obvious that something was bothering her friend. "How are the children?" she asked.

"They're all good," Mary replied. "Georgie, or rather, George, Junior, and his wife have invited me to join them on their holiday in Portugal at the end of the month. I'm sure they're only taking me so that they have someone to watch the kids, but I don't mind in the slightest. I love my grandchildren and I'll take any chance I can get to spend time with them."

"I'm sure Portugal will be lovely," Bessie said.

"I went with them last year as well," Mary told her. "They'd only just had the baby, and they really needed the extra help. Although I suppose with a six-year-old and a one-year-old, they still really need extra help."

"Will George be going as well?"

"Oh, good heavens, no," Mary said, shaking her head. "He'd go crazy sitting on a beach for a fortnight and he doesn't really have a lot of patience with the grandchildren, either. No, he'll stay here and pretend to be retired while working sixty hours a week, just like normal."

Bessie pressed her lips together while she struggled to find an appropriate reply. "What a shame he doesn't enjoy the grandchildren," she said finally.

"Yes, well, he found our three quite hard work when they were small, as well," Mary said in a confiding tone. "He gets along with them better now that they're all adults, of course."

"How are Michael and Elizabeth, then?" Bessie asked.

"Michael is well. His little one is turning into quite the handful and the doctors are beginning to suggest he might be autistic or something, which is, of course, worrying for Michael and Jenny."

"And for you," Bessie suggested.

"Oh, yes, he's such a lovely little lad most of the time, but he does have some rather, well, interesting behavioural issues." She shook her head. "And they have another baby on the way, which is wonderful, but also an additional source of stress."

"It sounds like they need a holiday in Portugal as well," Bessie said.

"They had a week across in June, before the school holidays started, and I think Jenny is going to take little Robert across for a week or two with her mum either later this month or early next. With Michael working for George, of course, he doesn't get nearly enough holiday time."

"I thought George was retired," Bessie said. "How can Michael work for him?"

Mary sighed. "George is 'semi-retired,'" she replied. "But he's far too involved in to many things to actually stop working. He keeps investing in different schemes that his friends come up with and a few mad ideas of his own. Michael is now working full-time just trying to keep up with George."

"I didn't realise," Bessie said. "How exhausting for you."

Mary smiled. "It is, rather, not that George sees it that way."

The waiter interrupted with their tea and treats and the two women oohed and aahed over the delicious-looking cakes and biscuits.

"We should do this more often," Mary said, after her first bite of cake.

"Indeed, we should," Bessie agreed.

"Anyway," Mary said, after a sip of tea, "Elizabeth is fine, too. She's finally dating a man whom George didn't hate on sight, which makes a nice change. I don't think he's going to be around for a terribly long time, but he's pleasant enough and at least he has a job. If he has any tattoos, they're well hidden, as well."

"Is she working for George as well?" Bessie asked.

"Oh, no, Elizabeth isn't working at all right now. She's decided that she needs some time to find her place in the world. She's dropped out of university, for the third time, and she's spending most of her time in her suite of rooms at our house watching telly and complaining about the state of the world."

"Oh, dear," Bessie muttered.

"She just needs some time to think," Mary said. "George is

always so driven and logical and unemotional and Elizabeth is more creative. I'm sure she'll find a way to make a difference, hopefully soon. The boyfriend is on summer holidays from studying medicine. He's busy working part-time at Noble's. I'm assuming he'll soon grow tired of Elizabeth's demands, maybe even before it's time for him to head back across to finish his course. They aren't at all well-suited, but Elizabeth loves making odd choices."

Bessie laughed. "Sometimes I think I was wise to not have children."

Mary shook her head. "I wouldn't change my three for anything," she told Bessie firmly. "Even if they can be difficult."

Bessie ate a tiny chocolate biscuit thoughtfully. "Thank you for having George ring me back," she said after a moment.

"Oh, it was no problem," Mary said with a wave of her hand. "He always enjoys talking with you."

"He didn't know any more about Island Choice Properties than you did, really," Bessie remarked. "He said the company is Grant Robertson's."

Mary made a face. "Yes, so I gather."

"I take it you don't like Mr. Robertson?" Bessie asked.

"Grant's fine," Mary said, the expression on her face at odds with her words. "I sometimes feel like he takes up too much of George's time, that's all."

"I didn't even realise the two knew each other until recently," Bessie told her friend.

"Oh, yes, they go way back," Mary replied. "They used to work together, many years ago now, of course."

"I didn't know that," Bessie said, hoping more information would be forthcoming.

"This was all before I met George, of course," Mary replied. "I gather, from what George has said, that he worked with Grant at the bank for a few years."

"I didn't know George worked in banking," Bessie said in surprise. "I thought he'd always worked in sales."

"He has since I've known him," Mary said. "And we've been married for twenty-eight years. I guess he was in banking for a few years after university. After a short time, where he earned a couple of good bonuses, he moved across and started his first business, selling cars. That's where we met, actually."

"You wanted to buy a car?" Bessie asked.

Mary laughed. "No, I wanted a job," she explained. "It was the late nineteen-sixties and I was determined to support myself and be an independent woman. George needed a receptionist at the car dealership and I applied. He didn't give me the job, but he asked me to have dinner with him. The rest is history, I guess."

Bessie chuckled. "Imagine how different your life might have been if he'd given you the job, instead."

Mary laughed. "I often wonder about that," she confessed. "He hired a really pretty and fairly stupid woman for the job and I used to tease him that I'd have done it better. He used to tease me that he'd mixed up the applications and meant to hire me and marry her."

"Did he ever explain why he hired her?" Bessie asked.

Mary flushed. "She was, um, she had, well, she had a very generous figure," she explained. "George used to have her wear short skirts and low-cut blouses. He always said she brought in a lot of business."

Bessie frowned. "Really?" she muttered.

"Things were very different in those days, of course," Mary reminded her. "That sort of thing wouldn't be acceptable today."

"And George and Grant stayed in touch all those years when George was across?" Bessie asked, changing the subject somewhat.

Mary blinked and then swallowed some tea. "I suppose they did," she said after a moment. "I'm not entirely sure how often they spoke, but I gather George did all of his banking through the bank here, rather than one across. For the business, as well as his personal accounts."

"And now they're buying up local businesses together?"

"I guess so," Mary shrugged. "George has never been one to talk about his work with me, but I gather he's put a lot of money into different schemes that Grant has suggested."

"Including Island Choice Properties," Bessie said.

"Yes, although George tried to persuade me to invest in that one as well."

"You?" Bessie asked.

"I have some money of my own," Mary explained. "My parents were quite comfortable and I was an only child, you see. I helped fund a lot of George's early businesses over the years, and, luckily, we've always ended up making money. George is actually very good at making money."

"But you didn't invest in Island Choice Properties?" Bessie asked.

"No, I don't invest in Grant Robertson's projects," Mary told her. "No matter how many times George asks." Mary flushed and then popped a cake in her mouth.

Bessie leaned over and patted her friend's hand. "Nothing you say to me will ever be repeated," she assured Mary.

"Thank you for that," Mary replied. "I haven't any real reason to dislike Grant, actually," she told Bessie. "There's just something about him that makes me uncomfortable."

"Sometimes we just don't take to people," Bessie said. "You can't force yourself to like someone if you don't."

"No, I know, but George thinks I'm just being stubborn," Mary said with a sigh.

"Because you wouldn't invest in the estate agency or because you don't like Mr. Robertson?"

"Both, I think," Mary said. She shrugged. "I'm pretty sure he's over the whole estate agency thing, actually. He found a few other investors to go in with him and Grant, so that's okay. He just really wants me to be friends with the man and I simply can't be more than polite to him."

"I don't know him at all," Bessie said. "What's he like?"

"Superficially, he's very polite and very professional," Mary told her. "But there's an undercurrent there that bothers me. I just don't trust him, even though, as far as I know, he's always been totally honest in every dealing we've had with him."

"George suggested that I come to a party you're having next week so that I can meet him for myself," Bessie said.

"Oh, yes, the barbeque," Mary replied. "I was going to invite you anyway, not to meet Grant, but because it might be fun."

Bessie looked closely at her friend. "You're saying fun, but your expression isn't saying fun."

Mary laughed. "I'm sure it will be fine," she said. "George likes to throw these big parties every few months for everyone he knows or has ever met." She shook her head. "I know opposites attract, but I hate big gatherings and George thrives on them. If he has to go more than few days without a social engagement he gets grumpy and starts talking about moving back across."

"Oh, I hope you won't do that," Bessie exclaimed.

"We won't," Mary assured her. "Not if I have any say in the matter, at least."

"So you're having a barbeque?" Bessie asked.

"George saw something on telly about a party in Texas where everything was cooked on these huge barbeque grills and he's been talking about it ever since. He's found a local caterer that is willing to have a go at recreating everything that was at the party on the television. George is beyond excited because there'll be fire and smoke and all sorts of food. He's invited at least half the island, I think."

Bessie laughed. "Surely you have room for half the island," she said. George and Mary lived in a huge mansion on the outskirts of Douglas, with many acres of land around it.

"I just hope it doesn't rain," Mary said. "They're meant to be setting up a bunch of marquees for people, in case it rains, but I'm sure everyone will end up in the house if the weather gets bad." She sighed. "I don't mind hundreds of people in the garden, but I'd rather not have them all in my home."

Bessie patted her hand again. "I know exactly what you mean," she told the other woman. With a public beach right outside her back door, Bessie had long ago grown accustomed to having people in what was effectively her garden. She was selective as to whom she welcomed into her home, though.

"You will come to the barbeque, won't you?" Mary asked. "I won't know more than a handful of the guests, well, aside from the children, of course. I'd love it if you could be there."

"I can't see why I couldn't be there. Do you think I could bring a friend?" Bessie asked, wondering if Doona might like an American-style barbeque.

"Oh, by all means, bring everyone you know," Mary said, a bit desperately. "I can't imagine anyone would notice if you brought a dozen friends."

"I won't bring that many," Bessie assured her. "But I might bring one."

Mary nodded. "When George first started talking about the barbeque, it was going to be a party for Mack Dickson," she told Bessie in a quiet voice.

"For Mack? Why?" Bessie asked. Mack was a brilliant archeologist and historian who'd recently been murdered. Bessie knew that George had been acquainted with the man; indeed, she'd been told that Mack had been blackmailing George, but Bessie wasn't sure how trustworthy her source was. The idea that George had been planning a party for Mack was surprising to her.

"I don't know all the details," Mary said with a shrug. "But the first I heard about the idea was when Mack had lunch with George and Grant the day of his lecture."

"Mack had lunch with George and Mr. Robertson the day of his lecture?" Bessie asked.

Mary laughed. "Yes, but I don't know why or what was discussed. The three of them ate in the small dining room and I wasn't invited to join them."

Bessie frowned. "Is that normal?" she asked and then flushed. "Sorry, that was a rude question," she said, sipping the last of her tea to hide her discomfort.

"It's fine," Mary answered. The waiter appeared at Bessie's elbow, offering more tea, which both women were happy to accept. Once he'd gone, Mary smiled at Bessie.

"Everyone's marriage is different," she said after a moment. "George has never involved me in his work, so yes, it is quite normal for him to have a meal with guests and not invite me to join them. I assumed at the time that he and Grant were discussing working with Mack on some project. Once Mack made his big announcement about Roman finds, I sort of figured that he'd been talking to George and Grant about that, but I've really no idea."

"That certainly makes sense," Bessie said, her mind racing.

"Sadly, nothing ever came of it, of course," Mary said.

"Indeed," Bessie replied.

"But that's enough about George and Grant," Mary said, picking up her last tiny biscuit. "What's this about you moving to Douglas?"

Bessie smiled at her friend. She'd been waiting for this opportunity. "I don't know," she said. "One of my friends lives in the building on Seaview Terrace that Alan Collins took me around. He's the agent from Island Choice Properties. She keeps talking about all the advantages of living in Douglas. Her building has grocery delivery and it's close to everything in Douglas, which makes it seem quite tempting, really."

"And you'd be closer to me," Mary said happily. "But you'd miss your little cottage by the sea."

"I would," Bessie agreed. "That's why I'm so uncertain as to what to do."

"It is a huge decision," Mary agreed.

"I'm afraid I'll sell my little cottage and buy a flat in Douglas and then hate it," Bessie said in a confiding tone. "And by that time some developer will have torn down my cottage and replaced it with a block of rental cottages or something."

Mary shook her head. "They couldn't tear down your cottage, could they? It's adorable."

"And desperately in need of modernisation," Bessie said with a shrug. "At least I'm sure that's what Alan Collins would say, if he got a look inside. I'm pretty sure the land is worth a lot more than my old cottage. Apparently sea views are a big selling feature."

"I suppose," Mary said slowly. "It's too bad you can't keep the cottage and simply rent a flat in Douglas for a while."

"That's a thought," Bessie said, as if the idea had never occurred to her. "I wonder if the people who own the flat at Seaview Terrace would be interested in renting it out for a while."

"You should ask Alan Collins," Mary suggested. "He should have some way to contact the owners."

"I might just have to do that," Bessie mused.

"I'll talk to George," Mary offered. "He knows more about the property market in Douglas than I do. Maybe he'll know of some other flats that are available."

"I'd appreciate that," Bessie said. "Although, I was really taken with the one at Seaview Terrace. If I am going to buy something, I think that might be the place for me."

"I'm sure George can help in some way," Mary said. "He knows everyone."

Bessie nodded. Although he'd only been back on the island for a year or so, it did seem as if George knew everyone, at least everyone who mattered, from the governor to the members of the House of Keys and anyone else who had any influence on the island. Sometimes Bessie wasn't sure why he'd bothered to become friends with her.

The pair finished their second round of tea with a more general chat about their lives. Mary was very excited at the thought of Bessie moving into Douglas and Bessie did her best to encourage her enthusiasm. While she had no intention of actually moving, she was very interested in seeing what might would happen if she showed real interest in the Seaview Terrace flat.

After tea, Mary drove Bessie home so that she didn't have to get a taxi back.

"I do love your little cottage," Mary said as she walked Bessie to her door. "I suppose I can see why you're tempted to stay put."

Bessie nodded. "Come and have a walk on the beach with me. You'll want to stay, too."

The pair took a short walk on the beach, stopping before they went too deeply into the crowds from the rental cottages. They returned to the relative quiet behind Bessie's cottage, and Bessie settled in on her rock.

"Have a seat," she suggested.

Mary perched tentatively on the rock and stared out at the sea. "We're on the sea as well, of course," she remarked. "But on a cliff above it, so you can't easily and safely get down to the water. George keeps talking about having steps put in, but he never gets around to doing it."

"I love being close to the water," Bessie told her. "But you do have the most amazing views."

Mary laughed lightly. "I think I'm just impossible to please," she said. "If we were right on the water, I'd probably complain about that, but since we aren't, I wish we were. I know I'm very lucky that we have a large home, but I love your cosy little cottage." She sighed. "I think I just need more sleep," she said after a moment.

"Perhaps your holiday in Portugal will do you some good," Bessie suggested.

Mary's face brightened. "I'm sure it will," she agreed. "I shall thoroughly enjoy spending time with the grandchildren. They're wonderful when they're small and still want to cuddle and play. All too soon they grow into teens and then adults and everything changes."

"Would you like to come in for a cup of tea or coffee or something?" Bessie asked after a while.

"No, thank you," Mary replied. "I've had quite enough to drink for now. It's just so very peaceful here on this rock with the sea whispering in and out. I think I might just sit here for a bit, if you don't mind."

Bessie took that as a hint that her friend wanted to be alone. "I'll leave you here, then," she told Mary. "If you change your mind, just knock whenever. I'll be home all night."

Bessie went into her cottage. She caught up on paying a few bills and then returned a few phone calls that were of no consequence. When she next looked out her back window, Mary had gone.

CHAPTER SIX

The next few days passed quietly. Bessie ignored the answering machine message from Alan Collins, who said he was just checking to make sure she didn't have any questions. She talked to Doona a couple of times, but Doona was working extra hours to help cover for some of the staff who were taking summer holidays. Spencer rang to let Bessie know that he'd made the shortlist for one of the jobs he'd been interviewed for, and Bessie was very pleased for him. By Friday, she was happy to get into Ramsey for some shopping, as she felt as if she'd been at home alone rather too much lately.

The feeling only lasted for a few minutes once she was out and about, of course. It was a rainy day and after Bessie had been "accidentally" elbowed into a puddle by a large woman with a huge umbrella, who was determined to walk as close to the shops as possible, regardless of who might be already in that space, Bessie was longing for her small, but blessedly empty, cottage.

ShopFast was quieter than normal, presumably due to the rain, and Bessie collected what she needed for the week without having to answer more than a few nosy questions from acquaintances. She'd almost made it out of the store before Maggie Shimmin spotted her.

"Ah, Bessie, there you are," Maggie's voice boomed across

the front of the store.

Bessie turned from the frozen foods and gave Maggie a smile. "Hi, Maggie, how are you today?"

"I'm well, but how are you?" the woman replied.

"I'm fine," Bessie replied.

Maggie came around her shopping trolley and took Bessie's hands in hers. "No, really, Bessie, how are you?" she asked intently.

"I'm fine," Bessie assured her, trying to pull her hands away.

"Bessie, we're friends as well as neighbours, you can tell me what's going on," Maggie said, staring hard at Bessie.

"I'm sure I don't know what you mean," Bessie replied, feeling confused.

Maggie sighed deeply. "I guess, if you don't feel you can talk to me, I mustn't be pushy," she said, letting go of Bessie's hands and turning away. "I thought we were friends, but you have to make that decision, I suppose."

Bessie put her hand on the woman's shoulder. "Maggie, we are friends," she said firmly. "And I have no idea what you're talking about."

Maggie stared at her for a moment. "I heard how you've put your house on the market so you can move into a flat in Douglas with medical staff on call," she said after a moment. "I know you're a very private person, so I guess I can see that you don't want to talk about your health problems."

Bessie just looked at her for a long time and then she began to laugh. Maggie was starting to look offended before Bessie got her laughter under control.

"Sorry," Bessie said, wiping her eyes. "It's just so ridiculous that I had to laugh."

"What's ridiculous?" Maggie asked.

"All of it," Bessie replied, shaking her head. "I have not put my house on the market. I am not moving into a flat in Douglas with medical staff on call. And, as far as I know, I'm in perfect health, as well."

Maggie sighed. "My sources are impeccable," she said stiffly.

"Well, in this instance, they're also wrong," Bessie told her.

"Would you like me to tell you what's really happening?"

Maggie nodded eagerly.

Bessie hid her grin. "I am giving some serious thought to moving into Douglas," she told the woman. "While I love my little cottage, living in Douglas has many advantages and I'm curious what living there might be like. Upkeep on the cottage is costly and time-consuming as well, while a little flat would make my life much easier. For right now, I'm thinking about it and exploring different options, but that's all I'm doing."

Maggie didn't look as if she believed Bessie, but she nodded. "Well, that's good to hear," she said.

"I just saw my doctor last month and there's absolutely nothing wrong with my health, by the way," Bessie added. "I have no interest in a flat with medical staff available. I'm actually looking at a flat on Seaview Terrace. My friend, Bahey Corlett, lives there."

"I remember Bahey," Maggie said. "She's older than I am, of course. She worked for the Pierce family, right?"

"She did," Bessie agreed. "Anyway, if I did decide to put my cottage on the market, you'd be the first to know."

"Well, thank you for that. I'm glad your health isn't a problem," Maggie said. "Now I really must be off."

Maggie was gone before Bessie managed a reply. Bessie shook her head and then checked her trolley. She'd completely forgotten what was on her mental shopping list or even what was already in her trolley. The chat with Maggie had amused and upset her in nearly equal measure. She really hated being gossiped about, but it was worse when the gossips got so much of it wrong.

After grabbing a few more things, almost at random, Bessie headed to the tills and then out to find her taxi. Back at home, she put the shopping away before playing through her answering machine messages.

"Ah, Bessie, it's Mary. Can you give me a ring when you have a minute? I have some news for you about that flat on Seaview Terrace."

Bessie reached for the phone. This should be interesting.

"Mary? It's Bessie, ringing you back."

"Hi, Bessie. I'm sorry I didn't ring you sooner, but George has been working a lot lately and I didn't get a chance to talk to him until yesterday afternoon. Then he had to talk to Grant, who had to talk to Alan." Mary laughed. "I suppose you don't need all the boring details, though, do you? You just want to know what I've found out."

Bessie laughed. "I don't mind hearing the whole story," she assured her friend. "You can tell me whatever you like."

"Thank you," Mary said. "George is always telling me to get to the point when I waffle about all over the place. Anyway, George talked to Grant, and you'll never guess what he found out."

"You don't really expect me to guess, do you?" Bessie asked.

"Oh, no, you'd never manage it anyway," Mary said with a laugh. "When the poor old dear who lived in number ten died, her family was rather desperate to get rid of the flat. They all live across and didn't have any island connections, so they just wanted it sold quickly. To help them out, Island Choice Properties bought the flat from them at just below market value."

"Really?" Bessie asked. "Is that typical for estate agencies? I have no idea how they work."

"I'm not totally sure," Mary said. "I don't think it is, really, but I'm sure Grant bought the place out of his spare change, if you know what I mean. The freehold on the property is owned by one of Grant's companies anyway. If they were willing to sell at below market value, he probably thought it would be a good chance to make a quick profit."

"But now the flat has been sitting on the market for months," Bessie said.

"And that's why they're happy to let you lease it," Mary told her.

"Are they indeed?" Bessie asked.

"Apparently George had to twist Grant's arm a little bit," Mary said in a confiding tone. "But you know George would do anything for you."

Bessie laughed. "I rather think that George would do anything for you and he's doing it for your benefit."

"Maybe," Mary replied. "But regardless, the good news is that you can move in whenever you like."

"As quickly as that?" Bessie asked, suddenly quite sure that she really didn't want to move at all.

"Shall I arrange a moving truck for you?" Mary asked. "We have an account with Island Movers. They moved us from across, not just me and George, but all of the children as well. They're very good and I'm sure they'll give you a bargain price."

"That's very kind of you," Bessie said, thinking quickly, "but I'm sure there are things that have to be arranged first. There must be a lease agreement or something that I need to sign and other paperwork as well."

"Oh, I don't know," Mary said. "I suppose I should have George ring you."

"That might be best," Bessie said, swallowing a sigh.

"Of course, your new flat is smaller than your little cottage. You'll have to choose what furniture you take with you very carefully," Mary said thoughtfully. "We have lots of furniture pieces in storage. If you think you'd like to have something different, I'd be happy to take you to have a look around."

"Why do you have things in storage?" Bessie asked, thinking about the huge mansion that Mary lived in. Surely there was plenty of room for a lot of furniture.

"George likes to redo rooms every so often and when he does, he clears out everything and starts from scratch. I can't bring myself to just throw away perfectly good furniture that's often only a year or two old, so I put it all in storage. Sometimes I can sneak a piece or two back in, in a different room or something, but usually I just leave it all in storage until I find someone who can use it. The boys have both furnished their entire houses from our storage units and Elizabeth redoes her rooms every couple of months or so. You're more than welcome to whatever you think you might find useful."

"Thank you, but I think I have more than enough furniture for that little flat," Bessie said, shaking her head. The rich really were completely different to her.

"Well, the offer is certainly open, if you want to reconsider."

After the call, Bessie spent several minutes just sitting at her kitchen table, looking out the window. She knew she wasn't seriously moving, but the whole idea still filled her with dread. She's slept in the bedroom upstairs just about every night for many more years than she was willing to admit to and she wasn't sure she was ready to leave it, even if it was only temporary. She sighed. This had all started out as a little favour for a friend, but it was turning into much more than that. She'd been thinking about a holiday, she reminded herself. She would simply have to think of her stay in Douglas as just that, a nice holiday.

George rang just after lunch.

"Ah, Bessie, Mary asked me to ring," he said, sounding distracted.

"Thanks for doing so," Bessie replied. "She said that you'd managed to arrange for me to lease the flat on Seaview Terrace."

"Yes, I talked to Grant yesterday and he's fine with you moving in whenever you want."

"What about a lease agreement or some sort of legal documentation?" Bessie asked.

"Oh, I don't think we need to bother with such things, really. You can get the keys from the building manager and move in whenever you want. If you decide you want to buy it, let me know. Otherwise, just let me know when you move out."

"Oh, but that seems very informal," Bessie protested.

"It's all between friends," George replied. "Must dash."

Bessie stared at the phone after he'd hung up. She felt very uncomfortable about the whole arrangement. With a sigh, she dialed her advocate. Doncan always had good advice for her.

She was delighted that he had time to talk when she rang. She quickly summarised the situation for him.

"So they're going to let you move into the flat and stay as long as you like?" he asked when she'd finished.

"That's what it sounded like to me," Bessie replied.

"How much rent will you be paying?"

"George didn't say," Bessie said.

"I've worked with George Quayle's advocate, Richard Hart,

many times. Let me give him a ring and see what's going on."

It was nearly time for dinner before he called Bessie back. "Sorry it's taken so long to get back to you," he told Bessie. "Richard had to ring Grant Robertson's advocate, Scott Meyers, and apparently neither of them knew anything about the arrangement, so many calls to both Mr. Quayle and Mr. Robertson were also needed."

"Oh, dear," Bessie said. "I hope George isn't upset with me for stirring up all this trouble."

"I'm sure he understands that you need to know what's happening. So here's what we've come up with. We're going to have you sign a standard lease agreement that will be open-ended so you can move out whenever you like. Similarly, they can ask you to leave with thirty days notice."

"That seems reasonable," Bessie said. There was no way she intended to stay for thirty days, anyway, even if she did try it out for a week or two so she could look into Bahey's concerns. Really, a fortnight's holiday in Douglas might be just the thing to shake her out of her occasional blue mood.

"You'll be charged ten pounds a month rent for the first three months," Doncan continued. "If you decide to stay after that, the rent will go up to a fair market rent that will be agreed on in advance. At any point, if you do decide to purchase the flat, everything you've paid in rent will be deducted from the agreed purchase price."

"That seems more than fair," Bessie said. "Have you any idea what the flat should be renting for?"

Doncan named a figure that had Bessie shocked speechless for a moment. "House prices are going up all the time," Doncan told her. "And so are rental rates."

"I had no idea," Bessie said. "They should be charging me more than ten pounds a month, surely."

"I gather Mr. Quayle is quite keen to help you out, or rather Mrs. Quayle is quite keen and Mr. Quayle is willing."

"Yes, but still, they should make me pay a fair amount," Bessie argued.

"Mr. Meyers would certainly agree with you," Doncan said

dryly. "However, Mr. Quayle wouldn't hear of it. You can argue with him the next time you see him, I suppose."

"I certainly will," Bessie replied.

"Anyway, I have all of the paperwork here. You just need to stop in and sign it at your convenience. The building manager has the keys, so once you've signed the paperwork, you can move in whenever you like."

Bessie took a deep breath that seemed slightly shakey. "Great," she said without enthusiasm.

"Bessie, I think when you come in, we'd better have a nice long chat," Doncan told her. "I want to make sure I understand everything that's going on."

"We can chat," Bessie replied. "But really, there isn't anything going on, other than my wanting a small change. Maybe, with all the sad things that have been happening lately, I just need to do something different for a bit. I can't really imagine selling my cottage, but I do need a change. It's more like an extended holiday than a move though, unless I truly do fall in love with Douglas."

"I'll transfer you to Breesha and she can make an appointment for you to come in and see me early next week," was Doncan's reply.

Breesha was strictly professional, but Bessie fancied that she could hear an undercurrent of disapproval in the woman's tone. Bessie hung up on a sigh. While she wasn't exactly lying to anyone, she was stretching the truth a great deal more than she was comfortable with. Bessie was beginning to wonder if she were taking things rather too far in her efforts to help Bahey.

The next morning was rainy and cool and Bessie stomped up and down the beach in her raincoat and Wellington boots, feeling cross with the whole world. Back in her small kitchen, Bessie felt as if the walls were closing in on her. For some reason, her little cottage felt cramped and claustrophobic today. She knew she was grumpy and out of sorts and she knew exactly why, but that didn't improve her mood.

Bessie usually spent Saturdays at home, often preparing and cooking things like soups, some of which could be enjoyed at once, the rest frozen for another day. Today she didn't feel like cooking or cleaning, so she curled up with a book and tried to get lost in it. She was meeting with mixed success when someone knocked on her door.

"Hugh? But how nice to see you," Bessie said in surprise when she opened her door.

"It's good to see you, too," the young constable replied.

Bessie stepped back, opening the door wide to let the man in. "It's nearly time for lunch," she said, glancing at the kitchen clock. "Would you like to join me? I have some soup in the freezer. It won't take ten minutes to warm it up."

"That would be great," Hugh replied, his brown eyes lighting up.

"You sit down," Bessie told him. "I'll get the soup started and then you can tell me why you're here."

Hugh took a seat at the small kitchen table while Bessie bustled around pulling containers of soup from the freezer and getting them ready to heat.

"It's always so comfortable in here," Hugh said, making Bessie smile.

"You've heard I'm thinking of moving and you've come to talk me out of it," she guessed.

"Not at all," Hugh said, flushing under Bessie's gaze.

Bessie smiled. The man was in his mid-twenties, but he still looked no more than fifteen. His brown hair always looked as if it hadn't been cut or even combed recently and he still didn't seem to have become entirely comfortable with his height or his broad shoulders.

"No, really," he said insistently. "I don't reckon I have any right to be giving you advice. I just, well, I just couldn't help but comment on how nice your cottage is. It's always been a place to come to get away from the rest of the world. I'll be sad to see you go, if you do move, that's all."

Bessie nodded. "I know what you mean," she assured him. "I've lived here for many more years than you've been alive, and leaving isn't going to be easy. That's why I'm only planning on leasing in Douglas, so I can just give it a try and see what it's like.

Who knows, by the end of the month I might be right back here with no intention of ever leaving again."

Hugh shrugged. "After everything that's happened lately, I can certainly see you needing a change. Really, I want you to be happy, even if that means you moving to Douglas."

Bessie smiled. "Thank you," she told him. Hugh was really turning out to be a nice young man. "I must admit, I'm a little excited about the thought of something so new and different," she told him, feeling somewhat surprised when she realised that it was true.

"I can see that," Hugh replied. "Excited but scared as well, right?"

Bessie nodded. "Exactly right," she agreed.

"That's how I feel about Grace," Hugh said with a sigh.

Bessie patted his back before pulling soup bowls from the cupboard. She carefully poured hot soup into two bowls. Hugh jumped up and carried the bowls to the table, while Bessie sliced a loaf of bread and put it and a plate of butter in between the bowls.

"What would you like to drink?" she asked Hugh.

"Oh, something cold would be great," he said happily.

Bessie handed him a fizzy drink and then switched the kettle on. The last thing she wanted with soup was something cold. She sat down across from Hugh and the pair ate for a few moments.

"Ah, Bessie, this is really good," Hugh said after several mouthfuls.

"I'm glad you like it," Bessie said, patting his hand as she got up to fix her tea. "So how are things with you and Grace?" she asked.

"Oh, things are good," Hugh said, ducking his head and staring at his bowl.

"I'm glad to hear that," Bessie said, rejoining him at the table. "I hope she'll stop by again soon. I like visiting with her."

"Yeah, well, that's one of the reasons I stopped by," Hugh said. "See, Grace and I are going away for a fortnight and I wanted to tell you so you wouldn't think I was ignoring you or something."

Bessie smiled. "You and Grace are having a holiday together?" she asked.

"Yes, but it isn't what you think," Hugh said, blushing brightly. "I mean, it isn't just me and Grace. I'm actually joining Grace's whole family on holiday. We're going across to one of those holiday park places where you can do sports and things for a week and then we're travelling down to Cornwall to visit with some of Grace's extended family."

"Grace's whole family?" Bessie asked.

"Yeah, her mum and dad and her younger brother and sister," Hugh explained. "Gus is sixteen and Pru is thirteen."

"That sounds exhausting," Bessie said, bluntly honest.

Hugh laughed. "Yeah, it will be interesting," he agreed. "I'm taking my car so Grace and I can travel together, but we'll be following Mr. Christian all around the country, which could be, um, well, interesting."

Bessie laughed. "What are the children like?" she asked.

"Gus is okay. He's a good kid and he isn't into drink and girls, at least not yet. He's really into football, which is why we're going to the holiday camp. Apparently there's some sort of training camp that week that he's been picked for, and we're all going to cheer him on, like."

"And Grace's sister?"

Hugh blushed again. "Ah, she's okay," he said, taking a big drink from his can.

"What aren't you telling me?" Bessie asked.

Hugh shook his head. "Pru has a little bit of a crush on me, that's all. She sometimes follows me and Grace around and keeps talking to me. Grace gets really fed up, and I end up feeling like I'm caught in the middle. I can't be horrible to Grace's little sister, can I?"

Bessie laughed. "No, you can't be horrible to her," she agreed. "Poor Grace, it must be very frustrating for her."

"Yeah, and for me," Hugh said grumpily.

"You must make sure to fill up the back of your car so that there isn't any room for passengers," Bessie told him. "Make sure there's only room for you and Grace and find a reason why you must take Grace and not Pru in your car."

"I hadn't thought of that," Hugh said. "My car's a bit of a mess anyway. I'm doing it up. Perhaps I'll take the backseat out of it so no one can ride back there at all."

Bessie laughed. "That might be a bit extreme," she said.

"Anyway, I'm sort of looking forward to the holiday and dreading it as well," Hugh confided. "I just have this feeling that it's going to be a real test of how Grace and I feel about each other."

"I'm sure it will be," Bessie said. "You've a ferry crossing each way, long drives and multiple nights staying with other people in strange places to get through, not to mention meeting Grace's extended family. The holiday may just reveal a lot about your true feelings."

Hugh frowned. "I've always hated tests," he said. "In school and in real life."

"You should talk to Grace," Bessie suggested. She got up and brought more soup to the table, carefully adding it to Hugh's nearly empty bowl. "I'm sure she's just as nervous as you are."

"Really?" Hugh asked. "I didn't think about that."

Bessie shook her head. The poor man had a lot to learn about women. "I'm absolutely certain of it," she said. "And the more you two can talk about such things, the stronger your relationship will be."

Bessie dug out a tub of ice cream, grinning as Hugh helped himself to a couple of huge scoops. Clearly his worries about the coming holiday hadn't affected his appetite.

"Anyway, Bessie, I want you to take good care of yourself while I'm gone," Hugh said as he helped clear away the dishes.

"When do you leave?" Bessie asked.

"We're on the overnight sailing tonight," Hugh replied glumly. "I hate sailing, especially when I should be sleeping, but Mr. and Mrs. Christian prefer late sailings."

"Well, I hope you have a wonderful time," Bessie told him, giving him a hug. "You must come and visit me as soon as you get back and tell me all about it."

"But will you be here or in Douglas?" Hugh asked.

Bessie opened and closed her mouth several times before she could reply. "I suppose I shall be in Douglas," she said eventually, as reality sank in. "I suppose I must have a housewarming or something."

"The inspector will be back by then as well," Hugh told her. "You can have us both over and Doona as well."

"That sounds like a plan," Bessie said faintly, feeling as if her life was getting rather out of control.

With one last quick hug, Hugh left. Bessie quickly cleared away the washing up and tidied her kitchen. When she was finished, she headed out to the rock behind the cottage. The rain had stopped, but the day was still somewhat cooler than was normal for August. The beach was quiet as a result. Bessie sat for several minutes, watching the tide as it made its way in. Hugh was exactly right; she felt excited and scared at the same time.

CHAPTER SEVEN

Bessie spent much of Sunday trying to figure out what furniture she should take with her and what she should leave behind. As she pictured the rooms in the new flat, everything in her cottage seemed the wrong size, the wrong shape or the wrong style. By Sunday evening she had just about decided that she was going to buy brand-new everything for the flat.

There were many reasons why the idea appealed to her. For a start, it had been years since she had been furniture shopping and the idea of a spree made the thought of moving far more exciting. Besides, it was difficult for her to picture any of the furniture she loved in a different location. If she bought everything new, the move would feel even more like a holiday or a temporary arrangement. Once she was ready to come home, she could sell everything she'd purchased.

She checked her bank balance. She could certainly afford some inexpensive furniture for the little flat. And inexpensive furniture was perfect for her little adventure. With that decided, she headed for bed on Sunday night feeling far more at peace with what was to come.

Monday morning was her appointment with Doncan Quayle to sign the lease agreement. Bessie was dreading it, but a last-minute problem with someone's will meant that the man himself wasn't even in the office when she visited. Instead, Bessie met with his young son, also called Doncan, to sign the papers.

"I know my father wanted to talk with you about this," the young man said. "But he didn't leave any instructions other than where to have you sign."

"Then I'll just sign it all and be on my way," Bessie told him.

Even though he was fairly inexperienced, young Doncan wasn't the type to let Bessie just sign the papers. He spent an hour taking her through each document and making sure that she understood exactly what she was agreeing to on every page.

"Your father explained all of this to me on the phone," Bessie told him at one point.

"And he'd fire me in an instant if he discovered that I didn't go back over it all with you in person," Doncan had told her.

Breesha, who had been the older Doncan's secretary for many years, brought in tea after the first twenty minutes.

"I figured you'd be needing this about now," she said, winking at Bessie. "The young man is good and thorough, he is."

"Oh, aye," Bessie said with a sigh. "Too thorough."

"No such thing in legal work," Doncan told her cheerfully. By the time Bessie left, she felt as if she'd had quite enough of advocates for a good long time.

Back at home again, she fixed a quick lunch, planning on starting to think about shopping and packing once she'd eaten. The phone interrupted her plans.

"Hello, Bessie, it's Mary Quayle. How are you?"

"I'm fine," Bessie replied. "How are you?"

"Oh, I'm very well, thanks," Mary said lightly. "You know I'm off to Portugal with Georgie and Diane in a few weeks. I really want to help you get settled into your little flat before I go."

"Oh, Mary, that is kind of you. I've signed all the paperwork, and I was just going to start thinking about packing and furniture shopping when you rang."

"You mustn't go furniture shopping," Mary said firmly. "I'll pick you up tomorrow and we'll go out to our storage units and you can pick out whatever you like. There's enough out there to furnish at least ten flats. I'm sure you'll find plenty you can use."

"Mary, I can't let you lend me furniture on top of everything else you've done," Bessie replied.

"Bessie, please, it's all just sitting out there, going to waste. The best thing you could do for me is borrow all of it and then ruin it so I don't have to store it anymore. I can't bring myself to get rid of it, but I'll never use it again."

Bessie was going to argue further, but she didn't get the chance.

"I have to dash," Mary said. "George just walked in. I'll see you around one tomorrow."

Bessie hung up the phone slowly, feeling both annoyed with Mary and grateful to her. Before she could decide what to do next, the phone rang again.

"Bessie? It's Bahey. What's going on?"

"Whatever do you mean?"

"The flat next door to me, the one you looked at, it got a fresh coat of paint yesterday. Now today, they've had some man here all day, working on the lift, and they've painted the lobby and the corridors as well. What have you done?"

Bessie shook her head and then laughed at herself. "I'm shaking my head," she told Bahey. "I don't know what's going on, or rather, I don't totally know what's going on. I've arranged to lease the flat for a short time, but I can't see why that would cause all of that activity. I certainly didn't expect them to paint for me."

"You're moving in?" Bahey asked.

"Yes, probably later this week," Bessie replied. "I've just been to see my advocate to sign the papers. I guess I can move in whenever I'm ready."

"Hurray!" Bahey shouted down the phone. "Things are getting weirder and weirder around here. I'm sure there was someone in the flat below me last night, walking around and talking loudly. I was going to go down and knock on the door, but the lift was out of order and I don't like to take the stairs at night. They aren't well lit."

"Is that all that's going on?" Bessie asked.

"My welcome mat disappeared a couple of days ago," Bahey told her. "I'd only just bought it and put it out in front of my door and the next morning it was gone."

"Did you ask the building manager about it?"

"I did, but he didn't know anything about it. I kept walking around the building, looking to see if it turned up in front of another door, but then this morning, it was back in front of my door."

"Really? That is rather strange, but at least you got it back," Bessie said.

"Yeah, but now I can't decide if I should leave it out there or bring it inside. I'm afraid it might go missing again."

"Ah, well, I guess you'll have to decide whether it's worth the risk. Is that all that's been strange?"

"Well, number ten hasn't received any post lately, but yesterday I was sure I saw something in the box for number five. That's the empty flat under mine."

"Could it have been an advertising circular?"

"I don't know. I could only just make out that there was something in the box."

"I suppose, if someone does own it, they have a right to get post to that address," Bessie suggested.

"I guess so," Bahey said. "It just feels off, that's all."

"I suspect there are perfectly logical explanations for everything that's going on," Bessie told her friend. "But this is the perfect time for me to have a complete change of scenery, so I'll move in and see what I can find out."

"Are you okay?" Bahey asked.

"I'm fine," Bessie assured her. "But life has been rather stressful lately and a change is as good as a rest, they say. Besides, August in the worst month for tourists on Laxey beach. It gets really noisy and at least one cottage always seems to have a party late in the evening just about every night. A stay in Douglas might be exactly what I need."

"It'll be great to get to spend some time with you," Bahey said. "But don't let me become a nuisance. I'm rather busy with Howard most days, anyway." Bahey laughed. "I'm sorry, I'm just so surprised that you're coming that I can't even think straight."

"You did suggest it," Bessie reminded her.

"But I never imagined that you'd actually do it," Bahey admitted. "I was just talking, like."

Bessie laughed. "Well, whatever your intentions, I'm doing it. I'll probably be moved in by Friday, although I have a lot to arrange before then. I think maybe I'll have a housewarming party on Saturday afternoon. I can invite the neighbours and get to meet them all."

"Why would you want to do that?" Bahey asked. "I mean, I'm sure they're nice and all." She sighed. "I'm not really a people person," she told Bessie. "I'll come to the party, since it's you having it, but I don't expect to enjoy it."

Bessie laughed. "Well, that's very honest, anyway. I guess I am a people person, and besides, I want to find out if anyone else has noticed anything strange going on. You said one of the neighbours mentioned seeing Alan Collins every time the lift catches on fire. I want to find out what else your neighbours know."

"See, this is why I rang you in the first place," Bahey said. "Because you're smart and you think of things like that. I never even thought about asking the neighbours."

"I'll let you know when I'm actually going to arrive," Bessie told her.

"Wait until I tell Howard you're coming," Bahey said just before she hung up. "He'll never believe me."

Bessie wasn't sure what Bahey meant by that, but she hung up the phone feeling a little bit more excited about her impending move.

She spent the afternoon doing laundry so that she'd have plenty of clean clothes to pack. There was no point in taking anything more than summer clothes at this point, so she would only need a few suitcases for them. It was strange to think of her little cottage sitting empty while she was in Douglas, but she supposed she could visit once in a while. There had been a small combination washer and dryer in the flat, but if she didn't like the way it cleaned her clothes, she might decide to head home once a week to do laundry at the very least.

Stop trying to find excuses for coming back to Laxey, she told herself sternly as she looked around the kitchen. She'd need plates and cups and flatware and pots and pans and the toaster and the kettle. She sighed deeply. She'd accumulated an awful lot of things over the years. Choosing what to take and what to leave behind was going to be an interesting exercise.

Doona rang while she was looking through the wardrobe in the spare bedroom.

"How are you?" Doona asked when Bessie picked up.

"I'm fine, just thinking about what I should take and what I should leave behind when I move."

"You're really going, then?"

"I am," Bessie said firmly, hoping to convince herself as well as Doona.

Doona sighed. "When?"

"I'm not sure. I'll have to get a truck booked, I suppose."

"Let's have dinner tonight and talk it all through," Doona suggested. "My treat, wherever you like."

They agreed on *La Terrazza*, which was Bessie's favourite. "I'll meet you there," Bessie told her friend. "I can walk or grab a taxi. You don't need to come for me."

With dinner plans sorted, Bessie headed back up the stairs. A few minutes later she was certain that there was nothing in the spare bedroom that needed to go to Douglas with her.

I should just give the entire room to a charity shop, Bessie thought to herself as she headed into her own bedroom. Or maybe a museum, she sighed.

After spending most of the day pottering around doing nothing much, Bessie decided to walk to the restaurant. She left early to allow herself plenty of time to get there and walked at a leisurely pace, stopping to chat with friends and acquaintances as she passed them along the way. It seemed as if everyone in Laxey was outside, enjoying the sunshine, as she made her way towards *La Terrazza*.

Doona was just pulling into the car park when Bessie arrived, and Bessie greeted her with a quick hug when she emerged from her car.

"I feel as if I haven't seen you in ages," Doona said. "I made a booking and requested a quiet corner so we can catch up."

The pair were well-known in the small restaurant and even

though there were many people waiting for tables, the host was quick to show them to a small table in the back corner of the room.

"Andy's still making our puddings," he told them as they took their seats. "But only for a few more weeks. He's off to culinary school across before the first of September."

"We must save room for it, then," Bessie said with a smile. Andy Caine, Anne's son, had been the primary beneficiary of the family's recent good fortune. Bessie knew he was planning on taking a two-year course that covered everything from cooking and baking to restaurant management and taxes. If everything went to plan, he was hoping to open his own restaurant on the island when he finished the course.

With drinks and food ordered, Bessie sat back and smiled at her friend.

"I'm going to miss seeing you regularly," she said with a small sigh.

"Tell me what's going on," Doona suggested.

Bessie brought her friend up to date, first explaining about the flat rental and then telling her about Bahey's newest revelations.

"It all sounds odd to me," Doona said when she'd finished. "Maybe Bahey is imagining things."

"Maybe, or maybe there are perfectly logical explanations for everything that feels slightly odd." Bessie shrugged. "Whatever, Bahey is getting herself all upset about it. I'm hoping I can figure enough out to help put her mind at rest. She loves her little flat and I would hate for her to move just because of a few odd experiences."

"I think moving is a pretty big thing to do, just to set a friend's mind at ease," Doona said.

Bessie shook her head. "I'm not really moving," she replied. "I'm just going to stay in Douglas for a while. It's more like an extended holiday."

"Where you take all your furniture with you," Doona said dryly.

"Oh, I'm not taking my furniture," Bessie said, chuckling as Doona gave her a confused look. "I was planning on going shopping for some inexpensive new pieces, just for the flat, but I think I'm going to borrow at least some of what I need from Mary

Quayle."

"Mary Quayle lends furniture?" Doona asked, looking even more befuddled.

Bessie smiled. "Apparently George likes to redecorate quite frequently and when he does, Mary puts all of the old furniture and things into storage. She said she can't bear to get rid of things that often aren't particularly old and haven't been much used."

"I want to be that rich," Doona said with a sigh. "Imagine redecorating whenever you feel like it. I had to save up for a year to replace my three-piece suite."

Bessie laughed. "As some of my furniture pieces are considerably older than you, I quite agree. Although if I were that rich, redecorating would come well below some other things."

"Like what?" Doona demanded.

"The first thing I would do is build an extension for a massive library," Bessie told her. "And then I'd fill the shelves with books on every subject imaginable. Whatever I felt in the mood for, I'd have a whole shelf of books about it. I'd add a few incredibly comfortable chairs and a fireplace and I'd probably never leave the room."

Doona laughed. "That sounds lovely, and just like you," she said. "I do enjoy a good book, but I'd rather have a fancy bathroom, with a huge tub with jets and whatnot and a big built-in vanity where I could fix my hair and makeup."

"Perhaps we should both be playing the lottery," Bessie teased.

"I do," Doona told her. "I won ten pounds last week."

They both laughed. "Well, that might pay for a few tiles for your dream bathroom," Bessie suggested. "You should put your winnings away and try to add to them every chance you get."

"Too late," Doona replied. "I treated myself to a box of champagne truffles and ate them in the tub last night."

"Well, at least you got some pleasure from the windfall," Bessie said.

The food was as delicious as ever and both women thoroughly enjoyed every bite. Dessert was sticky toffee pudding with cream for Bessie, while Doona had a mini Bakewell tart.

"I don't know why Andy's going away to school," Doona said as she scraped the last crumbs from her plate. "He's already a genius with puddings."

"But I need to learn how to make more than just sweets if I'm going to have my own restaurant someday," the man himself said. Neither woman had noticed his approach, but now Bessie stood up to give him a hug.

The handsome young man hugged Bessie back tightly. "I hope you enjoyed your meal," he said after he let her go.

"It was delicious as always," Bessie assured him.

The trio chatted for a just a minute before Andy had to get back to the kitchen.

"It's always such a pleasure to see him," Bessie said after he'd gone. "I'm going to miss him when he's across."

"And when you're in Douglas," Doona pointed out.

Bessie frowned. "Yes, of course," she muttered.

Doona insisted on driving Bessie home, even though it wasn't dark yet. "Let's sit on the rock and chat," she suggested when she'd parked.

It seemed a good idea, but the beach was rather crowded with families from the area as well as the people staying in the holiday cottages. Bessie and Doona perched on the large rock and stared down the beach.

"Is it always this loud?" Doona asked after a moment.

Bessie nodded. Several teenagers were playing music on large radios and they seemed to be having a contest to see who could get their machine to play the loudest. Large family groups were having picnics and playing games and seemed to cover nearly every inch of the sand in front of the rental cottages. Several games involving balls and flying discs were taking place, and more than one such object flew past Bessie and Doona as they watched the chaos.

"It can get pretty loud," Bessie replied as a very tall teenaged boy dashed past them to retrieve a ball. He shouted back at his friends as he threw it in their direction.

"Maybe a month in Douglas isn't such a bad idea," Doona said a moment later, after they were both forced to duck when a flying disc whizzed past their heads.

"It's sounding better all the time," Bessie replied as a large and grumpy-looking woman stomped over and retrieved her disc. She gave Bessie and Doona a dirty look as she splashed past them on her way back to her family.

"I guess I should have tried to catch it and throw it back to her," Doona said, shaking her head.

"She needed the exercise," Bessie whispered in reply.

"This isn't any fun," Doona said a moment later, as a group of small children began a game of tip all along the beach around them.

"Let's go inside," Bessie suggested, climbing carefully down from her seat. The pair walked quickly up the beach, trying to stay out of the way of the game.

"Okay, I think I'm beginning to see the appeal of the Douglas flat," Doona said with a laugh as she sank into a chair at the table in Bessie's kitchen.

"I am rather beginning to think of it as a holiday," Bessie told her. "You know my life has been quite stressful lately. I think I need a holiday."

"I'm not going to disagree with that; it's the strange happenings that are worrying me," Doona replied. "I still think Bahey should be talking to the police."

"Maybe," Bessie said. "But it won't hurt for me to have a little poke around. I won't do anything stupid, just talk to the neighbours and maybe the building manager. If I start to suspect that there really is something wrong, I'll ring the police right away."

"I want you to ring me every night," Doona said sternly. "I want daily updates."

"I think I can manage that," Bessie said. "Although I hate when you fuss."

"I'm not fussing," Doona told her. "I'm just keeping an eye on you."

And there's another advantage to the temporary move, Bessie thought. She knew Doona meant well, but her friend had a tendency to treat her like a small child at times.

After Doona left, Bessie got ready for bed slowly. The beach was still noisy, as childish shouts were slowly replaced with more adult party sounds. She settled into bed with a book and read until she felt tired enough to sleep regardless of noise. After a restless few minutes, she slept well.

Tuesday morning was sunny and bright and Bessie enjoyed her morning walk on the beach. The only sour note was the pile of discarded drinks cans and crisp packets and the like that were scattered behind a few of the cottages. Seagulls were diving on and off the sand, chasing down the crumbs that remained in the waste. Surely people ought to know better than to leave such a mess, she thought to herself as she walked.

When she got home, she made a quick call to Thomas Shimmin.

"I know it isn't your fault," she told him. "But the beach is covered in rubbish and the gulls are dragging it everywhere. I don't know what you can do about it, but I thought you should know."

"I'll be right over," he assured her. "I have a very strict clause in my rental agreements about rubbish on the beach. I'll do a spot inspection and fine anyone who has left a mess, as well as get them to clear it up."

"I hope they won't think I put you up to it," Bessie said worriedly.

"No worries about that," he replied. "I'll tell them the Laxey Commissioners have complained. They won't have any idea what that means."

Bessie laughed and hung up feeling better. Thomas was a good man and if she ever did decide to sell her cottage, she would give him first refusal. Bessie stayed off the beach for the rest of the morning, concentrating on clearing up a bit of research work that she'd been neglecting. By midday, when she sat down for lunch, the beach was spotless. Mary knocked on her door just as she was finishing the washing up.

"Bessie, how wonderful to see you again," Mary gushed after she'd given Bessie a hug. "I can't tell you how happy I am that you might be willing to take some of my furniture for me."

"I'm not sure about that," Bessie said cautiously. "You should let me pay rent for it or something."

Mary laughed. "I wouldn't have the first idea what to charge you, and anyway, I certainly don't need the money. Honestly, it's such a small favour as far as I'm concerned; you really mustn't worry about it."

"Maybe you won't have anything appropriate, anyway," Bessie said.

"Wait until you see what I have," Mary said with a smile. "I probably have more than most small furniture stores. You'll be hard pressed to convince me that none of it will work."

"The flat isn't very large," Bessie said. "I won't need much and I guess small pieces would be best."

"George has given me the specifications for the flat," Mary told her, patting her handbag. "I have a tape measure as well, so we can measure everything and be certain it will fit."

"You're very efficient," Bessie said admiringly.

"I do this with the children all the time," Mary explained. "Georgie and Diane like to change their house around almost as much as George does. And I've already told you that Elizabeth changes her suite almost monthly. It will be so nice to think of someone using the furniture who might actually appreciate it. The children are too spoiled."

"But how nice for them to not have to worry about buying expensive furniture pieces when they need them," Bessie commented.

"I'm sure it is," Mary replied. "But it also means they don't understand the value of such things, either." Mary sighed. "But today isn't about complaining about my children. Are you ready to go?"

"Let me just grab my handbag," Bessie replied. She stuck her head in the small downstairs loo and checked her hair. It looked fine, but she added a quick coat of lipstick to her lips before grabbing her bag and rejoining Mary.

"All set," she said.

Mary was driving a large luxury vehicle and Bessie felt rather lost in the huge bucket-style leather seats.

"My goodness, I think this is the most comfortable car I've

ever sat inside," she told her friend.

"It is rather nice," Mary said absently. She pulled away from Bessie's cottage and headed north.

"I never did ask where you store all of your furniture," Bessie said.

"There's a huge facility in Jurby that we use," Mary replied. "We started with two units and we now have an entire row of six. I told George we aren't renting any more. We'll have to start selling or donating some of our things once we fill up the last unit."

Mary took the coast road into Ramsey while the two chatted about Mary's grandchildren. From there, she headed west across the island and Bessie enjoyed looking at the farmlands and wetlands as a change of scenery.

"I don't know why there aren't more direct routes to places on the island," Mary said as they followed a particularly circuitous road through the countryside.

"I suspect if someone set out to build the roads today, they'd do them very differently, but many of these roads were originally nothing more than paths through the country. In those days no one could have imagined the motor car, let alone planned for it."

Mary laughed. "I shouldn't be impatient, I should be enjoying the scenery."

"And watching for wallabies," Bessie suggested.

"Pardon?"

"Wallabies," Bessie repeated. "There's a small but thriving population of wild wallabies in this part of the island. Apparently a breeding pair escaped from the wildlife park and they and their descendants have been living out here ever since."

"When did they escape?"

"Sometime around nineteen-seventy," Bessie replied.

Mary laughed. "I was expecting you to say something considerably more recent. I guess the park has stopped trying to catch them, then."

"I guess so," Bessie said. "Last I heard they estimated the population as somewhere around a hundred animals. As far as I know, there aren't any plans to try to round them up."

"Now I feel sorry for the ones in the park itself," Mary said. "I took my oldest grandson to see them the other day, but I didn't realise they had wild relatives so nearby. I'd love to see them."

"I gather they're nocturnal," Bessie told her. "I don't know many people who have actually seen them in wild."

"It's still quite amazing," Mary replied. "It makes me happy for some strange reason."

Bessie smiled. "I'm awfully glad I told you, then."

A few minutes later they turned down a long and narrow road. As the land was very flat, Bessie felt as if she could see for miles. There seemed to be nothing around anywhere. In the far distance, she could just make out several large single-storey buildings. As they got closer, she saw that each larger building was divided into several smaller, numbered sections. Each section had its own garage-style door.

"Ah, good, Jack's already here," Mary said as she pulled up in front of one of the buildings. Bessie looked at the large truck labeled "Island Movers" and swallowed hard. Maybe she was moving sooner than she realised.

CHAPTER EIGHT

Bessie followed Mary out of the car. "I didn't even know this was here," she told the other woman.

"It's fairly new, but as everyone in the world tries to accumulate as much as they can, such facilities will be probably start popping up everywhere."

Bessie nodded. Having "things" seemed to be the trend at the moment, even if the "things" in question were fairly useless or did nothing different from some other things you already had. That was quite different to having lots of books, of course there was absolutely nothing wrong with having lots of books.

"Let's just start in here and work our way down the row," Mary suggested, waving towards the first door. "I wish I could say that the units are organised in some way, but they aren't, and I can't for the life of me remember what's in any of them."

Mary pulled out a ring of keys and flipped through them. Bessie could see that they were all marked. She joined Mary in front of the first door.

"Ah, here we are," Mary said, holding up a key. She inserted the key into the padlock on the door and unlocked it. One of the men from the moving truck quickly came forward and slid the overhead door up for them. A light flickered on inside the unit and Bessie nearly took a step backwards as she tried to take in the vast quantity of furniture that was crammed into the small space.

"There is rather a lot," Mary said, her tone apologetic.

Bessie shook her head. "Most of these pieces look like antiques," she said. "I can't possibly borrow anything this valuable."

Mary stepped forward and then wandered back and forth, looking into the room. "I think this is all the furniture from George's mum's place," she said eventually. "That would make sense, since we moved back over here to look after her when she was, well, rather ill. We stayed with her for a short while, and then, when she passed away, we bought our house. George didn't want to use any of this furniture in our new place, so we put it all in storage."

"I see. Well, it simply wouldn't do for me to borrow it then, would it?" Bessie asked.

Mary shrugged. "You're more than welcome to it," she said. "Especially that armoire at the back. I really hate that armoire."

Bessie looked at the piece and laughed. "It is somewhat, well, ornate," she said. "I'd rather not borrow it, thanks anyway."

Mary nodded. "I keep trying to get one of the boys to take it. I keep hoping that their kids will destroy it. It was one of George's mum's favourite pieces, of course, so we can't just get rid of it."

Bessie looked again at the overly decorated piece. "It really isn't to my taste," she told Mary.

"That's because you have taste," Mary replied with a laugh. "Let's move on; there will be more suitable things here somewhere."

An hour later, Bessie was exhausted, but it seemed like Mary was just getting started. They had made it as far as the fourth unit and Mary plunged inside while Bessie looked hopelessly at the two moving men.

"You must be bored paralytic," she remarked.

"I never complain about getting paid to stand around," one of them told Bessie.

Bessie flushed. She hadn't even thought about it, but of course they were getting paid, and since Bessie was the one moving, she would be the one paying their bill. She strode purposefully into the unit, determined to find what she needed and put the men to work.

"Here, Bessie, what about this?" Mary called from the back of the room.

Bessie carefully picked her way through the packed piles of furniture and boxes until she found her friend.

Mary was standing in front of a three-piece suite in a sandy brown colour that Bessie instantly loved.

"Sit down and see how it feels," Mary suggested.

Bessie sank down on the sofa and sighed. It was even more comfortable than it looked. "It's wonderful," she said.

"I remember it being rather nice," Mary said. "We had it in the little sitting room off the master bedroom suite. I can't think why we got rid of it. It must have been when we had the new carpets laid. George insisted we replace all of the furniture when the new carpets were put in."

"I can't imagine getting rid of this lovely couch," Bessie told her.

"There are matching tables and lamps," Mary said. "I'll have them load up the lot."

"Are you sure?" Bessie asked. The reality of the situation seemed to hit her suddenly and she felt very nervous about borrowing all of the beautiful and undoubtedly expensive furniture.

"You're doing me a favour," Mary insisted. "I hate the thought of it all just sitting here going to waste. If you do decide to buy the flat, you can purchase it from us or I'll take it all back, whatever you like, but for now, while you're just renting, there's no point in buying lots of furniture, is there?"

"If I do decide to buy it, I'll have to move my furniture from the cottage there," Bessie told her.

"Oh, I guess I thought you'd keep the cottage anyway," Mary said.

Bessie smiled. "I can't pay for the flat if I don't sell the cottage," she pointed out gently.

"Oh, of course," Mary said, her cheeks turning pink. "I don't know what I was thinking."

For a moment Bessie wondered how it would feel to be rich enough to have storage units full of furniture and the ability to buy a spare flat or two just because you wanted them. She shook her head. She wasn't rich, but she was definitely comfortable and from everything she'd seen in life, extra money brought a lot of extra troubles.

She and Mary made their way out of the unit and the two movers headed in. While they carefully loaded the suite, with its matching tables and lamps, onto their truck, Mary and Bessie moved on to the next unit.

There, Mary found a small bedroom set that was perfect for the cosy bedroom in the flat. "There's a bed frame, two chests of drawers, a bedside table and a wardrobe," Mary showed Bessie. "What do you think?"

"I think it's perfect," Bessie said, admiring the solid oak furniture. "I just hope there's room for it all."

Mary took out her measuring tape and measured the pieces, making careful notes. Then she pulled out the specifications for the flat. On a piece of scrap paper, she quickly sketched the room with the furniture in two different arrangements.

"It would all fit if you arranged it either of these ways," she told Bessie, showing her the drawings. "Or you could do something else altogether."

"You're very good at this," Bessie said. "I think that's perfect." She pointed to one of the sketches, which seemed to best suit the room's layout.

"That would be my choice," Mary agreed. "You'll get the best light from the window if you do it that way."

The movers had joined them and now Mary pointed out which pieces to take, giving one of the men her sketch. "This is how it should be arranged in the flat," she told him.

"Yes, ma'am," he said.

Bessie and Mary moved out of the way while the two men got to work.

"That isn't a bad dining table," Mary said, pointing to a small table near the door. "It has four chairs that match. I think it used to be in one of the children's rooms, although it is full-sized."

"It looks just right," Bessie agreed. She couldn't help but feel as if she should have simply stayed at home and let Mary furnish the flat for her. Not only did Mary have wonderful taste, Bessie didn't feel as if she should argue since Mary was doing her such a large favour in lending her the pieces in the first place.

The dining table and chairs quickly joined the rest of the choices on the truck.

"Is that it?" Bessie asked, feeling as if they'd been there for many hours.

"What about kitchen things?" Mary asked. "I have boxes and boxes full of plates and glasses and flatware. You're welcome to whatever you'd like."

"I was simply planning on taking my everyday plates and glasses and whatnot," Bessie replied. "They'll only fill a couple of boxes."

"I suppose," Mary said. "Although I do have a set of plates that I'd love to lend to you. I'd consider it an enormous favour if you could manage to break every single plate, cup and saucer in the set."

Bessie laughed. "Let me guess, you inherited them from your mother-in-law."

"Exactly," Mary laughed. "And they're absolutely ghastly."

"Then I definitely don't want them," Bessie said firmly.

Mary sighed. "Oh, well, I tried."

With the last of the furniture loaded up into the moving truck, Bessie and Mary climbed back into Mary's car.

"We can follow them into Douglas and make sure they put everything in the right place," Mary suggested. "And then I'll buy you dinner to celebrate."

"I think I should buy you dinner," Bessie objected. "I can't imagine how much it would have cost to purchase all of that furniture. And the pieces you're lending me are so much nicer than what I would have bought, as well."

"It's nothing," Mary said, waving a hand. "I'm glad to help, really I am."

Even though Bessie knew that Mary was sincere, she still felt a bit guilty. "At least let me buy dinner," she repeated herself.

"If you insist," Mary said with a laugh. "Maybe I'll have someone drive us and then we can have a bottle of wine or two as well."

"That sounds perfect," Bessie told her friend.

The moving van pulled away and Mary followed them. They drove back across the island to Ramsey and then headed across the mountain road into Douglas.

"I never get tired of the scenery," Mary told Bessie as they turned the last corner on the mountain road and Douglas lay before them.

"Me either," Bessie replied. "I don't come over the mountain all that often, but whenever I do, I try to memorise the views."

Mary laughed. "I do that," she said. "But they're ever so much more spectacular in real life than in my memory."

"Especially when the sun is shining," Bessie added.

The two movers had made better time than Mary and they were already unloading the furniture when Mary and Bessie arrived at Seaview Terrace. Mary pulled into the building's small car park and she and Bessie made their way inside through a door that was again propped open, presumably this time by the movers.

"Ah, Mrs. Quayle, what a pleasant surprise." The building manager jumped up from his seat and rushed towards them. Bessie took a step backwards as the man approached.

Mary smiled tightly. "Mr. Green, how nice to see you again. You've met Bessie Cubbon, haven't you?"

"Oh, aye, well, just a bit, when she came to look around, you see," he said, thrusting his not entirely clean hand at Bessie. Bessie shook it reluctantly.

"I didn't know she was a friend of yours, though, or I'd have made sure she got the VIP treatment, you know?" he continued.

"I should have thought all potential purchasers would get the VIP treatment," Mary said coolly. "Regardless of who they know."

"Well, yeah," the man said quickly, his face flushing. "I mean, well, what I meant was, I'd have given your friend the extra special VIP treatment, like."

Mary nodded. "Well, I expect nothing less while she's staying here," she told the man. "I assume you've given the movers the keys to the flat?"

"Yes, ma'am," he said.

"We'll just go up and see how they're getting on, then." Mary turned and walked down the short corridor to the lift, with Bessie on her heels.

Inside the lift, Mary blew out a long breath. "What a disagreeable little man," she said. "I'm sure I don't know why Grant hired him."

"He seemed eager to please," Bessie replied.

"Because of who I am," Mary said, "or rather, who I'm married to. I think you'll get treated well because of your connection to George. I'd love to hear how he treats the other residents, though."

"I'll let you know," Bessie promised.

The lift was slow, but seemed to be working properly. The door to number ten was open and Bessie could hear the movers inside the flat. She peeked inside and smiled. The movers had already arranged all of the furniture in the large main room, and thanks to the new coat of paint that was a slightly less boring shade of beige, and the gorgeous furniture, the flat looked comfortable and cosy.

"Oh, Bessie, it's adorable," Mary said with a smile.

"It does look rather charming," Bessie agreed. She peeked into the bedroom, where the movers were assembling the bedframe. "I think I'll be quite comfortable here, really."

"I do hope so," Mary said. "I'm actually feeling a bit jealous. Maybe I need a little flat of my own where I can get away from everyone."

"Surely, in a house as large as yours, you have lots of places you can go to get away?"

"You'd think so, wouldn't you?" Mary asked with a wry grin. "But George always finds me, or one of the staff does. Someone always needs something. A flat of my own would be ideal."

"If I decide I don't like it, you should buy it," Bessie suggested, only half-joking.

Mary looked thoughtful for a moment and then laughed. "What a silly idea," she said.

"So, you're the new neighbour, then?" a voice came from

behind the women. Bessie turned around and smiled brightly at the man in the doorway.

"I'm Elizabeth Cubbon," she said, walking towards him. "Everyone calls me Bessie."

"Hi, Bessie," he said with a wink. "I'm Bertie Ayers. I'm right across the hall."

Bessie offered her hand and studied the man while he shook it. He was just about her height, although she imagined he had been taller in his youth. He had a few stray grey hairs sticking out in all directions on his head, but not enough to trouble anyone. His brown eyes were all but hidden behind thick glasses that had a hearing aid attached on each side. While his clothes didn't look expensive, they were clean and had obviously been ironed as well.

"I'm a bachelor," Bertie announced. "I'm going to be seventy-three in a few months and I'm not looking for a girlfriend."

Bessie laughed. "I've never married, either, my age is none of your business and I'm not looking for a boyfriend."

Bertie laughed until he began to wheeze. "Sorry," he said when he'd caught his breath. "I was a smoker back when we didn't know any better. Anyway, it's a real pleasure to meet you, Bessie. I like a woman who tells it like it is. Are you moving in today, then?"

"No, probably not for a few days," Bessie replied. "I'm having a housewarming on Saturday afternoon, though, so make sure you plan to stop in."

"There's nothing on the telly on a Saturday afternoon," Bertie said. "So I'll probably be able to make it."

"What are the other neighbours like?" Bessie asked. "I do know Bahey in number eleven and Howard in number twelve."

"I like Bahey a lot," the man confided. "If Howard hadn't seen her first, I might have had to change my mind about the girlfriend thing."

"Does that mean you don't like Howard?" Bessie had to ask.

"Oh, no, he's an okay chap," Bertie said. "I've no complaints against him. That just leaves Ruth and Muriel on this floor. They're both okay, too."

"Just okay?" Bessie pressed him.

"They both seem to think I need a girlfriend," Bertie said. He leaned in towards Bessie. "If I do, it wouldn't be either of them," he whispered. "But you'll get to meet them all soon enough, I reckon. They'll both be over to check out the competition."

"Competition? For what?" Bessie asked.

Bertie laughed. "Well, Howard's pretty well taken, I guess, but I'm single and so is Simon, although I suspect he might be more interested in me than you, if you catch my drift."

Bessie nodded.

"Anyway, the big prize at the moment seems to be our friend Mr. Green. All the ladies in the building seem to be chasing after him."

"Mr. Green? The building manager?" Bessie asked, stunned.

"Yeah, that's the bloke. And don't ask me what they see in him, I'm just telling you what I've seen. Anyway, I have to go. It's time for my next programme."

He was gone before Bessie could press him for more information. She turned to Mary. "Why on earth would anyone chase after the building manager?" she asked.

"I've no idea," Mary replied with a shrug. "Maybe our Mr. Ayers is just a touch confused."

"Maybe," Bessie replied, thoughtfully.

The movers soon had the bedroom finished and Bessie was delighted with the end result. The small room felt almost as cosy as her bedroom at home.

"I'll need a mattress, of course, and bedding," Bessie said.

"Oh, I have...." Mary began, but Bessie held up a hand.

"You've already done far too much," Bessie said firmly. "I'll buy a mattress and bedding and whatever else I need."

Mary opened her mouth to object, but Bessie gave her a stern look. "Okay," Mary said. "Would you like to go shopping for those things now?"

Bessie glanced at her watch. They had just about enough time to pick up a few things before dinner. "If you have the time," she said, hesitantly.

"Of course I do," Mary told her.

Half an hour later, at a small shop nearby, Bessie had everything she needed picked out and paid for.

"We'll get it all delivered tomorrow," the shop assistant promised as Bessie handed over her credit card.

"Well, I'd call that a good day's work," Mary said as the pair headed back to Mary's car. "Let's stop at my house and see if we can get someone to drive us to dinner."

"Perfect," Bessie said with a satisfied smile. Her little flat was now furnished and almost ready for her and she was really starting to look forward to moving in.

Bessie caught her breath as Mary turned up the drive to her mansion. No matter how many times Bessie saw the place, she was always surprised by the sheer size of it. Now she tried to see it through Mary's eyes, as home, but it simply wasn't possible. There was nothing about the sprawling mansion that seemed "homely" to Bessie.

"I'll just be a minute," Mary told Bessie as she led her into the enormous foyer of her home. "Do you want to wait in the library?"

"I'd love to," Bessie replied. The library was the only part of the house that made Bessie feel the tiniest bit jealous. The large room had bookshelves from floor to ceiling on three walls. The fourth wall was nearly all windows, so that if you looked up from your book you could spend some time admiring the incredible sea views. Bessie sank down into one of the comfortable leather chairs that were dotted around the room. The tables on either side of it had neat piles of books on them, and Bessie happily amused herself by flipping through them, reading back covers and scanning first pages.

"Ah, Bessie, Mary told me you were in here," George's voice boomed from the doorway. "I thought I ought to entertain you while you wait for her to get ready."

Bessie bit back a sigh. The last thing she needed in a library like this was anyone to "entertain" her. "Hello, George," she said politely. "Thank you so much for arranging the Seaview Terrace rental for me. I'm looking forward to the change of scenery."

"Ah, yes, well, it wasn't any problem at all," George replied. "It's just sitting there empty, after all."

"Well, I'm very grateful," Bessie said.

"I do hope you're joining us on Friday?" George changed the subject abruptly. "Grant is looking forward to having a chance to get to know you a bit better."

"I am planning on coming," Bessie said. "And I'd love the chance to thank Mr. Robertson as well."

George nodded. "Well, I suppose I'll see you then," he said, looking as if his mind was elsewhere. "What are you and Mary doing tonight, then?"

"I'm taking her to dinner to thank her for loaning me some furniture for the flat," Bessie explained.

"Oh, are you making use of some of our things?" George asked. "That's good of you. And I'm ever so glad you and Mary are friends. She needs more friends."

"I do hope you weren't planning on having dinner with her yourself," Bessie said, feeling awkward. "I mean, you're more than welcome to join us, of course."

George shook his head. "Oh, no, I'm having dinner with Grant. We have a lot of business to discuss. No, if my dear wife were staying at home tonight she'd be having a quiet dinner on her own. I'm afraid I often have dinner meetings."

"Mary said you had lunch with Mack Dickson the day of his talk," Bessie said, hoping she didn't sound too interested in George's reply. Having heard the Mack was blackmailing the man, she was very curious as to what he'd say.

George narrowed his eyes. "Did I?" he asked. Bessie fancied he sounded nervous. "Oh, yes, well, Grant and I did, I think." He cleared his throat. "I'd quite forgotten about that afternoon. Well, not what happened later, of course, but the luncheon, I'd quite forgotten about that."

"I hope you had an interesting conversation with him," Bessie remarked.

"Oh, yes, it was quite interesting," George replied. "If I remember correctly, Mack was advising a young man at some university who was working on a history of banking. He wanted to find out about the early days of the Manx National Bank and Mack was hoping to get him an interview with Grant."

"Oh dear, I hope Mack's death didn't upset the young man's plans."

George shook his head. "I've no idea if Grant ever followed through or not. I should ask him later."

"Ah, Bessie, I do hope my husband hasn't spoiled your enjoyment of the library," Mary said as she walked into the room.

Bessie smiled at her. "We're having a lovely visit," she told her friend with a wink.

Mary laughed and gave George an affectionate pat on the shoulder. "I told you to just let Bessie enjoy the books," she chided him gently.

"But I wanted to say hello," George protested. "And I didn't want her to get bored."

Mary laughed again, but shook her head. "Of course, dear," she said gently. "Are you ready for some dinner, then?" she asked as she turned to Bessie.

"I'm afraid I'm underdressed," Bessie replied.

Mary had changed into a lightweight summer suit in a soft pastel pink. Mary's shoes and handbag matched exactly and Bessie guessed that the outfit probably cost more than she spent on clothes in a year.

"You look lovely," Mary said with a wave of her hand. "I'm just using tonight as an excuse to fuss a little bit. I rarely go out in the evening."

Bessie stood up and tried to smooth out the wrinkles in her shirt. "Maybe I should at least run a brush through my hair," she suggested.

"Only if you want to," Mary said. She showed Bessie to a loo across the hall.

Bessie shut the door and stood still in the middle of the room for a moment. The loo was larger than Bessie's sitting room and Bessie couldn't help but wonder why it needed to be so large. She dug around in her handbag, pulling out a comb and a lipstick. She did the best she could with her appearance, feeling somewhat intimidated by the enormous and ornate mirror that reflected her image. After another attempt to mitigate a few of the wrinkles in her outfit, Bessie gave up and rejoined her friend.

"I look a mess next to you," she remarked as she followed Mary back towards the front door.

"I look stiff and stuffy next to you," Mary countered. "Let's just go and have fun and not worry about it."

Bessie laughed. "You are a very wise woman," she told her friend.

"Where should we go?" Mary asked as the two women settled into the back of one of Mary's luxury cars.

Bessie named one of her favourite Douglas restaurants.

"Oh, that's rather expensive," Mary said. "Are you sure I can't treat?"

"I'm very sure," Bessie said firmly. "Tonight is my treat, and you can choose the restaurant, if you don't like my suggestion."

"Oh, I'm happy anywhere," Mary assured her. She leaned forward and told the driver their destination. The car moved quickly and quietly through the streets of Douglas.

"I'll ring you when we're ready to be collected," Mary told the driver as he helped them from the car.

"Yes, ma'am," he replied, nodding at Bessie before he climbed back behind the wheel.

Inside the restaurant, the host was quick to find them a quiet table.

"Ah, Mrs. Quayle, what an enormous pleasure and surprise it is to see you," he said, fawningly.

Within moments their waiter was ready to take their drinks order and Mary was quick to order a bottle of wine.

"I never get service like this," Bessie whispered to her as the waiter rushed away to get the wine.

"I always do," Mary said with a sigh. "It's quite tiresome."

Bessie laughed. "It seems quite delightful," she disagreed.

Mary shrugged. Before she could reply, the waiter was back with the wine. Once he'd poured them each a glass, he recited the specials.

"We'll need a moment with the menu," Bessie said.

"Just wave when you're ready," he replied.

After a quick discussion of the specials, the two women made their selections. Bessie set her menu down and looked around.

Their waiter rushed over before she'd even managed to catch his eye. Once the food was ordered, Bessie turned to Mary and shook her head.

"I'm beginning to see your point," she told her friend.

The wine was excellent and the food arrived quickly and was perfectly prepared and presented. One bottle of wine turned into two as Bessie and Mary enjoyed talking about anything and everything together.

"Crème brulee," Mary announced as the waiter cleared her plate. "I absolutely need crème brulee."

"Oh, me too," Bessie said. "That's sounds just perfect."

"What's it like living on your own?" Mary asked Bessie as they waited.

"I'm not sure I know how to answer that," Bessie replied. "Especially since I've had a great deal of wine."

Mary laughed. "When I drink I start to wonder why I married George," she told Bessie in a whisper. "Sometimes I think living all alone must be wonderful. I'm quite jealous of your little flat."

"But you love George," Bessie objected.

"Yes," Mary said slowly. "I suppose I do."

Bessie wasn't sure how to respond to that. She didn't want to encourage Mary to tell her things she might regret talking about later.

"I lived with my parents until I married George," Mary said now. "And once we were married, we had Georgie six months later. After the children came the staff, as well. The more money George made, the more staff he wanted around. I'm afraid I've quite forgotten how to cook or clean or iron."

"You're welcome to come and clean my cottage any time you like," Bessie offered with a laugh.

"To be honest, I'm not very good at it," Mary confided. "My parents had staff as well. When George and I were first married, we could only afford part-time help and I had to do some bits and pieces, but that didn't last long. And once the children started coming, I didn't have time to do anything but look after them, anyway."

"I suppose it's lucky George was so successful, then," Bessie suggested.

"Yes, well, some of the money is mine," Mary said. "But then George only married me for my money."

Bessie gasped. "You don't mean that," she said.

Mary shrugged. "It's probably the wine talking," she admitted. "But I do wonder. We're nothing alike, George and I, and I can't imagine why he married me sometimes."

"Opposites attract," Bessie put forward.

"I was so madly in love that I never thought about it," Mary confided. "He completely swept me off my feet. He was so charming and smart and funny, and I was overwhelmed. I was deliriously happy in those early days."

"I'm told that sort of love never lasts," Bessie said cautiously.

"No, I suppose it can't," Mary said. "But we were always very happy, anyway."

"And you still are," Bessie said, anticipating the reply she would get.

"Yes, well, I don't know about that," Mary said.

"Mary, I'm happy to listen to anything you want to tell me, but I'm not sure I'm the right person to talk to about this. Maybe you should talk to one of your friends who's married herself."

Mary shook her head. "You're the perfect person for me to talk to," she told Bessie. "Because you have a totally different and unique perspective on things. And because I know you won't repeat anything I say."

"That's true," Bessie acknowledged.

"Anyway, I'm not telling you anything I haven't told George a dozen times this week. We're drifting apart and it bothers me. The last year has been, well, difficult for me and for us as a couple, but George doesn't seem to notice or mind."

"So you've only been having problems since you moved to the island?" Bessie asked.

Mary shrugged. "We weren't as close as I might have liked before, but it's much worse now. George is working at least as much as he did before he 'retired' and he's spending a lot of time with Grant Robertson, even though he knows I don't like the man."

"You said they're old friends, right?"

"Yes, from before George moved to the UK. Although I don't know how close they were. I never met him before we moved here."

"Really?" Bessie asked. "Did they stay in touch over the years?"

"I have no idea," Mary said with a sigh. "George never mentioned him, but he was one of our first visitors when we moved back." She shrugged. "I just don't like him, but I pretend to for George's sake."

"That can't be easy," Bessie murmured.

"I'm looking forward to hearing what you think of him, after Friday," Mary continued. "I think you're a very astute judge of character."

Bessie shook her head. "I don't know about that," she said. "I've been introduced to him once or twice before. I'm certainly not looking forward to getting to know him better, after everything you've said."

"But it might just be me," Mary said. "He does take George away from me a great deal. Maybe I'm just jealous," Mary tried to laugh, but the sound was choked.

"I thought you moved back here so George could retire," Bessie said.

"So did I," Mary replied. "For the first few months, George only worked a few hours a week and we spent a lot of time together. He even started to show an interest in the grandchildren. Since then though, things keep cropping up. George calls them 'little projects,' and they seem to take more and more of his time. It seems like every time Grant visits, a new 'little project' is added to George's work load."

Bessie shook her head. "And you've told George how you feel?"

"I have," Mary said, draining her wine glass. "He keeps telling me to be patient, that he's just helping Grant out on a few things, but now he's gone and hired Michael to help him as well. I know Michael needed the work, but surely he could have gone to work for Grant, not George?"

Mary sighed. "I'm sorry, I didn't mean to complain all night," she said quietly.

"You haven't been complaining all night," Bessie said. "And even if you had been, that's what friends are for. I'm just sorry I can't help in any way."

"At least after Friday you can share you thoughts on Grant with me," Mary said, a forced smile on her lips. "I'm hoping you hate him."

"I'll hate him," Bessie told her. "Just for you."

Now Mary managed a genuine smile. "That's good of you," she replied. "But I don't think you'll have to do it for me. He's a really unlikable person."

"So why is George friends with him?"

"That's an excellent question," Mary said. "He's usually a better judge of character."

The conversation turned back to more general topics as they women finished the last of the second bottle of wine. Mary rang for their car as Bessie settled the bill.

"He's on his way," she told Bessie. "Maybe we should wait outside. I probably could use some fresh air."

Bessie nodded. "We did drink rather a lot of wine," she said. "Fresh air sounds wonderful."

The women made their way very carefully out of the restaurant. The evening was still warm and they enjoyed the short wait for the car. They chatted lightly about nothing as the driver made his way to Bessie's cottage.

"I had a wonderful time," Mary told Bessie as she walked her to her door.

"I did as well," Bessie replied. "Once I'm in Douglas, we'll have to do this more often."

"I'd really like that," Mary said with some intensity.

Inside her little cottage, Bessie quickly got ready for bed. With all of the borrowed furniture in place in her little flat in Douglas, all she needed to do was pack her clothes and her kitchen things and she could move in. She fell asleep thinking that there was no reason to delay. Tomorrow would be moving day.

CHAPTER NINE

When she woke up the next morning with only a slight headache, Bessie decided that she'd been right the night before. If she started finding excuses to delay the move, she would never actually do it. After a quick breakfast of cereal and tea, she took a short walk on the beach. It felt different today, knowing it would be her last walk on this particular beach for a while.

The holiday cottages were, for the most part, still quiet, but Bessie saw a few lights on in a few windows. A small child was drawing a picture on the wall in one cottage and Bessie could only hope that he wasn't using permanent markers. Thomas painted all of the flats every autumn, after the rental season; he wouldn't want to have to do it mid-season as well.

Once she'd reached the stairs to Thie yn Traie, she turned around. On her way home, she spotted Spencer on his patio and she gave him a friendly wave.

"Oh, Bessie, it's good to see you," he called across the sand.

Bessie stopped as he was walking towards her. "Good morning, Spencer," she said. "How are you this morning?"

"I'm wonderful," he replied with a bright smile. "I was offered the perfect job yesterday. Not only is it in my field, doing what I love, but they've offered to pay some of the cost of moving me back to the island, as well."

"Oh, Spencer, how wonderful," Bessie said, delighted for the man.

"And I have you to thank for it," Spencer continued. "One of the names you gave me, well, when I rang him, he gave me the lead on the job."

"I'm glad I could help," Bessie said.

"You were wonderful and I owe you a huge favour," Spencer said. "What can I do for you?"

Bessie laughed. "I can't imagine," she said.

"I can," Spencer grinned. "Do you need a ride anywhere today, for instance? I don't have any plans for the day and I have my car full of petrol and ready to go."

Bessie started to shake her head and then stopped. "I don't want to impose," she began.

"Oh, please, impose," Spencer said with a laugh. "I owe you a lot. Not only did you help me find the perfect job, but, well, I met someone special as well." He flushed and looked at the sand.

"Someone special? Do tell," Bessie said.

"When I went to the interview for this job, she was there. She was actually interviewing for a different job at the same company. We were both really early, and we started talking about how we both always feel like we need to be early for things. Anyway, after I had my interview, I waited for her to come out of hers and we got a coffee. Her name is Beverly and she's really sweet."

"How wonderful for you," Bessie said, feeling happy for Spencer and relieved for Doona. Bessie knew her friend had been feeling bad about dumping the extremely nice man, even though they weren't well suited.

"As it happens, she didn't get the job she interviewed for, but she was offered a different one elsewhere that she's really excited about. We're having dinner tonight to celebrate both of our new positions."

"It all sounds wonderful," Bessie replied.

"But that leaves me with my whole day free to help you with whatever errands you need to run," Spencer continued. "Where can I take you?"

Bessie hesitated for just a moment. "Would you like to move me to Douglas?" she asked.

Spencer quickly nodded. "I'm happy to do it, but I only have a sedan. I'm not sure how much furniture will fit in it."

Bessie laughed. "All of the furniture is already in Douglas," she assured the man. "I just need to move my clothes and my kitchen things. I can probably manage that in just a few boxes and a suitcase or two."

"In that case, we might be able to do it in one trip," Spencer said. "Are you ready now?"

"No, not yet," Bessie replied, feeling a strange mix of excitement and dread. "How about if you come over for lunch? I should be able to get everything packed by then and I'll make us a quick lunch from everything perishable in my refrigerator. Then we have the afternoon to move me, if that works for you."

"It's perfect," Spencer assured her. "Are you sure you don't want some help with packing?"

"I can manage," Bessie insisted. "I'll see you around midday."

Bessie walked back to her cottage with a bit more urgency in her step. There was no going back now; she was moving today, ready or not.

By the time Spencer arrived for lunch, Bessie had everything she wanted to take to Douglas packed up and ready to go.

"I hope sandwiches are okay for lunch," she told the man after she'd answered his knock. "And I hope paper plates are acceptable, as well. I've packed my everyday dishes."

Spencer laughed. "I live alone. Paper plates are about all I have."

Bessie pulled out all of the sandwich fixings, and the pair quickly put their lunches together. "Would you like tea or coffee?" Bessie offered.

"I'll just have something cold," Spencer replied. "You probably want to pack your kettle."

"I already did," Bessie admitted. "But I know exactly where it is. I could have grabbed it back out if you wanted a hot drink."

"With the temperatures where they are today, the last thing I want is a hot drink," Spencer said.

After lunch, where Bessie filled Spencer in on all of her plans, she quickly tidied her small kitchen. She tied up her rubbish bag and put it in the bin outside her back door.

"What day do the bin men come?" Spencer asked. "I'll pop over and put your bin out for you."

"Ah, thanks," Bessie replied. "But they'll grab it from behind the cottage. They always do."

Spencer loaded the boxes full of kitchenware into the boot of his car and then carefully added the two suitcases full of clothes as well. "Is that everything?" he asked.

Bessie frowned. "It doesn't seem like much," she said, with a bit of a catch in her voice.

"But it's only a holiday, right?" Spencer asked gently. "If you decide to move properly, you'll have ever so much more to take."

Bessie nodded. "I suppose so," she said.

"Shall we go, then?"

Bessie took a deep breath and then took a long look around her kitchen. She felt tears beginning to fill her eyes and shook her head. "This is silly," she said loudly. "I can come home any time I want."

"Of course you can," Spencer replied. "I'm not even clear on why you're going in the first place."

Bessie laughed. "Neither am I," she said after a moment. "But I must think of it as an adventure."

"Let's get the adventure started then, shall we?" Spencer held out an arm and Bessie took it with a shaky smile.

"Let's do that," she agreed.

Spencer chatted all the way to Douglas about all sorts of inconsequential nonsense. While the non-stop noise was irritating, Bessie was grateful that he didn't give her time to think about what she was undertaking. By the time he pulled up at Seaside Terrace, Bessie was focussed on helping Bahey and enjoying the change of scenery.

Spencer found a spot in the small car park and followed Bessie up to the building. She pushed the main doorbell and then pulled the door open when the lock release buzzed.

"Ah, Ms. Cubbon, so nice to see you again." The building manager jumped to his feet and rushed over to the door to greet Bessie obsequiously.

"It's good to be finally moving in," Bessie said with forced enthusiasm. "I'll just need my keys."

"Of course, of course," the man said, beaming at her. He went back behind his small table and dug around in a box on top of it. After a moment, he pulled out a small key ring.

"Here you are," he told Bessie, handing her the ring. "The large key is the front door to the flat. The slightly smaller one opens the front door to the building. The smallest key is the key to your postbox."

"Thank you," Bessie said politely. She turned and headed for the lift, with Spencer on her heels. It arrived quite quickly and seemed to working much more smoothly than it had been when she'd visited with Alan Collins.

"There was something about him I didn't like," Spencer told Bessie as they rode the lift up to the first floor.

"Can you be more specific?" Bessie asked.

Spencer shrugged. "Not really, just something bothered me for some reason. Maybe it was the ill-fitting suit or the greasy hair. Maybe it was because he smelled like cheap cologne. I just wouldn't trust him if I couldn't see him, and even then I'd worry."

Bessie smiled. "I feel much the same about him," she replied.

On the first floor, Bessie quickly unlocked the door to her borrowed flat. She walked in and gave her new home a good look.

"It's nice," Spencer said from behind her. "Okay, the views aren't great, but the layout is efficient and the furniture is all gorgeous."

"The furniture is all on loan from a friend," Bessie told him. "I'm sure it's all much nicer than my own things."

Spencer shook his head. "You have amazing antiques," he said. "These are all much more modern, but they're very well made and they really suit the space."

Bessie laughed. "I only have antiques because I bought all sorts of new furniture when I first bought my cottage. I guess that makes me an antique as well."

"I'd call you a classic," Spencer told her with a wink. "And before I get myself into any more trouble, I'll go and get your things."

While Spencer made several trips from the flat to his car and back again, carrying in all of Bessie's belongings, Bessie took another look at her new home. In the bedroom she patted her new mattress that had already been put into place on the bed frame. There was a large bag in the corner from the same shop and Bessie checked that the bedding she'd purchased had been delivered as well. At some point, she'd get the bed made up but for now she headed back into the main room.

It felt reasonably spacious, or at least not cramped, but that was mostly because she had a limited amount of furniture. Compared to her cottage, it was considerably smaller. She found the box with the kettle in it and immediately set it up on the kitchen counter. Once she'd filled it and switched it on, she located mugs and teabags. The kettle boiled just as Spencer carried in her last suitcase.

"Just in time for tea," Bessie told him.

"Perfect," Spencer replied.

"Unfortunately, I don't have any milk to go in it," Bessie said with a frown. "I wonder if Bahey is home and could lend me some?"

Bessie made the quick trip down the hall, knocking on both Bahey's door and Howard's, but neither was at home.

"No time like the present to meet the neighbours," she muttered to herself as she knocked on the door to number nine, which was right across the hall from Howard's flat. After a few moments, the door opened slowly.

"I'm not interested," the woman who looked out said flatly. "And how did you get in here anyway? We're supposed to have security."

"Oh, but I'm not selling anything," Bessie said, feeling a bit flustered by the unexpected response to her knock. The woman had opened the door with a security chain in place, so Bessie could only just see a tiny sliver of a rather thin and unhappy looking older woman.

"I'm Elizabeth Cubbon," she said. "I've just moved in to number ten and I was hoping you might be able to lend me a small amount of milk so I can have a cuppa."

"Never touch it," the woman replied. "No tea or coffee or dairy products. Try her next door. She'll eat anything."

Before Bessie could reply, the door was shut firmly in her face. "That went well," Bessie muttered to herself, turning to the next door in the hall. No one answered her knock there, so she tried the final door, number seven. After a few moments, she could hear movement inside the flat. It was at least a minute later that the door finally opened.

"Ah, Bessie, wasn't it?" Bertie Ayers smiled out at her. "Are you moving in today, then?"

"I am," Bessie told him. "Actually, I've just finished and I was going to have a cuppa, but I don't have any milk. I don't suppose you could spare a little bit?"

"Oh, I'd love to come over for a cuppa," Bertie told her. "Just let me find the milk and I'll be right over."

He shut the door in Bessie's surprised face. She shook her head and then turned and went back into her own flat. Her new neighbours were turning out to be rather interesting.

Bessie smiled at Spencer when she walked back into her flat. "Milk is on the way," she told him. By the time she'd filled the teapot, someone was knocking on her door.

"Ah, Bertie, do come in," Bessie said, as she pulled the door open.

"I brought the milk," he told her. He held up a pint container.

"Excellent," Bessie replied. "This is my friend, Spencer," she told him when they'd reached the kitchen. "He helped me move in."

"Oh, I didn't realise you had company," Bertie said, looking flustered. "I hope I'm not interrupting anything."

"Oh, goodness, no," Bessie laughed. "We were just going to have a quick cuppa before Spencer has to get back to Laxey." She poured the tea and everyone added milk and sugar to taste.

"I have a date tonight," Spencer told Bertie. "But I was happy to help out Aunt Bessie."

"Oh, she's your aunt. That makes sense," Bertie said.

"She isn't really my aunt," Spencer replied. "Everyone in

Laxey calls her Aunt Bessie, though."

Bertie frowned. "Why?"

"Since I never had children of my own, I'm sort of an honourary auntie to many of the children in Laxey," Bessie explained. "They know I always have biscuits and cakes and I'll always listen to their complaints about their parents."

"I do hope you aren't planning on having lots of small children visit you here," Bertie said. "I'm not fond of small children."

"Oh, I'm sure things will be very different here," Bessie said, trying not to sound as sad about that as she suddenly felt.

"Do you have children?" Spencer asked the man.

"No, I never married," Bertie replied. "I managed to avoid getting caught and I'm not letting my guard down, even now. There are some women in this building who would like very much to be Mrs. Bertie Ayers, I can tell you."

Spencer chuckled. "I hope I'm in as much demand when I'm your age," he said.

"Widowed women are everywhere when you get to my age," Bertie said, shaking his head. "And they all seem to want to get married again."

"How unpleasant for you," Bessie murmured, wondering who on earth would want to marry this rather odd little man.

"Oh, it's not all bad," Bertie said in a confiding tone. "I get a bit spoiled at Christmas time and the like. Muriel and Ruth seem to try to outdo each other and I end up with all sorts of things I wasn't expecting."

"Like what?" Spencer asked, clearly fascinated.

"Oh, Muriel bakes. She'll make me a Christmas cake and mince pies and all sorts of delicious treats. I usually have Christmas dinner with her, as well. She's a wonderful cook. Ruth, on the other hand, has allergies or sensitivities or something, so she eats only very plain food and nothing with any sugar in it. She knits or something with yarn, so I get scarves and jumpers and mittens and hats and all sorts like that from her."

"How very kind of both of them," Bessie said.

Bertie flushed. "I know they mean to be kind," he answered. "But it does get rather tiresome. I only have the one head and two hands, so I don't really need four pairs of mittens or six hats, and a dozen or so mince pies is really my limit."

Spencer laughed. "Perhaps I need to meet them," he said. "I could use a winter hat and some mittens, and I've never met a mince pie I didn't like."

"You're too young for either of them," Bertie said with a laugh. "Otherwise, I'd tell you to go for it. Although you're not much younger than the building manager, and he seems quite keen on both ladies."

"Whatever do you mean?" Bessie asked, trying to sound less interested than she was.

Bertie shrugged. "He just seems to spend a lot of time talking to them both, that's all. He's much more friendly with them than he is with me."

Bessie finished her tea and set her cup down on the kitchen counter. "So Muriel is in number eight and Ruth is in number nine?" she asked Bertie.

"Yep, and you said you know Bahey and Howard, right?"

"That's right," Bessie agreed.

"So that's everyone up here," Bertie said. "Have you met anyone from the ground floor yet?"

"Just the building manager," Bessie replied. "Who else is there?"

"Well, Nigel, the manager, has his mother living with him," Bertie told her. "She's not well, either physically or mentally, but I'm never sure which. Anyway, she doesn't leave their flat very often and when she does, she just sits and stares into space."

"Oh, dear, I wonder what's wrong with the poor woman," Bessie said.

Bertie shrugged. "Nigel might tell you, if you ask. I never have."

Bessie nodded. She'd be sure to ask the man the next time she saw him. "Who else lives on the ground floor, then?"

"Simon O'Malley is in flat number one," Bertie replied. "Muriel and Ruth went crazy for him when he first moved in, but he's not much interested in the ladies. He moved here from Ireland after working for one of the big department store chains over there for many years. He did windows, or something like that."

"Washed them or installed them?" Spencer asked.

"Neither," Bertie replied. "He decorated them, like. The big display windows that they do up at Christmas and that sort of thing."

"Oh, I see," Spencer replied.

"Anyway, Mabel Carson lives next to him in number two. "She was a nurse and a midwife in Leeds and she has family here and there, so she isn't around all that much. She seems really nice, when I've spoken to her."

"I hope she'll be able to make it to my housewarming," Bessie said.

"Oh, slip a note under her door and she'll probably stop by. She's plenty friendly enough; she's just quite busy. It's the one after her you probably don't want to invite."

"Oh, dear, who's in number three, then?" Bessie asked.

"A lady named Annabelle Hopkins. She's retired from the civil service and she doesn't like anything or anyone. She could complain for England, she could. If you do invite her, she won't like anything you have to eat or drink. Don't take it personally. She hasn't been happy since before the war, I reckon."

Bessie shook her head. "Life's too short to be miserable all the time," she said thoughtfully.

"Anyway, Tammara Flynn lives across from Annabelle. She's in number six. She's Irish like Simon, and they seem to do things together quite a bit. I don't really know her, but she seems pleasant enough."

"What about number five?" Bessie asked, curious what Bertie would say about the flat she knew was empty.

"It's empty," he replied. "From what I understand, someone bought it a while back, but they haven't moved in yet." He shrugged. "I'm sure someone will move in eventually. I can't imagine whoever it is can afford to have two places forever."

"And Nigel and his mother are in number four?" Bessie checked.

"Yep, and I'm not sure how they manage it," Bertie replied. "These flats are comfortable enough for one person, but they aren't big enough for two."

Bessie glanced around her compact space. "I'd have to agree with that," she told her new neighbour.

Spencer left after he'd finished his tea. Bessie knew he was eager to get back to Laxey to get ready for his date. Bertie proved harder to get rid of. He drank his tea and told Bessie all about his life while Bessie smiled politely and tried to figure out how to get him to leave.

"Well, it's getting late," he said finally, just as Bessie was wondering how best to fake a heart attack. "Did you have plans for dinner?"

Bessie took a deep breath, trying to figure out the best possible response. Before she'd managed it, Bertie continued.

"I'm not asking you out," he said hastily. "I mean, like, not on a date or anything. I just think I need to make sure you understand that. But I thought, if you didn't have plans, maybe we could go somewhere together. I don't have plans, you see, and I don't really like to cook. We would each pay for ourselves, you understand. It isn't a date or anything."

Bessie bit back a laugh. "That's very kind of you," she said. "But I do have plans. A dear friend is coming over and I need to run to the grocery store and do some shopping before she gets here."

"Oh, I'll just get out of the way, then," Bertie said. "Maybe we could do dinner another night."

"Maybe," was as far as Bessie was willing to go. "But don't forget my housewarming on Saturday," she told him as she walked him to the door. "I'm hoping to get to meet all the neighbours."

"I expect most of them will turn up," Bertie replied. "We're all pensioners on fixed incomes, so if there's food on offer, we'll be here."

Bessie laughed. "There will be food," she assured him. "And drinks as well."

"If you can manage a nice bottle of gin, I'd love a gin and tonic," Bertie told her, his eyes shining with anticipation. "I haven't had one since Christmas."

Bessie nodded and added gin to her mental shopping list. This little gathering was starting to seem like an expensive proposition. Still, she wanted to meet the neighbours; she just hoped it would be worth the fuss and bother.

As soon as Bertie left, Bessie grabbed her handbag and headed out to the nearest grocery store. It was just a short walk away, and Bessie was quite pleased with the easy convenience of it. While she was walking, she made a quick call to Doona, inviting her dinner. She felt lucky that Doona was not only available but also happy to make the short drive to Douglas to see Bessie.

Mindful that she had to carry all of her shopping back with her, Bessie limited her purchases to things she felt she absolutely needed. Bertie had insisted that Bessie keep the rest of the container of milk he'd brought, so she bought him a replacement carton. She also bought what she needed for a simple dinner with Doona and a ready-made apple crumble.

She enjoyed her walk back to Seaside Terrace, in spite of having to carry the shopping bags. She'd have to get a taxi or a friend to drive her when she shopped for the party, though. There was no way she would be able to carry everything she needed for that, unless she made several trips.

Nigel Green jumped up when Bessie walked back into the building's foyer. "Oh, you should have told me you needed shopping," he exclaimed. "We have a service for that. We could have picked up everything you need for you."

"I needed the walk almost as much as I needed the shopping," Bessie told him. "But I might have you get me some things for Saturday. I'm having a little housewarming, or should I say, flat warming? I do hope you and your mother will be able to attend."

"Oh, I'd love to come," he replied, seeming overeager to Bessie. "But I'm not sure about mother. We'll have to see how she's feeling, won't we?"

"Will we?" Bessie asked.

"Well, yes, of course," he said, frowning.

Bessie smiled to herself as she boarded the lift. Back in her flat, she quickly put away the shopping and threw the beef stew ingredients into a pot. Once it was simmering nicely, she settled down to write out invitations to her flat warming.

Hoping that she was remembering all of the names correctly, Bessie wrote out the same invitation eight times and then addressed each envelope. After dinner, she would go door to door and pass them out. She'd only just finished the last one when someone knocked on her door.

"Doona, how wonderful to see you," Bessie said when she'd opened the door.

"You sound a little desperate already and you've only been here since midday," Doona replied, as she greeted Bessie with a hug.

"It's such a huge change," Bessie said. "I feel a little desperate."

"Maybe you should just move back to Laxey," Doona suggested.

"I have to give Douglas a fair try," Bessie said firmly, as she pulled Doona into the flat. "Besides, look at the lovely furniture I've borrowed."

Doona admired the pieces that Mary Quayle had lent Bessie with genuine enthusiasm. "I wish I had rich friends who would lend me things like this," she said, running her hand across the luxurious sofa.

"I feel quite guilty about it," Bessie admitted. "Mary is really pleased that I might be moving to Douglas for good and I feel bad that I'm deceiving her."

"Are you certain there's no chance of you moving for good?" Doona asked.

Bessie shook her head. "I can't imagine living here permanently," she told her friend. "It doesn't feel at all like home."

"You've only just moved in," Doona pointed out. "Maybe you need to give it a chance."

Bessie nodded slowly. "I suppose you're right, although I'd rather figure out what's going on that's spooking Bahey and then go home."

Doona laughed. "I won't argue with that," she told her friend.

"I'm really going to miss you."

"But you're coming with me to the barbeque at the Quayles' on Friday and you're coming to my housewarming on Saturday," Bessie reminded her. "Honestly, I think you're going to see more of me than normal in the next few days."

"Possibly," Doona conceded. "But it won't feel the same."

"No, it won't," Bessie agreed.

"I thought I'd be helping you move, as well," Doona said as Bessie went into the kitchen to start serving the stew.

"Spencer moved me over this afternoon," Bessie explained. "He fit everything in one trip."

"That was kind of him," Doona said.

Something in her voice had Bessie looking at her carefully. "I thought you didn't really like Spencer," she said after a moment.

"I don't," Doona said with a deep sigh. "But it turns out I like being chased. It was lovely having someone who wanted to be with me all the time, even if I did feel smothered by it."

Bessie shook her head. "He's not the right man for you," she reminded her friend.

"I know that, but I miss the attention," Doona replied. "I miss having someone, even the wrong someone. I feel like I've been on my own for a very long time."

Bessie laughed. "Speaking as someone who really has been on her own for a very long time, a few years is nothing. You need to learn to be happy by yourself and then, when you least expect it, someone wonderful will come along."

"That sounds good," Doona said. "But there aren't any guarantees, and I'm not getting any younger."

"No, but if you learn to be happy on your own, you won't care if someone special doesn't turn up," Bessie replied. "Anyway, you're too special to be alone forever. Someone out there is looking for you, even if he doesn't know it yet."

Doona sighed. "I hope you're right," she said after a moment. She took a deep breath. "Okay, sorry, how are you? How are you finding the new flat? How are the neighbours? Has anything strange or unusual happened to you yet?"

Bessie laughed. "I'm not sure I can answer all of that," she said. She set two very full bowls of stew down on the small table. "I'd offer you wine, but you're driving," she said.

"I'd better have a fizzy drink," Doona replied.

Bessie got them each a can of something fizzy and brought them to the table with glasses. "Let's eat while I try to remember and answer everything you asked," Bessie said.

"This is delicious," Doona told Bessie after her first bite.

"It isn't bad," Bessie said with a shrug. The flat's cooktop was much more efficient than her old one at home, and Bessie had already realised that she was going to have to pay more attention to her cooking until she got used to the difference. No doubt the modern fan-assisted oven would bake very differently to her much older model at the cottage as well. She'd put the apple crumble in to warm; now she got up to check on it.

"What's wrong?" Doona asked.

Bessie explained about the differences in the old oven at her cottage and the much more modern one here. "But the crumble looks fine," she told Doona as she sat back down to finish her stew.

"Oh, good," Doona replied with a smile. "It's an apple crumble kind of night."

"But you were asking about the flat and my neighbours," Bessie recalled. "The flat seems fine, so far. It's going to take a lot of getting used to, but I'm determined to think of it as an adventure. Nothing unusual or strange has happened yet, at least not that I've noticed. As for the neighbours, why don't you come with me after dinner and you can meet them for yourself."

"What you are doing after dinner?" Doona asked.

"I thought I'd hand deliver the invitations to Saturday's party," Bessie answered, her eyes twinkling. Whatever else, she was excited to start trying to figure out what was happening that was upsetting Bahey.

After generous helpings of apple crumble with cream, Bessie and Doona quickly tidied up the tiny kitchen space.

"Well, that didn't take long," Doona said, as she put away the last of the dried dishes.

"No, it seemed to go faster than at home, but I'm sure it's my imagination," Bessie remarked.

"Or maybe it's because it was just the two of us, and in Laxey you often have Hugh and John over when I'm there as well," Doona suggested.

"That could be it," Bessie agreed. "Shall we play postman, then?"

"Lead the way," Doona invited. "I'm almost as excited as you are to meet everyone."

Bessie knocked on Bahey's door, but no one answered. She shrugged at Doona. "Maybe she's at Howard's," she suggested.

"Ah, Bessie, you didn't move in today, did you?" Howard demanded when he opened the door to his flat a moment later. "Bahey and I would have helped, if you'd let us know."

Bahey walked up to the door, a glass of wine in her hand. "Bessie? I thought you were moving in tomorrow? Did I get it wrong? We would have been happy to help."

"I was going to move in tomorrow, but then I had an offer of help today so I decided not to wait," Bessie explained. "I was just dropping around with invitations for my housewarming on Saturday afternoon."

"Oh, but come in and have a glass of wine," Bahey suggested.

"I really need to get these invitations out," Bessie demurred. "And I have a friend with me as well."

"Well, pass out the invitations and then come back," Howard said firmly. "And bring your friend. We have plenty of wine."

Doona spoke from behind Bessie. "I'm driving, or I'd take you up on that for sure," she told the man.

"Please do stop back," Bahey said to Bessie. "I feel as if I haven't seen you for a long while."

"Well, the good news is, I'll be right next door, at least for a while," Bessie told her. "Anyway, I'll stop back after I've been around the building. We have a lot to talk about."

Howard shut the door as Bessie turned to number nine. "I met the woman who lives here earlier," Bessie told Doona. "She wasn't terribly welcoming."

She knocked on the door with more enthusiasm than she felt.

After a moment, the door swung open as far as the security chain would allow.

"I still don't have any milk," the woman told Bessie through the crack.

Bessie forced herself to chuckle. "I'm just dropping off a party invitation," she told the woman. "I'm having a housewarming on Saturday so that I can meet all my new neighbours. I'd love it if you could come."

"I suppose you'll be expecting fancy presents," the woman sniffed. "I'm on a very tight budget. You probably won't be wanting to invite me now."

Bessie shook her head. "I don't want presents," she replied. "In fact, I said that very thing on the invitations. I just want a chance to meet everyone in the building. I've lived alone in a little cottage in a somewhat remote area my entire life. I'm looking forward to having neighbours and getting to know them all."

She held out the invitation towards the woman. After a moment, Ruth reached a hand out through the crack and took it from her.

"I hope to see you Saturday," Bessie said cheerfully as the hand snaked back inside the flat.

Bessie could just make out the "maybe" that was said before the door slammed shut in her face.

"Lovely," Doona muttered from behind Bessie.

"Maybe she's just lonely," Bessie suggested.

"Maybe everyone leaves her alone for a reason," Doona shot back.

Bessie laughed and then knocked firmly on the door to number eight. After a few moments, the door swung open and Bessie blinked at the plump and friendly-looking woman who was now standing in the doorway.

"Oh, good evening, I'm Bessie Cubbon," she began. "I've just moved into number ten and I'm having a housewarming on Saturday. I do hope you can make it."

She handed the woman the invitation with her name on it. The woman took it and looked it over for a moment, giving Bessie time to study her. She had to be in her sixties, at least, and she was very generously built. Her hair was grey and pulled back into an untidy bun at the back of her head. Her clothes were the sort that could be bought at any shop on the high street in the section marked "plus sizes," but they were reasonably well-fitting and looked clean and neat.

"So, who's been telling you about me, then?" the woman demanded now in a thick Scottish accent.

"Bertie was kind enough to supply everyone's names," Bessie explained. "And I'm friends with Bahey and Howard as well."

"Aye, so you'll be knowing everyone's business before you've even unpacked, won't you?"

Bessie shrugged. "I'm not really interested in prying into people's private lives," she said. "I just want to get to know my new neighbours."

The woman nodded. "Well, I'd be delighted to come to your little gathering. Especially if Bertie is going to be there." She looked at Bessie for a moment and then narrowed her eyes. "You aren't going to be interested in my Bertie, are you? He's too young for you, anyway."

Bessie laughed. "I'm not interested in Bertie," she assured the woman, whose bright smile had now disappeared. "I'm quite happy on my own."

The woman nodded slowly. "Well, then, I'll see you Saturday," she said, slowly shutting her door.

Bessie turned away before the door was shut in her face.

"My, what interesting neighbours you have," Doona muttered, as they headed for the next door.

Bessie laughed and knocked on Bertie's door. After a moment she looked at Doona and shrugged. "Maybe he's gone out," she said. She waited a moment longer and then sighed. "I'll just slip his invitation under the door."

Having done so, the pair crossed to the lift and headed down to the ground floor. Nigel Green was still sitting behind the small desk in the foyer.

"Ah, Ms. Cubbon, I hope you're settling in okay," he said, giving her a huge smile.

"I am, thanks," Bessie replied coolly.

"And who is this?" he asked, turning towards Doona and extending his hand.

"I'm Doona Moore, one of Bessie's closest friends," Doona replied, taking the offered hand reluctantly.

"Well, any friend of Bessie's is definitely a friend of mine," he said, raising Doona's hand to his lips.

Doona pulled her hand away just before it reached his mouth. "Yeah, whatever," she muttered.

"I have an invitation for you and your mother for Saturday," Bessie told the man, handing him the envelope. "I do hope you'll be able to make it."

"Will you be there?" he asked Doona, winking at her.

"I'm hoping to be there with my boyfriend," Doona replied.

Nigel frowned and then shrugged. "I might make it," he said noncommittally.

"Well, you and your mother are both very welcome," Bessie said, putting emphasis on the 'your mother' part of the sentence. She was very eager to meet the woman for some reason.

"We'll see," was all that she received as a reply.

Bessie headed past him now, down the hallway between the ground floor flats. Outside the first flat, there was small, framed mirror hanging next to the door.

"I wonder if this is the mirror that Bahey says keeps moving," Bessie whispered to Doona.

"It doesn't look terribly exciting," Doona replied, glancing at it.

Bessie shrugged and knocked on the door to flat number one.

"One minute," someone called from inside. A moment later the door swung open and Bessie drew a deep breath. The man who stood looking out at her was one of the most attractive older men she'd ever seen. He must have been somewhere in his sixties, but his silver hair and artfully arranged wrinkles simply made him look distinguished rather than old.

"Oh, what a pleasant surprise," he said in a lilting Irish accent. He gave Bessie a perfect smile. "Two lovely young ladies on my doorstep. To what do I owe this unexpected pleasure?"

Bessie opened and then closed her mouth, for a moment unable to speak.

"Bessie's just moved into the building," Doona spoke for her. "She's having a housewarming on Saturday and wanted to invite all of her new neighbours."

"Oh, how delightful," the man said, clapping his hands together. "I've always thought it was a shame we didn't do more as a building. It will be such fun to get together with everyone."

Bessie gave herself a mental shake and then handed the man his invitation. "I do hope you can make it," she said politely.

"Oh, I'll be there," he assured her. "I never miss a party." He gave Bessie a wink and then slowly shut the door. Bessie turned to Doona and surprised herself by giggling.

"He's gorgeous," she gasped.

"And you're not his type," Doona replied dryly.

"But he's made the whole building feel much more scenic," Bessie replied with another giggle.

No one was home in number two or number three, so Bessie simply slipped their invitations under their doors. At number six, she was happy to finally find someone at home.

"Can I help you?" the woman asked in an Irish accent that made Bessie smile.

"I've just stopped by to invite you to my housewarming on Saturday," she explained as she studied the other woman.

"Oh, how lovely of you," Tammara replied. She, too, looked to be somewhere in her sixties, with long grey hair and matching eyes. She was slender and very elegantly dressed. "It would be nice if the whole building was friendlier," she told Bessie. "I do feel rather isolated down here in my corner sometimes."

"Well, I'm doing my best," Bessie replied.

Bessie couldn't resist knocking on the door to number five, even though everyone said it was empty. She waited a moment, listening intently. After several seconds, she was sure she heard movement within the flat. She knocked again, but this time the only sound she heard was from the foyer.

"Aye, that flat's empty, you know," Nigel called from the entrance to the hall. "No point in knocking there, or on my door, either. Mother will be dead to the world by this time of night."

Bessie figured she wouldn't get any more snooping done with

Nigel watching, so she gave him a bright smile and then she and Doona headed towards the lift. Bessie thought about asking him about the missing man, but he disappeared into his own flat before she managed to do so.

"Well, that was interesting," Doona said as they walked back into Bessie's flat. "But I'm going to have to call it a night. I have to work tomorrow."

Bessie was sorry to see her friend leave, but she knew Doona's job demanded a great deal of her. Doona needed to be well rested, especially with Inspector Kelly in charge.

"Are you turning in now?" Doona asked as Bessie showed her out.

"I think I might just pop over to Howard's for a quick glass of wine," Bessie replied.

CHAPTER TEN

Howard was happy to pour Bessie a glass of wine.

"Come and sit down and tell us what you've been up to," he said, waving towards the comfortable looking sitting area past his kitchen.

Bessie sank down in one of the overstuffed chairs and grinned. "This is very comfortable," she said.

"I love this furniture," Bahey told her friend. "I spend most of my spare time over here, sitting on Howard's lovely furniture."

"And all this time I thought it was me that was the draw," Howard said, making a sad face.

Bahey flushed. "You know what I mean," she scolded the man.

He laughed. "I do," he agreed. "And I know it is wonderful furniture as well, so I suppose I wouldn't blame you if it were part of the attraction."

The trio drank wine and chatted about nothing much for several minutes. "I suppose I should get back to my flat," Bessie said after a while. "I'm not sure how well I'll sleep. The first night in a different place is always strange."

Bahey nodded. "It took me a few weeks to feel comfortable here," she told Bessie. "And now, with all the odd things going on, I'm not sleeping well again."

"Has anything else happened since we last talked?" Bessie

asked.

"Aside from hearing noises from the flat below me, not really," Bahey said. "Although the mirror has disappeared again. It was outside my flat for about a week and now it's gone."

Bessie described the mirror she'd seen outside of Simon's flat. "Is that the one you're talking about?" she asked.

"It is indeed," Bahey confirmed.

"Then I've seen it," Bessie told her. "It's outside flat number one at the moment."

Bahey shrugged. "I'm sure Simon enjoys having it there," she said. "If I had his gorgeous face, I'd look in the mirror all the time."

Bessie smiled. "He is very attractive," she agreed.

"Should I be getting jealous?" Howard asked, giving Bahey's hand a squeeze.

"Not even a little bit," Bahey answered, blushing.

"Have you heard any more about the mystery man?" Howard asked.

Bessie shook her head. "I gather he left Noble's and disappeared. I assume you haven't seen him around since?"

Both Bahey and Howard shook their heads.

"No sign of him," Bahey said.

"Thank you for the wine," Bessie said, standing up reluctantly. The chair truly was incredibly comfortable. "I'd better go before I fall asleep in your chair."

"Oh, but I have a little present for you," Bahey said. She followed Bessie to the door. "I'll just get it for you."

Bessie tried to protest, but Bahey waved her words away. "It isn't really a present so much as an experiment," Bahey told Bessie as she unlocked the door to her flat. Bessie waited in the hallway as Bahey rushed inside and then back again. She handed Bessie a bag with something flat inside of it.

Bessie peeked into the bag and then laughed. "A welcome mat?"

"I thought you could put it outside your door and we could see if it disappears like mine did," Bahey told her. She flushed. "I will get you a proper housewarming gift, too. This is just a little something."

"It's lovely," Bessie said. She pulled the mat from the bag and smiled. The dark mat was covered with a bright floral pattern that spelled out "Welcome." While it wasn't anything Bessie would have bought for herself, its cheery colours were perfect for the somewhat dimly lit hallway.

"Anyway, I don't want any presents," Bessie told Bahey sternly. "This is wonderful as it's bright and cheerful and will be an interesting test of what's going on here, but nothing else, okay?"

Bahey shrugged. "Do you have plans for the rest of the week?" she asked.

"I thought I'd spend tomorrow playing tourist in my new town. On Friday, I need to get the shopping done for Saturday in the morning and then I'm going to a barbeque in the afternoon. That will probably run into the evening as well."

"Would you like a ride to the shops on Friday?" Bahey offered. "We usually go out to the ShopFast in Onchan at least once a week anyway. They have a bigger selection than the one down here."

"That would be wonderful," Bessie told her. They agreed to meet at nine and then Bessie opened the door to her flat. Before she headed inside, she carefully put the mat in front of the door with the "Welcome" facing out to greet visitors.

Inside her flat, she made sure everything was tidied and put away from dinner and then made her way into her bedroom. She'd already unpacked the two suitcases of clothes that she'd brought; now she changed into her favourite nightgown. In the loo, she brushed her hair and teeth and washed her face before heading back into the bedroom.

She'd only brought a single box of books for now, so she quickly flipped through it until she found something that appealed to her. She crawled into bed and adjusted the small reading lamp she'd brought. After only a single chapter, she decided to try to get some sleep. In the dark, she found herself listening carefully to all the unfamiliar noises that surrounded her. Someone was running water somewhere in the building and at one point she was sure she could hear footsteps in the hallway outside her flat.

It felt like hours to Bessie before she finally drifted off to sleep.

It was a restless and interrupted sleep as well, as doors opened and closed outside her flat and below her. She could hear traffic noises from the car park below her and perhaps even from the promenade that wasn't terribly far away. By the time six o'clock arrived, Bessie was ready to give up on trying to sleep. She took a quick shower and then, once dressed, looked out the window at a lovely sunrise. A morning walk along the promenade and Douglas beach would no doubt improve her mood.

She pulled her door open and stopped short as she met her own eyes in the mirror that was now hanging in the hall outside her door. She blinked and then reached out and ran her hand down the frame. It appeared to be the exact same mirror that she'd seen hanging outside Simon's door the previous evening. Shaking her head, Bessie turned and locked her door. She took a few steps and then stopped as her tired brain registered another anomaly. Her brightly patterned mat was right where she'd left it, but the word "Welcome" was now facing inwards, as if welcoming Bessie into the hallway rather than welcoming her guests to her flat.

Bessie frowned and continued down the hall towards the lift. She was certain she'd put the mat the other way around and she knew that that mirror hadn't been there when she'd gone to bed the night before. Perhaps Bahey was right. Perhaps there was something mysterious going on at Seaview Terrace.

In spite of feeling slightly out of place on the unfamiliar beach, Bessie greatly enjoyed her walk. Although the beach was strange, the sea was an old friend and Bessie felt invigorated by the fresh salty air that she filled her lungs with as she strolled. The beach was still very quiet at this hour, though Bessie did nod and smile at a few other earlier morning walkers.

When she went back into her building, she peeked down the corridor on the ground floor. The mirror that had been outside Simon's flat was missing. Back upstairs, Bessie turned her welcome mat back around and then found a pen in the handbag she'd taken with her. She took down the mirror and quickly made a small mark in a corner on the back of the mirror's frame. She rehung it and then let herself into her flat.

She'd had toast and tea before her walk now she brewed herself some coffee, feeling as if the extra jolt of caffeine would be welcome after her restless night. As her time in Douglas was meant to be a holiday, Bessie decided to spend the day playing at being a tourist. She headed back down to the promenade and bought a ticket for the horse trams. She joined several families as they rode up and down the street behind "Matthew," who didn't seem the least bit bothered by the weight he was pulling.

Bessie briefly considered a short trip on the electric railway, but as that would take her out of Douglas, it didn't appeal. Instead, she made her way into the city centre, spending hours window shopping and buying herself tea at one of the town's small cafés. An hour in the new bookstore rounded out the day nicely and Bessie returned to her flat feeling almost as if she were on a proper holiday.

She fixed herself a light meal, still feeling quite full after her afternoon tea, and then settled in to read until she was tired enough to sleep. Her sleep was restless, as she still hadn't become used to the strange noises in her new home. By six the next morning she was ready to be up and about.

After her walk, while she waited for Bahey, she made a shopping list of everything she thought she would need for the party the next afternoon. She would have snacks and drinks, she decided, rather than proper food. That way it didn't matter if people arrived all at once or just a few at a time. By the time Bahey knocked on her door, she had the list finished.

"Ready to go?" Bahey asked her friend.

"I am," Bessie replied. She followed Bahey down to the car park and Bahey led her to Howard's car, where he was waiting.

"Bahey said you're getting ready for Saturday," he said after they'd exchanged greetings. "Are you going to be able to get everything you need at ShopFast?"

Bessie shrugged. "I hope so," she replied.

"Well, I haven't anything better to do today, so if you need to stop anywhere else, just let me know," Howard told her.

The drive was a short one and the trio split up in the store, each with their own lists. Bessie smiled as she watched Bahey pull a paper list from her bag, while Howard headed off, presumably with nothing but a mental list to shop from.

An hour later, Bessie met the others at the tills. "I think I got everything I need," she told Bahey. "I hope so, anyway, since I'm tired of shopping and probably broke as well."

Bahey laughed. "Well, your trolley is just about overflowing, so I guess that means it's time to stop shopping."

For a moment Bessie wasn't sure that everything was going to fit in Howard's boot, but he managed to squeeze it all in. They made the short drive back to the apartment building and then Howard insisted on carrying everything in for Bessie and Bahey.

"You two go on up and get the kettle on," he said cheerfully. "I'll be done before it's boiled."

"Should we do tea in your flat or mine?" Bahey asked Bessie as they made their way into the building.

"Oh, let's do mine," Bessie replied.

With Howard following with some of Bessie's shopping, they made their way into the lift and up to the first floor. Bessie quickly opened her door and went inside, with Howard following with the heavy bags.

Bessie filled her kettle with water and switched it on. While Howard made several trips back and forth to his car, Bessie worked on putting away the shopping he'd brought up for her. Then she piled biscuits onto a plate and pulled out her tea things. By the time Howard had finished by bringing up the handful of bags that were his and Bahey's, the kettle had boiled. Bessie filled the teapot and set it on the table.

"Shall I be mother?" Bahey asked as Howard came in and sank into one of the chairs.

"Please do," Bessie said. She carried the plate of biscuits over to the table, along with small plates for each of them. Bahey poured the tea and everyone ate and drank quietly for a moment.

"I needed that," Bessie said, after she'd finished her tea.

"I did as well," Howard told her. "Shopping is very tiring."

"Especially when you have to carry in the shopping for three people," Bessie suggested.

"I didn't mind a bit," Howard insisted. "I'm always happy to help."

"Well, I'm hugely grateful," Bessie replied. "I wasn't sure how I was going to get all that shopping bought and into the flat. I'm far less worried about tomorrow now."

"What's the plan for tomorrow?" Bahey asked.

"I'm hoping to talk to all of the neighbours," Bessie told her. "I want to see if anyone else has noticed anything strange."

"I don't know," Bahey said. "Now that I've dragged you down here and made you move house and everything, I'm starting to think that I'm imagining things after all."

"Well, the mirror outside my flat isn't imaginary," Bessie told her. "And I didn't put it there. And I'm certain someone turned my welcome mat around as well. They're harmless enough things, but they're strange."

"I'm relieved it isn't just me that's seeing these things," Bahey told Bessie. "But now I'm worried that I've invited you into some sort of trouble."

"I'm only going to ask a few questions," Bessie said. "If I think there's anything other than a few odd pranks going on, I'll be straight on to the police."

Before they could talk further, Bessie's phone rang. She hadn't brought her answering machine with her, so she felt she had little choice but to answer it.

"Ah, Bessie, it's Mary. I don't suppose you were just sitting around feeling bored and would like nothing better than to come and spend the afternoon with me?" Mary Quayle said in answer to Bessie's tentative hello.

"I thought you'd be busy getting ready for the barbeque," Bessie said, trying to give herself some time to think before answering.

"George's assistant hired some sort of party planning person and she's done all of the work. All I have to do is turn up at four, ready to play at being the hostess," Mary said.

Bessie could hear dissatisfaction in her friend's voice. "That makes it nice and easy for you," she said.

"Yes, easy and boring and makes me rather unnecessary," Mary retorted.

"I'm just in the middle of putting away some shopping," Bessie said. "Give me a few minutes to finish that and I'll grab a taxi and head over."

"Don't do that," Mary said. "I'll send a car. He'll be there in fifteen minutes or so."

Mary hung up before Bessie could reply. She looked at the receiver in her hand and sighed deeply. She liked Mary a lot, but sometimes the woman could be a little bit too high-handed.

"Are you going out now, then?" Bahey asked.

Bessie sighed again. "I guess so," she said with a frown. "Mary and George Quayle are having a barbeque later this afternoon and I guess Mary is a bit bored waiting for it to start. She's sending a car to collect me."

"How very posh," Bahey said with a laugh.

"She's very wealthy," Bessie said, "but I don't think she's very happy."

Bahey nodded. "We both know money can't buy happiness," she said. "When I think about the Pierces, well, it's just very sad, that's all."

Bessie nodded. "It does often seem as if the wealthiest of families are the least happy," she said as Howard and Bahey helped her tidy up the tea things.

"I guess I should be grateful I've never had to worry about having money," Bahey laughed.

"My sister married into a quite wealthy family," Howard interjected. "They all hate each other and most of them haven't spoken in at least a decade. All over money, of course."

After she'd let Bahey and Howard out, Bessie changed into a summery dress and added a touch of makeup to her face. After combing her hair, she rang Doona at the police station in Laxey to let her know about the change in plans.

"I don't need you to pick me up," she told her friend. "You can just go straight to the Quayle mansion after work. I'll already be there."

"I was going to ring you anyway," Doona replied. "It looks like I might have to work later than I'd planned. I should be at the barbeque by half five, but probably not any earlier."

Bessie made sure that her friend knew exactly where she was going, and then rang off. She was going to check her hair again when someone knocked on her door.

The uniformed chauffeur made Bessie feel slightly uncomfortable, but she quickly had him chatting about his childhood and his family as he drove her to the Quayle mansion. He'd grown up in Port Erin, and Bessie ran through a list of everyone she knew in the south of the island until they found a few mutual acquaintances.

"Thank you kindly for collecting me," she told him when he pulled up to the front door of the enormous home.

"Happy to do it," the man replied with a bow. He helped Bessie from the car and then escorted her up the handful of steps to the front door. "Enjoy your evening," he said, winking at her before he headed back to the car.

The front door was pulled open by Mary herself. "Oh, there you are," she said, sounding anxious. "I'm just a bundle of frizzled nerves for some reason."

Bessie gave her a hug and then followed her into the house. "Let's have a walk in the garden and chat," she suggested. "Maybe a glass of wine would help as well."

Mary laughed uncertainly. "That sounds great," she said. She led Bessie through the foyer and down a long hallway, ducking into a huge kitchen that was full of gleaming appliances. Bessie couldn't imagine what some of them were even for.

"Can we open a bottle of wine, please?" Mary asked one of the kitchen staff.

"Of course, ma'am," the woman said smartly. "What would you like?"

Mary shrugged and looked at Bessie, who laughed. "White?" Bessie asked. "I don't know anything about wine, really, but generally I prefer white to red."

Mary smiled and then had a short conversation with the woman about wine types that Bessie didn't understand. After a moment the woman nodded and disappeared. She was back only a few seconds later with a bottle of wine in her hand.

"Would you like to taste it before I pour?" the woman asked

Mary.

"Oh, good heavens, no," Mary laughed. "We're going to take a walk around the grounds, so maybe you should put it into large glasses."

The woman nodded and then poured the entire bottle of wine into two huge glasses. Mary picked them both up off the counter and handed one to Bessie.

"It isn't the most elegant way of serving it," she admitted after her first sip. "But this way we don't have to worry about topping up our drinks."

Bessie took her glass gingerly. She'd never been given half a bottle of wine in one glass before and she wasn't sure how much of it she actually wanted to drink. She took a cautious sip and then smiled at Mary. "This is delicious," she said, surprised at how crisp and refreshing it tasted.

"Let's walk," Mary said, leading Bessie back into the corridor. At the very far end of it, there was a door to the outside. Mary pulled it open and Bessie followed her out into the huge garden. It was meticulously manicured and felt almost too perfect to be natural.

"It's lovely," Bessie said.

"It's overdone," Mary said with a sigh. "George pays a small army of men a fortune to make sure that every leaf and flower grows in exactly the right place. Nothing is allowed to just go crazy and grow as it pleases."

Bessie made her way down the brick path that meandered through the shrubs and flowers. She sipped her wine and sighed. Maybe being very rich did have its advantages, she thought, as she wound around into another section of the grounds. Here everything was flowering and as Bessie looked from left to right, the colours moved from white, though the lightest of pinks, darker and darker until, at the walled edge of the section, dark red flowers bloomed.

"The next section does something similar in shades of blue and purple," Mary told her in a bored voice. "And then there's a rainbow section. That's where the barbeque is being held."

"How wonderful," Bessie said, feeling slightly breathless.

Mary laughed. "I suppose it is," she said. "I'm rather jaded by now, I'm afraid. When George and I were first married, we lived in a little house and I did all of the gardening. My efforts were amateurish, at best, but I loved our little garden and our little house. This house and these grounds, they suit George, but they aren't really me."

Bessie smiled sympathetically at her friend. "They are rather grand," she said. "I feel as if I'm visiting a stately home in England, rather than a family home where real people live."

Mary nodded. "That's exactly it," she said sadly.

The pair sipped their wine and walked slowly around the beautiful grounds of the estate. Mary seemed lost in her own thoughts and Bessie was happy to let her own mind wander as well.

"Oh, goodness," Mary said suddenly. "It's nearly time for things to get started. I'd better get inside and finish getting ready."

Bessie looked at her friend's gorgeous dress and perfectly done hair and makeup. "You look fabulous," she told Mary.

"I'm sure I need a fresh coat of lipstick, and my hair will need combing," Mary said, running her hand over her hair. "I'll just leave you in the library for a few minutes, if that's okay?"

"It's more than okay," Bessie said with a laugh. "You know that."

Mary showed Bessie to the library and then rushed away. Bessie sighed happily as she made a slow circuit of the room, pulling out books at random for inspection.

"Ah, Bessie, tucked up in the library again?" George's voice boomed from the doorway.

Bessie slid the book she'd been looking at back into place and turned to greet the man. She smiled brightly at him so that he wouldn't know how annoyed she was at being disturbed yet again.

"Good afternoon," she said. "Are you all ready for your barbeque?"

"I think so," George replied. "The staff are handling everything, of course. I just sign the cheques."

Bessie smiled, noting that George was carrying a glass with some amber-coloured liquid in it. He took a sip and then shrugged at Bessie.

"It's a party," he said. "I thought a drink was appropriate."

"Mary and I have been drinking wine all afternoon," Bessie replied.

"I'm glad you were able to spend some time with her," George said. "She's ever so worked up about this party for some reason."

"I'm sure we'll all have a wonderful time," Bessie murmured.

"Of course we will," George said firmly.

A woman in a dark suit now appeared in the doorway next to George.

"Mr. Quayle, the guests have begun to arrive," she said.

"Oh bother," George said with a sigh. "I guess I have to go and play host, then."

He turned and strode away, leaving Bessie on her own to wonder at his words. She'd never known him to shy away from hosting duties in the past.

Mary dashed in only a few moments later. "People are arriving," she told Bessie. "Are you ready to come and be sociable? I don't have a choice, of course."

Bessie smiled. "I suppose, as it's a party, I should make the effort. I'd rather stay here and read, though, really."

"Me, too," Mary said. The smile she gave Bessie looked forced. "Off we go, then."

The pair made their way through the house and out the back door again. Now Mary led Bessie down a different path and into a section of the grounds that she hadn't seen before. They walked through a small gate in a long fence and Bessie felt as if she'd been transported somewhere else altogether.

"It's an American theme," Mary muttered to her.

Bessie shook her head. A large barn had been erected in the middle of the grass, but it looked as if it were hundreds of years old, with weathered boards that seemed to have been painted a very long time ago. There were gaps between some of the boards and some were missing altogether. The roof looked as if it were only just barely intact.

She made her way into the barn and looked around. There were tables and chairs set up along one side of the barn and a large platform, presumably for dancing, was in place on the other side. A huge bar was set up in the back of the space. It appeared to be made entirely of bales of hay. Behind it, several young men dressed as cowboys were serving drinks to the small crowd that had arrived early. Through the gaps in the boards on one side of the barn, Bessie could see several large barbeque grills had been set up nearby. She could just smell the smoke as the men behind them fired them up.

"Come on over to the bar and I'll introduce you to Paul," Mary told her.

Bessie followed her friend to the bar. Mary waved to one of the "cowboys" and he quickly made his way over to them.

"Good afternoon, ma'am," he greeted Mary. "What can I get for you?"

"Gin and tonic," Mary answered. "But first, this is Bessie."

Bessie held out her hand and the man took it, giving Bessie a huge smile. "Very nice to meet you, Bessie."

"Paul is our butler, household manager and a dozen other things," Mary told Bessie. "If there's anything you want or need, just let him know."

"I'll keep that in mind," Bessie said. She smiled at the man. "I suppose a gin and tonic would be a good start."

"Right away," Paul said. He was only gone for a moment or two and when he returned, he was carrying their drinks.

"Here we are," he said, handing the drinks over. "Let me know if there's anything else you need."

"I think we're good for now," Mary replied.

Bessie took a sip of her drink and smiled. She hadn't had gin and tonic in many years and she'd forgotten how much she liked it.

"I have to go and play hostess," Mary said to her quietly. "Are you going to be okay on your own?"

"Of course," Bessie answered firmly. "Anyway, Doona will be here soon."

Mary slipped away. Bessie knew Mary was painfully shy and that the day would be something of an ordeal for her. She watched as Mary joined George in a small group near the barn's entrance. He was quick to put his arm around his wife, and Bessie hoped he would look after her all evening.

Bessie was chatting happily with Mary's daughter Elizabeth when Doona finally arrived nearly two hours later.

"There you are," Doona said, giving her friend a hug as Elizabeth slipped away. "I wasn't sure I'd ever find you in this crowd."

Bessie looked around. The spacious barn was feeling quite crowded as more and more guests had arrived.

"Maybe we should go outside," Bessie suggested.

The pair made their way to the front of the barn. The gardens around it seemed to spread out in every direction and for a moment Bessie was tempted to just start walking. "We can't just sneak away," she said firmly to herself.

"I wasn't suggesting we should," Doona said, looking at Bessie in surprise.

"Oh, did I say that out loud?" Bessie asked with a laugh. "Maybe I've had more to drink than I should have."

"Bessie, there you are," George's voice boomed across the garden. "You must meet Grant."

Bessie forced a smile onto her lips before she turned around. "George, what a lovely party," she said. "You remember my friend, Doona?"

"Of course, and you look lovely tonight." George took Doona's hand and held it tightly for a moment. "If only I had time to stay and chat with you. Unfortunately, I'm rushing about making sure everyone is having fun." He dropped Doona's hand and then turned back to Bessie.

"Come and meet Grant," he insisted. He took Bessie's arm and led her across the grass and back into the barn. Doona followed as they made their way to the bar.

Bessie recognised the man more from photos she'd seen in the local papers over the years than from previous encounters. He looked even more slick and polished in person that he had in the photos. Grant Robertson had to be in his sixties, but his dark and perfectly styled short hair didn't seem to have a single grey strand. He was tall and lean, and as George introduced them,

Bessie felt his cool and calculating eyes assessing her.

"I can't believe we've both lived on the island all these years and we've never become friends," he said in a deep, silky smooth voice.

"I don't spend much time in Douglas," Bessie said, annoyed to hear that her tone was apologetic as she spoke.

"Or rather, you didn't," Grant suggested. "I understand you're trying out our fair city at the moment."

"Oh, yes, of course," Bessie replied. "And I can't thank you enough for renting me the flat at Seaview Terrace."

"Ah, I must confess to ulterior motives," the man said with a chuckle. "I'm tired of that flat sitting empty. I'm hoping you'll fall in love with it and buy it from me, you see."

Bessie smiled. "Anything's possible."

Bessie introduced Doona and then stood back to watch the man turn his considerable charm on to her. He held her hand for far too long after the introductions, staring into Doona's eyes as if she were the only woman in the room.

"And where have you been hiding all these years?" he asked Doona.

"Actually, we've met before," Doona said, pulling her hand away.

Grant frowned and studied her for a moment. "It was the grand opening of the Beachside Hotel, wasn't it?" he said after a moment. "You were with the hotel's district manager who'd come over for the event."

Doona nodded. "You have a good memory."

"I never forget a beautiful woman," he countered. "You aren't still with him, are you?"

"No," Doona said.

Grant smiled. "That's a very succinct answer. Why do I think there's a story behind it?"

Doona shook her head. "It's of no consequence," she said.

"But I'm intrigued by you," the man told her. "Maybe we could have a drink one night and you could tell me about the things that are of consequence to you?"

"I don't think so," Doona replied. "Thank you for asking, but

I'm otherwise involved."

Grant frowned. "How terribly disappointing," he said. He reached into his pocket and pulled out a card and a pen. After jotting something on the back of the card, he handed it to Doona.

"My card. The number on the back is my private mobile number. If you change your mind, give me a ring." He turned back to Bessie and smiled smarmily at her, reaching back into his pocket again.

"One for you as well. I'm sure you won't need my private number, but if you have any issues or concerns about the flat or anything, please don't hesitate to ring my office. My staff will look after you."

He gave them both a quick smile and then picked up his drink. "I must go and socialise," he told them, slipping past them.

Bessie turned to Doona and blew out a breath she hadn't realised she'd been holding. "Wow, he was, well, intense, I guess is a good word."

"Very," Doona agreed. "And creepy."

Fresh drinks in hand, the pair joined the queue for food and then found space at one of the picnic tables. Once they'd eaten, Bessie felt as if she'd had enough of the festivities and Doona was happy to agree.

They found George and Mary and quickly thanked them for the lovely party. Mary looked miserable, but she managed to smile when Bessie invited her to her housewarming the next day.

"I'll try to make it," she promised, as George pulled her away to greet someone else.

Bessie sighed deeply when she finally climbed into Doona's car. "That was something of an ordeal," she said to her friend. "Let's hope my party tomorrow is less stressful and more fun."

CHAPTER ELEVEN

Bessie slept slightly better on the third night in her new flat. She woke up once, around three, certain that someone was walking around outside her door. By the time she'd thrown on her robe and slippers, however, the noises she'd been hearing had stopped. She was reluctant to open her door at that hour of the night, but she stood behind it, listening for several minutes. When she heard nothing further, she took herself back to bed.

Awake again at six, she showered, dressed and ate a bowl of cereal with milk. The cup of tea she used to wash it down helped her feel more like herself. She headed out for her morning walk. The mirror that was still hanging outside of her door caught her frown. This morning her welcome mat was upside down. Bessie flipped it over and shook her head. While it was a harmless enough prank, it unsettled her. The "out of order" sign on the lift didn't improve her mood.

Bessie stomped over to the stairs, yanking open the fire door. The stairs were poorly lit, but Bessie didn't have a choice. She headed down them. At the bottom, she pulled on the fire door. It didn't budge. She frowned and tried it a second time, but it was no use. The door seemed to be locked. Surely that couldn't be right, she thought to herself. What if there was a fire? She made her way back up the stairs to the first floor and pulled on the door she'd just come through. It too seemed to be locked. Bessie sighed deeply and then turned and went back down. Ignoring the ground floor door, she headed down even further, into the building's lower, subterranean level.

She pulled on the fire door at the bottom of the last flight of stairs and was relieved when it opened easily. The room where she found herself wasn't large and it was only very dimly lit. Bessie walked carefully through it, heading towards what she hoped was a way out. There were several suitcases and boxes in piles all around the space and Bessie wondered who all of the things belonged to. If it had been better lit and less creepy in the space, she might have investigated further. As it was, she rushed through the room and then found herself in a short corridor. At one end of the corridor, she spotted a few steps that led up to a door that had to lead to the outside.

She felt a rush of relief as she pushed it open and found herself looking at the building's car park. As she let the door shut behind her, she heard an angry shout.

"Hey, what were you doing down there?" the voice yelled.

Bessie turned around and squared her shoulders as Nigel Green stormed towards her.

"I said, what were you doing in the basement?" he said, stepping right up to her and glaring down at her.

"I was trying to find a way out," Bessie replied, working hard to keep her voice level. "The lift is out of order and the fire doors are all locked. What was I meant to do?"

"There's nothing wrong with the lift," he snarled at her.

"Well, there's an 'out of order' sign on it," Bessie countered.

"And the fire doors aren't ever locked," he continued as if she hadn't spoken. "It's against the law to lock them."

"They were locked when I tried them," Bessie replied. "From the inside, anyway. I suggest you go and check the lift and the doors and stop shouting at me."

He opened his mouth, probably to argue, but then snapped it shut. "Thank you for alerting me to the problems," he said tightly. "I'll get right on fixing them." He spun on his heel and took a few steps away from her before turning back.

"There are some things of mine in the basement that

shouldn't be there," he said, giving Bessie a sheepish grin. "I'd appreciate it if you didn't mention that to Mr. Robertson or Mr. Quayle. It's just that my mother had so much stuff when she moved in with me, I didn't have anywhere else to put it. I'm working on getting rid of it all, but it's difficult."

Bessie shrugged. "It really isn't my concern," she said. "I'm far more interested in getting my morning walk in."

"Sorry," he said, flushing. "Off you go. I'll make sure everything's sorted out here before you get back."

The walk down to the beach only took a few minutes and Bessie strolled happily across the sand, enjoying the early morning sunshine and putting Nigel Green firmly out of her mind. The forecast she'd heard on the morning radio had suggested rain later, but it certainly didn't feel like it at the moment. After so many years walking on Laxey beach, the change of scenery had Bessie walking far further than she usually did. Almost without realising it, Bessie found herself standing in front of the Summerland complex.

For several minutes she stood and stared at the large building that now housed a roller-skating rink, a children's play area and a ballroom, among other things. She sighed deeply, remembering the original building that had stood there in the early nineteen-seventies. She'd only been inside that building a handful of times, but it had made an unforgettable impression on her.

The new building, although large, was smaller than the original that had housed a dance floor, restaurants and bars. The original centre had only been open for a few years before it was destroyed by fire. Bessie thought of the fifty people who had died in that fire, one of the island's most devastating tragedies. There was nothing about the replacement building that hinted at its tragic history. Bessie couldn't help but feel that some sort of memorial was appropriate. Perhaps she'd have a word with George Quayle; it seemed the sort of project he'd get behind.

With a sigh, she turned and headed back towards Seaside Terrace. It was a beautiful summer day and she didn't want to dwell on the past too much. At her age, it was only natural that she'd experienced a great deal of sorrow, she supposed, but the time in Douglas was meant to help her forget about recent events. Thinking about a long ago catastrophe wasn't going to help her feel better.

When she got back to the apartment building, Nigel Green greeted her with a huge, fake-looking smile. "Ah, Ms. Cubbon, I was starting to get worried about you," he said brightly. "Either that was some long walk or you stopped to enjoy the sunshine for a while."

"I walked down to Summerland," Bessie replied. "It was too nice a day to come back here straight away."

"It is a lovely day," Nigel agreed. "Anyway, I've checked and rechecked the lift and it's absolutely fine. I've no idea how the sign got on it, but there's nothing wrong with the lift."

"That's good to know," Bessie said. "And the fire doors?"

"Ah, I've checked them as well and I've made sure they're unlocked. I'm not sure how they came to be locked, but I can assure you it's been taken care of."

"Good," Bessie replied. "Did you ever find out anything about the man who was found in flat five?" she asked.

Nigel shook his head. "I gather the police think he was just some vagrant. He's long gone now, and I've been talking to Mr. Robertson about putting in some extra security. We can't have our residents being bothered by such things, can we?"

"I should think Mr. Robertson, with all his money, could do a good deal to help the island's homeless population. Then extra security here wouldn't be needed," Bessie suggested.

"Oh, yes, rather, well, I'm sure he's considering many things," Nigel replied.

"I'd better go and start getting things ready for this afternoon. I'm so looking forward to meeting your mother," Bessie said.

Nigel's smile faltered. "Yes, well, I'm not sure she'll be able to make it," he said. "She had a bad night. She might need a nap this afternoon."

"Well, I expect to be in all afternoon, so you're both more than welcome any time from two until six. I'm sure she can't nap for that many hours"

Nigel lips twitched into something like a smile. "That's kind of you," he said. "I hope we'll make it."

Bessie couldn't push things any further, she decided. Instead, she turned and headed towards the post boxes. She'd noticed the postman coming out of the building as she'd gone in and she'd realised that she hadn't actually checked her new postbox since she'd moved in. She carefully put her key into the lock on her box and turned it slowly. She pulled the door open and looked in surprise at the large pile of post.

A quick flip through it all showed her that nearly everything in the box was addressed to "Mrs. Hilary Montgomery." Bessie frowned. She'd never heard of the woman. She sorted out the two envelopes that were actually addressed to her and then put the rest back in the postbox. Perhaps the postman would take them back and redirect them if she left them in there.

Nigel was on the telephone when Bessie walked back past him, so she didn't have to speak to him again. The lift did seem to be in perfect working order when she took it to the first floor. Outside her flat, the mirror was still in place and the welcome mat was exactly how she'd left it before her walk. She let herself into her flat and immediately got to work.

By the time she was ready for lunch, Bessie had much of the food prepared for the party. She nibbled on a few of the snacks, reasoning that she needed to make sure everything tasted good and that there was no point in going to all the fuss of making herself a proper lunch. She made a small sandwich from the rolls and sliced meats she'd purchased and ate that while she arranged the "bar."

She'd bought several bottles of wine to go with the bottle of gin that Bertie had requested. Her refrigerator was fully stocked with a variety of cold drinks and mixers, as well as a few bottles of beer in case anyone fancied it.

After she'd cleared away the crumbs from her slapdash lunch, Bessie sat down with a book and tried to relax. Only a few minutes later, someone knocked on her door.

"Ah, Bessie, help," Mary said as a greeting when Bessie opened the door.

"What do you need?" Bessie asked.

"I need someone to eat and drink a whole lot," Mary said with a laugh. "We've been left with ever so much after last night. I've brought piles of food and drink with me for you to use for your party. I hope you don't mind."

Bessie took a deep breath. She did mind, actually. She'd spent the entire morning and a great deal of money getting everything just the way she wanted it. The last thing she wanted or needed was a bunch of leftovers from the grand barbeque the night before.

Mary must have caught the look on her face. "Oh, goodness, I'm sorry," she said now, her face bright red. "I didn't mean, that is, I'm sure you've put a lot of time and effort into getting things ready for the party. It's just that I don't know what to do with all this food." She gestured to several large boxes that were piled on the floor next to her.

"What have you brought?" Bessie asked, with a deep sigh.

"Just snacks and things," Mary said. She bent down and picked up one of the boxes. Bessie grabbed another and they carried them into Bessie's kitchen. Pulling open the one she'd carried, Bessie was confronted by huge tubs of various summer salads. Mary opened a box and Bessie looked at trays of sliced meat and cheeses and sighed.

"There are only going to be a handful of people here," she told Mary. "Even if I didn't already have food, there's far too much here."

"Maybe they'll all be happy to take some of it home with them?" Mary suggested. "I'm really sorry, Bessie. The caterers left all of this in the kitchen and our chef was screaming about it all morning. She hates mess in her kitchen, so I told her to box it all up and I'd take it with me. I suppose we can just throw it all away."

Bessie shook her head. "Don't be silly," she said. "That would be a terrible waste. We'll put some of it out for the party and then donate whatever's left at the end of the afternoon to one of the organisations that feed the poor. I know the woman who runs one in Laxey. I'm sure she'll be able to tell me who to ring here in Douglas."

"What a great idea," Mary exclaimed. "Why didn't I think of that?"

"I suspect you've rather too much on your mind at the moment," Bessie told her.

"We can't donate away the drinks, though," Mary said. "I've brought wine and beer and gin and scotch and vodka, and probably a bunch of other things as well that I can't even remember."

Bessie helped her carry in the smaller but heavier boxes that contained the various drinks.

"I'm sorry that I brought all of this," Mary said with a sad smile. "But I didn't really want it in the house."

Bessie looked at her sharply. "Why not?" she asked gently.

"George has been drinking a bit more than normal," she replied. "I thought it was best to eliminate some of the temptation."

Bessie nodded and stifled a sigh. It looked as if she now had a fully stocked bar. Well, her new neighbours would probably be impressed. Or think she was a drunkard.

Mary helped Bessie unpack all of the food. She just about managed to find space for everything in her small kitchen and dining room area. The boxes of cakes and pies which Mary had forgotten to mention, she carried into her bedroom and piled on the floor near the door.

"Do remind me these are here," she told Mary. "I'll start putting them out as people eat their way though the food."

"I'll try to remember," Mary said. "But if you forget to put out the chocolate cake, well, I'll happily volunteer to help you eat that tomorrow."

Bessie laughed. She couldn't stay angry at Mary, who was genuinely trying to be helpful. Besides, the food all looked delicious and it wouldn't hurt to be very generous with her new neighbours and her old friends.

With Mary's help, Bessie rearranged the bar area, until Bessie thought it looked like something that ought to be in a restaurant. There were bottles of things she was sure she'd never heard of before.

"I don't even know what half of these are," she told Mary.

Mary shrugged. "The theme was Texas barbeque, so the caterers brought in an expert on American cocktails. I haven't any recipes, though, just bottles and bottles of drink."

Bessie laughed. "I guess people will just have to mix up their own concoctions," she said.

"That's a thought," Mary said, studying the array of bottles.

"Oh, do help yourself," Bessie said. "Or just open a bottle of wine. Whatever sounds good."

Mary gave Bessie a wicked smile. "It's rather early to be drinking," she said. "But a glass of wine would be about perfect right now."

"We've worked awfully hard, setting everything up," Bessie said. "And it is a party, after all, or it will be soon."

"One of my staff brought me over and carried all of the boxes up for me," Mary told Bessie. "I didn't have the nerve to knock on your door until it was all up here, though. I was afraid, if my driver was still here, you'd send it all back with him."

Bessie gave her friend a hug. "Please don't ever feel uneasy about anything with me," she said. "We figured it all out. That's what friends do."

Mary selected a bottle from the table and found Bessie's corkscrew. Bessie pulled down wine glasses from her cupboard. "I suppose I should put glasses out," she said.

"Oh, I brought glasses," Mary exclaimed. She dug through the one box that Bessie hadn't opened. It was full of napkins, paper plates and plastic cups and glasses in every imaginable size. Mary pulled out a stack of wine glasses from the box.

"The very finest in plastic wine goblets," she said in a solemn tone before giggling.

"Those will be perfect for the guests," Bessie told her. "But until they get here, let's pretend we're grown-ups and use the real things."

Mary laughed and took the glass Bessie offered her. "Don't tell me you sometimes feel like you're just playing at being an adult," she said.

"Pretty much all the time," Bessie admitted. "Whenever I

chop anything with a sharp knife, I keep expecting someone to take it off of me."

Mary shook her head. "I thought I was the only person past fifty who felt that way," she told Bessie. "I'm still somewhat surprised that my children trust me to babysit my grandchildren. I never felt like I was grown-up enough to look after them."

Bessie laughed. "And I always thought I felt like a kid at heart because I never had children of my own."

A knock on the door startled both women. "I thought the party didn't start until two?" Mary said as Bessie headed towards the door.

"It doesn't," Bessie replied. "We should have another half hour or so to ourselves."

Doona grinned at Bessie when she pulled the door open. "I hope I'm not too early," she said. "I was bored."

Bessie laughed and pulled her inside. "Of course you aren't too early," she told her best friend. "Mary and I were just getting a little head start on the fun."

Doona greeted Mary warmly. The two women didn't know each other well, but as the wine flowed, they quickly became better acquainted. By the time two o'clock rolled around, the three were having a wonderful time and the first bottle of wine was empty.

CHAPTER TWELVE

Just minutes before two, Doona and Mary got busy in the kitchen, getting things that needed heating ready to go into the oven, while Bessie paced back and forth, waiting for someone to knock on her door.

"Where is everyone?" she asked her friends at five minutes past two.

"Be patient," Doona told her. "We're here, at least."

"And I'm ever so grateful for that. But we have enough food for an army," Bessie complained.

"And Hugh's away," Doona said with a sigh.

"More's the pity," Bessie replied. A moment later, a knock came and Bessie scurried to answer it.

"Ah, Bessie, I do hope I'm not first," Bertie said as he gave her a hug.

"Oh, no, a few friends came early to help," Bessie told him. She was sure he looked momentarily disappointed, but she didn't have time to worry about that. As she offered him a drink, someone else knocked.

Doona quickly offered to oversee the bar so that Bessie could handle the door.

Bessie pulled open the door and smiled at the woman on the other side of it. Muriel Kerry was just a bit too large to be what Bessie would consider "pleasantly plump." Her white hair was again piled into a messy knot that Bessie could only assume had started the day near the top of her head, but it had now slid both down and sideways so that it seemed to stick out from somewhere behind her left ear. Her glasses were huge, with black frames, and they seemed to dominate her face. She was dressed all in black, in a sleeveless shirt and long trousers.

"Hello, again," she said now, her Scottish accent unmistakable.

"Mrs. Kerry, I'm so glad you've come," Bessie replied.

"Ah, you must call me Muriel," the woman said.

"Of course, and I'm Bessie. Do come in," Bessie invited. "Bertie is already here."

"Aye, he would be," Muriel replied.

Bessie wasn't sure exactly what that meant, but before she could ask, she heard a door open in the corridor. A moment later Bahey and Howard were on their way towards Bessie.

Muriel wandered into Bessie's flat, while Bessie waited for her friends.

"You look lovely," she told Bahey, who'd obviously gone to some effort for the party. Bahey rarely wore makeup or fussed with her appearance, but today she'd not only put on lipstick, but she was wearing a pretty summer dress and a pair of low-heeled shoes.

"As do you," Howard told Bessie, after he'd kissed her cheek. He was looking rather dapper in a pair of dressy trousers with a shirt and tie. Bessie ushered them into the flat and left them in Doona's capable hands. Doona would make sure everyone was introduced to everyone else, Bessie was sure of that. Most of the neighbours ought to know one another, anyway.

Mary was bustling around arranging and rearranging the food, which kept her from having to talk to people. Bessie felt sorry for her shy friend, but before she could speak to her, someone else knocked.

Marjorie Stevens, Bessie's good friend from the Manx Museum Library, smiled back at Bessie when she opened the door.

"I can't believe you've actually moved into Douglas," she told

Bessie, giving her a huge hug.

"Neither can I," Bessie murmured.

Liz Martin, whom Bessie had met in one of Marjorie's Manx language classes, had come with her.

"Welcome to the neighbourhood," she told Bessie. "I'm only a few blocks away, so if you ever need anything, give me a ring. I'm home with the kids and I always welcome a few minutes of adult conversation."

Bessie laughed. "Thank you," she told the young woman. She escorted her friends into the flat. She'd just begun introductions when someone else knocked.

"Ah, yes, well, good afternoon," the woman at the door said stiffly when Bessie opened it.

Bessie hid a smile as she recognised the woman she'd seen through the crack that the safety chain allowed at flat nine. Bessie reckoned that Ruth Ansel was so thin that she'd seen just about all of the woman through the tiny crack. She was dressed in a summer suit that was spotless and immaculately ironed. As Bessie escorted her into the flat, she wondered if the suit would have the nerve to wrinkle if Ruth were to decide to sit down.

A few moments later, Simon O'Malley arrived, escorting Tammara Flynn. Bessie smiled at them both as she let them in.

"You're looking smashing," Simon told Bessie. "That colour is perfect for you."

"Oh, thank you," Bessie replied.

"So many women seem to be afraid of colour," Simon said softly. "But life's too short to wear black all the time."

Bessie's eyes inadvertently slid to Muriel, who was standing next to Bertie and seemingly hanging on his every word.

Simon sighed deeply. "I could help her," he whispered to Bessie. "But she doesn't want my assistance."

"Never you mind," Tammara said, slipping her arm around Simon. "You stick to helping me."

Simon laughed. "But you're already perfect," he told the woman.

"Ah, flattery will get you everywhere," she said, giving him a wink.

Bessie headed back to the door, expecting another knock, but all was quiet at the moment. By the time she'd walked the very short distance back, Doona had already supplied everyone with drinks and Mary was pulling the last of the food from the refrigerator.

"Who needs fancy caterers?" Bessie whispered to Doona as her friend handed her another glass of wine.

"I don't know," Doona said. "But I think I'd quite like someone to turn up in a few hours to clear everything away."

Bessie couldn't help but agree with that as she glanced around her little flat. It was already beginning to look a mess and the party had just started.

"Please make sure to eat a lot," Bessie told everyone. "There's far more food than we can get through."

Bessie let everyone mingle for a moment, while she sipped her wine. Then she wandered over to where Simon and Tammara were fixing themselves plates of food.

"Do you still have that mirror outside your flat?" Bessie asked after a few innocent pleasantries.

"Mirror?" Simon looked confused. "I'm not sure what you mean."

"When I stopped by the other day, there was a mirror hanging outside your flat," Bessie replied. "I'm only asking because it looked the same as the one that's now hanging outside my flat, but I don't know where that one came from or why it's there."

Tammara laughed. "That mirror!" she exclaimed. "The management keeps moving it around the building. I think they must have some sort of strange plan for where it goes, but I can't quite figure it out."

Simon shrugged. "I can't say as I really noticed it," he told Bessie. "But maybe it wasn't at my flat for long. I know Tammara mentioned something about it in the past, though."

"It was across the hall from my door for ages," Tammara told Bessie. "And just when I started getting used to it, it disappeared."

"Strange," Bessie murmured.

"It's the building manager who's strange," Tammara told her in a confiding tone.

"Why?" Bessie asked.

"He flirts with all of the women in the building, for one thing," Simon interjected. "They're all rather older than he is, but that doesn't seem to stop him. He was even dating Linda, the woman who used to own this flat. I can't imagine what she saw in him."

"Me, either," Tammara said. "He's creepy and odd."

"He does seem rather odd," Bessie agreed.

"He's actually a very nice man," Muriel said firmly as she began to fill her plate. "We've had dinner together once or twice, not that we're dating or anything, just as friends." She glanced over at Bertie to see if he'd heard her, but he was chatting animatedly with Doona.

"He didn't happen to explain why there's always noises in the middle of the night from flat five, did he?" Tammara asked.

Muriel shook her head. "We didn't talk about the building. We talked about ourselves. He's had a rough time of it, with his mother."

"She's not well," Simon told Bessie. "Sometimes she sits in the foyer with Nigel, watching the people go in and out, but mostly she's confined to his flat. She can't get around without a wheelchair and she's usually quite mentally unfocussed as well."

"It's very hard for him," Muriel said.

"Are you talking about poor Nigel?" Ruth asked. "I did suggest that he try modifying his mother's diet, but he doesn't like to risk upsetting her."

"He told me she has a terrible temper," Muriel said. "I've never seen any evidence of it, but that's what he said."

"He's so dedicated to her," Ruth said with a sigh. "The poor man never gets to have any fun."

"He so enjoyed dinner with me, the last time we went out," Muriel said. "And then, at the end of the evening, he'd forgotten his wallet. He was so embarrassed, but I didn't mind treating."

Ruth frowned. "He forgot his wallet when we had lunch together one day, as well," she said thoughtfully.

"You must be talking about Nigel," Bertie said, joining the conversation. "Linda said he forgot his wallet at least once a week when they were dating."

"How very careless of him," Bessie said quietly.

"As I said, I don't mind treating for a meal now and then," Muriel said, her tone defensive. "He has a difficult life, does Nigel, and I'm sure money is quite tight for him."

"He tried that trick on me as well," Tammara said with a laugh. "We'd only gone for a cuppa, but I wasn't falling for it. I waited in the restaurant while he went and got some money. Funnily enough, he hasn't asked me to have a drink with him again."

"He's never asked me," Simon said with a wicked grin. "I guess I should be grateful."

Bessie chuckled. "I don't think he'll be asking me, but if he does, I think I'll politely decline."

Another knock on the door interrupted the conversation. Bessie hurried to open it.

"Hello, you must be Bessie," the woman at the door said. She was sturdily built with a kind and friendly face. Her grey hair was cut in a short bob. The frames of her glasses were turquoise and matched her jumper almost exactly.

"I am, indeed," Bessie answered.

"I'm Mabel Carson, and I'm just on my way to watch my grandson at taekwondo, so I can't stay. I wanted to pop around and meet you, though, and welcome you to the building."

"That's very kind of you," Bessie replied.

"I wish I could stay and chat, although it sounds as if you have quite the party going on," Mabel said, waving a hand towards Bessie's flat. "Tell everyone I said 'hello,' will you? I'll try to catch you another time, but I'm rather very busy, really."

She turned and disappeared back down the corridor before Bessie could reply. Well, I guess I'm not going to learn anything from her, Bessie thought to herself as she shut the door behind Mabel.

"Who was that?" Marjorie asked when Bessie returned to the party.

"That was Mabel Carson. She lives in number two and is, apparently, incredibly busy."

"Oh, she is," Simon confirmed. "She's in and out all day, every day. She has a couple of children here and some across as well and about a hundred grandchildren that she minds on a moment's notice. Her kids take advantage of her, of course, but she seems to thrive on it."

"That's why I moved across the Irish Sea," Ruth said with a brittle laugh. "My children seemed to think I loved nothing more than minding their children while they went out and acted like they didn't have any responsibilities themselves. I love my grandchildren, but I wasn't about to rearrange my entire life so that I could watch them at the drop of a hat."

"Ah, Bessie, this has been lovely," Simon said, putting his arm around her. "But Tammara and I have to rush off, I'm afraid. We'd already made plans for this evening, before we knew about your little gathering. It's been wonderful to meet you and I hope you enjoy living in our little building."

"Thank you so much for coming," Bessie replied. "I hope we can get to know each other better, over time."

Tammara gave Bessie an awkward hug as she walked the pair to the door. Bessie pulled it open, startling a woman who was standing on the other side.

"Oh, my goodness," she gasped, looking from Bessie to the others and then back at Bessie.

"Hello, Annabelle," Simon said brightly. "Bessie, this is Annabelle Hopkins. She lives in number three."

He grabbed Tammara's hand and the pair quickly disappeared into the lift, leaving Bessie with the last of the neighbours whom she hadn't met before.

"It's very nice to meet you," she said politely.

"Yes, well, that was very rude of young Simon," Annabelle said sniffily. "Fancy rushing off like that."

"Apparently he and Tammara had plans for the evening," Bessie explained.

"At least that's what they told you," Annabelle said. She looked down her nose at Bessie, no easy feat as she was only an inch or two taller than Bessie's five foot three.

Bessie forced herself to smile, an effort aided by the quantity of wine that she'd already drunk. "I've no reason to doubt them," she said with a shrug. "But do come in and have a drink and something to eat," she invited.

"Oh, yes, well, I can't stay long," the woman answered. She strode into the flat, leaving Bessie to follow behind her. Bessie shut the door slowly. The newest arrival was almost as thin as Ruth Ansel, and looked even more miserable. Bessie wondered if she too had come to the island to escape from the demands of her adult children.

Back in the flat, Annabelle was shaking her head firmly at Doona. After a moment, Doona looked up at Bessie and shrugged. Bessie reluctantly joined the pair.

"Ms. Hopkins prefers a different brand of gin for her gin and tonics," Doona said in carefully measured tones.

"Ah, that is unfortunate," Bessie said, suppressing a deep sigh. "Perhaps you'd like something else, then?"

Annabelle shook her head. "I'll just have plain water, please. I assume you have something bottled."

Bessie forced herself to smile. Thanks to Mary, she had a ridiculous selection of different bottled waters for the disagreeable woman to choose from.

"What sort do you prefer?" she asked. There was no way she was going to list all of the options, only to have the woman claim the only one she drank wasn't on the list.

Annabelle pressed her lips together for a moment and then named an obscure and very expensive brand, giving Bessie a triumphant smile.

"Actually, we do have that," Bessie replied, turning her head so that the disagreeable woman wouldn't see the smile that rose to her own lips. Bessie dug around in the refrigerator until she found the right bottle.

"Would you prefer a glass tumbler, rather than plastic?" Bessie asked. She herself preferred water in a glass container.

"Yes, thank you," Annabelle replied, looking somewhat defeated.

Bessie got down a tumbler and then poured half of the contents of the bottle into it. "I'll just leave this in the refrigerator for when you want more," she told Annabelle.

"Thank you," the other woman murmured, taking a sip.

Bessie ignored the face the woman made, taking a moment to refill her own wine glass. She took a large sip, feeling as if she'd earned it.

"There's plenty of food," Doona suggested to Annabelle.

"Oh, no, thank you," the woman replied. "I never eat food I haven't prepared myself."

"Do you have allergies?" Doona asked.

"No," was the woman's reply.

Bessie bit back a dozen replies before Bertie interrupted.

"Ah, Bessie, my dear, I'm having such a good time," he said, fixing himself another gin and tonic. "You're going to be an interesting addition to this building, I can tell."

"Bessie, I'm sorry to interrupt, but we have to be going," Marjorie told her. "Liz's husband has just rung and there's some small crisis at their house."

Bessie gave each woman a hug. "I hope everything's okay," she said anxiously to Liz.

"We're potty training," Liz replied, rolling her eyes. "Dear hubby hasn't quite figured it all out yet. I'm sure there's just been another accident on the couch or something, but he's in a panic, so home I go."

Bessie showed the pair out, sorry to see them leave. Now Doona and Mary were the only people at the party from outside the building. Bessie didn't want her new neighbours to think she was lacking in friends. It was a shame that John Rockwell and Hugh were both away, she thought as she rejoined the group. She'd invited a handful of other friends as well, but it seemed like nearly everyone she knew was on holiday off the island at the moment.

She wandered back into the party. "When I went to my postbox earlier, I had some letters addressed to Hilary Montgomery," she said to no one in particular. "Does anyone know who that is?"

"Hilary?" Bertie asked. "She had this flat before Linda, but she passed on well over a year ago. Why on earth would she still be getting post here?"

"Advertisements keep coming forever," Annabelle said. "I still get catalogues addressed to the woman who used to have my flat and I've lived there for two years now."

"These weren't catalogues, though," Bessie said. "It was proper post, letters with stamps. Some of them looked quite important."

"You should ask Nigel about them," Ruth suggested. "He and Hilary were quite close."

"I wouldn't say that," Muriel said. "They were friends, that's all."

"What happened to her?" Bessie asked, interrupting Ruth before she could reply.

"She had a heart attack, didn't she?" Ruth asked. "I'm sure that's what Nigel told me."

"I know she died suddenly," Muriel said. "But I can't remember what happened exactly."

"It was pneumonia," Bertie said. "She was fine one day and then she started coughing and two days later she was gone."

"I don't remember her coughing," Ruth said, shaking her head. "I think you're confusing her with that woman who lived in number five for a few weeks. She was always coughing every time I saw her."

"Oh, her," Annabelle said with a frown. "She was terribly ill, I think. I tried to speak to her once about the amount of noise she was making in the corridor, and she was very rude to me."

"Who needs another drink?" Doona asked loudly. Several people rushed towards her with their nearly empty glasses, leaving Bessie alone with Annabelle Hopkins.

"Do you know anything about the mirror that seems to move around the building?" Bessie asked her.

Annabelle shrugged. "I don't know what you're talking about."

Bessie thought about explaining, but decided against it. "My welcome mat keeps flipping over," she said instead. "Any idea who might be wandering around at night playing little pranks on us?"

"Perhaps you're imagining things," Annabelle replied tightly. "I can't imagine that any of us have the time or energy to play pranks on one another."

Bessie didn't argue; it didn't seem worth it. Bertie wandered over to join them, a very full drink in his hand. It didn't stay full for long, though. He took a large swallow and then nodded at Annabelle.

"It's nice to see you again," he said. "You've been rather busy lately, haven't you?"

"I'm always busy," Annabelle replied. "I prefer to keep busy and active. Idle hands, you know."

"Yes, well, there is something to be said for enjoying one's retirement," Bertie suggested.

"I didn't particularly want to retire," Annabelle said. "I thoroughly enjoyed working and I'd go back tomorrow if there was a position open that suited me."

Bertie laughed. "Not me," he said firmly. "Oh, I didn't mind working, when I had to do it. But the day they said I could retire, I was happy to get out."

"I'm curious," Bessie said, as the conversation seemed to stop. "How long has flat five been empty?"

"I'm not sure it is empty," Annabelle told Bessie. "I know I hear noises coming from there once in a while and I'm sure I've heard the door open and close late at night. I suspect someone is using it as a little love nest for late night meetings that his wife doesn't know about."

Bessie immediately thought of George Quayle, and then gave herself a mental shake. He couldn't possibly be cheating on Mary. She glanced around to see where Mary was, but she was busy again in the kitchen and hadn't overheard Annabelle's comment.

"But you've never seen anyone going in or out?" Bessie asked.

"No," Annabelle admitted. "But that doesn't change the fact that someone is."

"Of course not," Bessie replied.

"Ah, is that the time?" Ruth said loudly. "I really must be going." She headed for the door, leaving Bessie to rush after her to thank her for coming.

"Oh, it was a lovely party," Ruth replied. "Next time I'll make sure I bring something with me that I can eat."

"Couldn't you find anything?" Bessie asked.

"Oh, there were a few things I might have tried," Ruth said. "But I simply wasn't sure. I've so many allergies and intolerances, it's simply easier to not eat."

"You should have given me a list of things you can eat," Bessie said. "Then I could have made sure I had something for you. I'll do that next time."

"Oh, I'd hate to have you fuss over me," Ruth replied, before striding off down the corridor.

No, it's easier to wait until it's too late and then complain, Bessie thought to herself as she returned to the party. It seemed as if things were suddenly winding down.

"Why don't we walk down to the café on the corner and have a cuppa?" Muriel was asking Bertie.

"After all that gin and tonic?" Bertie replied. "No, I think I'm overdue for a nap."

Muriel frowned at him, but he ignored her, turning to thank Bessie instead.

"Great party, great gin," he said. "Make sure you invite me to the next one."

"I certainly will," Bessie promised. It was an easy promise to make, as she had no intention of having another party, at least not in this flat.

Muriel followed Bertie to the door. "I guess I should be going as well," she said. "Thank you for a lovely time."

"You're very welcome," Bessie replied.

As Bessie shut the door behind them, she could hear Muriel trying again to persuade Bertie to spend some time with her. She sighed and returned to the flat.

"That was a deep sigh," Doona said.

"Muriel's trying so hard to get Bertie to do something with her and he just wants to have a nap," Bessie explained.

"I don't understand women," Bahey said. "Chasing after men like they can't live without them."

Howard chuckled. "I certainly know better than that," he said, slipping his arm around Bahey. "You've made it very clear you can live without me. That's part of why I worked so hard to persuade you to let me into your life."

Bahey flushed. "This dating thing is stupid, anyway," she said defensively. "I don't think I'll ever get the hang of it."

"I hope you don't," Howard told her. "I'm hoping you'll just stick with me."

"That's my plan at the moment," Bahey replied, briefly resting her head on Howard's shoulder. "But I'm not making any promises."

Bessie laughed.

"Anyway, as nice as this has been, we have to get going," Bahey told Bessie. "Howard has to ring his daughter and then we have dinner plans."

"Thank you for coming," Bessie said. "We need to get together soon to talk about things." Mary's presence in the kitchen meant that Bessie didn't want to discuss Bahey's concerns at the moment.

"Maybe you could stop over tomorrow morning," Bahey suggested. "Come after your walk, at nine, maybe, and have breakfast with me."

"I'd like that," Bessie agreed. That should give her plenty of time to think about everything that she'd heard at the party.

After they left, Doona and Bessie helped Mary pack up nearly all of the food that remained. Bessie rang a friend who worked for one of the island's charities for the homeless. He was delighted to learn that Mary would be dropping off several large boxes of food.

Mary called her driver and he carried all of the boxes down to her car. Then Mary gave Bessie a huge hug. "Thank you for helping me get rid of everything," she told Bessie. "We must have lunch next week. I'll ring you."

Mary was gone before Bessie could do much more than mutter a reply. Back in her flat, Bessie and Doona stood and looked at the table that held the drinks.

"What are you going to do with all of this?" Doona asked.

"I have no idea," Bessie said with a laugh. "They don't encourage drinking at the homeless shelters, but it will take me a dozen years to drink all of this."

"Maybe you should have another party."

Bessie shook her head. "I think I need some time to recover from this one first," she replied.

"Well, as it's Saturday, and I don't have to work tomorrow, I suppose I could help you get through a bottle or two tonight, as long as I can sleep it off on your couch."

"I don't know how comfortable the couch is for sleeping," Bessie replied. "But I'd love it if you'd like to stay. This place doesn't really feel like home, at least not yet."

Doona sat down on the couch and then lay down across it. "It's pretty darn comfortable," she said as she sat up. "I don't think I'll have any trouble sleeping, especially after a few drinks."

The knock on the door startled Bessie. She pulled it open and tried her hide her surprise as she greeted the man on the doorstep.

"Mr. Green, how kind of you to stop by," she said.

"I was gonna try to get up here earlier," he said. "But I got busy with stuff. Anyway, if the party isn't over, I brought mum up as well." He nodded towards the lift, and Bessie could see the wheelchair inside it.

"Oh, good heavens, bring her in," Bessie exclaimed. "Most people have left, but there's still plenty of food and lots of drink."

Nigel looked as if he was going to say something, but after a moment he turned and walked over to the lift. He pulled the wheelchair from the lift and turned it around, pushing it towards Bessie's door.

"Hello, Mrs. Green," Bessie said when they'd reached her. "It's very nice to meet you."

The woman in the chair blinked and gave Bessie a blank look. She was covered in blankets, leaving only her head visible, but Bessie got the impression of a very small and frail woman. She had long grey hair that was matted and tangled as if it hadn't been brushed or washed in many months. Her eyes were seemingly unfocussed as they gazed towards Bessie.

Bessie ushered the pair into her flat. She quickly introduced Doona to the new arrivals. "There's a lot of food left; just give me a minute and I'll put some out," she told Nigel.

"Oh, I'm fine," he told her. "I just wanted to stop by and make sure that you felt welcome in your new home, that's all. I can't stay long. Mum will need her nap."

Bessie smiled. "Well, at least have a drink," she suggested. She gestured towards the "bar" and watched Nigel's face.

"Wow, that's some selection," he said with an excited look on his face. "I suppose I could have one drink."

Doona joined him at the table and the two began to discuss the choices. Bessie took advantage of the opportunity to try to talk with Margaret Green.

"Mrs. Green, it's very nice to meet you," she began again.

The other woman tipped her head and looked at Bessie. After a moment, she grunted.

Figuring that was all the encouragement she was going to get, Bessie continued. "I understand you moved to the island from across. I do hope you're enjoying life here."

After a moment, the other woman nodded slowly.

"I understand you sometimes sit in the foyer; perhaps you'd like me to take you for a walk one day," Bessie suggested.

"Oh, mum can't walk," Nigel called, walking over to join them. He had a tall drink in his hand, but Bessie couldn't guess what was in it.

"I thought I could push her chair," Bessie told him.

"Oh, well, I don't know," the man replied, doubt in his voice. "Mum likes to stay close to me, don't you, mum?"

The woman in the chair definitely shook her head, which made Bessie smile. "Everyone likes a change of scenery once in a while," she told Nigel. "We should plan something soon."

"Yes, well, we'll see," he replied cautiously.

"I was going to ask you about Hilary Montgomery," Bessie said.

"What about her?" Nigel asked, looking nervous.

"There was some post for her in my postbox," Bessie explained. "I didn't know what to do with it."

"Oh, that sort of thing happens all the time," Nigel said. He took a long sip of his drink. "Just leave it in the box or give it to me and I'll talk to the postman the next time I see him."

Bessie nodded. "Did you say that number five is empty?" she

asked. "One of the guests said she sometimes heard noises coming from there."

Nigel frowned. "People should mind their own business more," he said grumpily. "The flat belongs to someone. What they choose to do with it is their business."

Bessie shrugged. "I guess people are just curious," she replied.

"Curiosity killed the cat," Nigel replied.

The woman in the chair made a noise that had everyone looking at her.

"What's that, mum?" Nigel asked.

She made another noise, but Bessie couldn't make words out of the sounds.

"I think mum is tired," Nigel said. While the woman shook her head, Nigel finished his drink quickly. "I'd better get her home."

Bessie walked to the door with them. "Thank you for making the effort to come by," she told Nigel. "It was nice meeting you," she said to his mother.

The woman made a sound and then her eyes met Bessie's. For a moment, the cloudiness in them seemed to disappear and Bessie was startled when the woman winked at her. Nigel pushed her out the door before Bessie could speak. She watched him push the chair towards the lift before he dashed back.

"I was wondering if you'd like to have a drink later," he said to Bessie. "I try to get to know all of our residents personally, you understand. Maybe after dinner? I could come up when mum's asleep and we could go down to the pub?"

Bessie shook her head. "I can't tonight," she said. "I'm having dinner and drinks with my friend. Maybe another time." She held her breath, hoping he wouldn't try to pin her down to anything. She didn't want to be rude, but she had no intention of going anywhere with the man.

The lift pinged and slid open. Nigel glanced at it and then back at Bessie. "Soon," he said. "I'd like to do it soon." He dashed back and pushed him mum into the waiting lift.

Bessie shut her door and headed back into her flat.

"Did I hear him asking you out?" Doona asked.

"You did," Bessie replied.

"I already told him we had plans for tonight," Doona said. "He asked me out as well."

"I suspect he had very different motives for asking you than for asking me," Bessie said.

"I don't know," Doona replied, shaking her head. "He seems like he's just desperate for female company."

"Other than his mother," Bessie added.

The pair feasted on leftover party food and shared a bottle of wine, enjoying one another's company. As she snuggled into her bed for the night, Bessie sighed. If she stayed in Douglas for long, she was really going to miss Doona.

CHAPTER THIRTEEN

The next morning, Doona was already awake when Bessie woke at six. They shared a pot of coffee before Doona headed for home while Bessie went out for her walk. Having been as far as Summerland the previous day, today she went in the opposite direction. Again, the change of scenery kept her walking longer than she might have otherwise, and she soon found herself at the Sea Terminal.

She looked out to sea for a while, watching the early morning ferry. Ferry staff were loading it up, ready for its departure. It didn't seem that many years ago that the terminal building had been built, but when Bessie did the math, she realised the building was over thirty years old. She frowned and turned to head back towards her flat, smiling when she spotted the Tower of Refuge in the harbour.

The tower had been built on a partially submerged rock as a safe location for people to shelter within if they hit the rock during a storm and couldn't get safely to shore. As it had been constructed in the eighteen-thirties, Bessie felt young by comparison. Back at her flat, she combed a few wind-blown tangles from her short hair and then headed to Bahey's flat next door.

"Ah, Bessie, come in and have some coffee," Bahey suggested as she showed Bessie into the flat.

"I've had rather a lot of coffee already today," Bessie replied. "If tea is too much bother, I'll just have a glass of water, please."

"Oh, tea's no bother," Bahey replied. "I'll even join you and leave the coffee for Howard."

"I think I need it today," Howard commented as he topped up his mug from the pot on Bahey's counter. "I didn't have a good night."

"Too much fussing over that daughter of yours," Bahey muttered under her breath. Bessie heard it clearly, but Howard either didn't or pretended he didn't.

"So, what's new with the investigation?" Bahey asked as they all sat down with their drinks.

"From what I learned yesterday, it does seem as if there are several odd things going on," Bessie told her friend. "And there is definitely someone using flat five, even if they aren't actually living there."

"So why does Nigel keep telling me it's empty?" Bahey demanded.

"He told me that someone is using it and that I should mind my own business," Bessie replied. "Someone else suggested that it's being used as a love nest."

"I suppose that's possible," Bahey said. "But what about all the other strange little things? And what about the post? And what about the mystery man?"

"As for the mystery man, I think that's going to have to remain a mystery. But I'm going to send myself a bunch of letters this week and see how long they take to get to me," Bessie told her. "And I'm going to start leaving notes on your door to see if you get them. The mirror is still in place outside my door and my welcome mat hasn't moved for a few days, so perhaps whoever was playing games has grown bored and stopped."

"I hope so," Bahey replied. "I haven't noticed anything odd in the last few days, either, now that you mention it."

Bessie smiled. "Maybe I can move back to Laxey sooner rather than later."

"I'd hate to see you go," Bahey replied. "Are you missing your home a lot?"

Bessie thought about her reply for a moment. "Yes and no," she said eventually. "I miss my privacy and my beach, but I'm quite enjoying the change in scenery. All of the little things going on here seem harmless enough, so it's sort of fun to play detective as well."

The trio finished their drinks while speculating on who might be using the ground floor flat.

"Maybe Nigel is using it for late-night meetings with some woman who's too embarrassed to be seen in public with him," Bahey suggested.

"I'll bet it's some Member of the House of Keys," Howard said. "Politicians all seem like the type to cheat on their wives."

Bessie shook her head. "Actually, most of the MHKs I've known over the years have been wonderful," she told the man. Of course, I don't actually know any of the current group."

"Maybe that Grant Robertson who owns the building is the real owner," Bahey said. "Although he isn't married, so I'm not sure why he'd need to sneak around in a tiny flat down here. He has a huge house in Onchan that overlooks the sea, anyway."

Bessie thought again about George Quayle, but she bit her tongue. She wasn't going to speculate about his private life. She could only hope, for Mary's sake, that it wasn't him using the flat.

With nothing else planned for the day, Bessie walked into town to do some more shopping. Not all the shops had Sunday hours, but there were enough stores open to allow her to get everything she was after. She returned home with a few new books and a box of expensive chocolates as a special treat.

There was a note stuck to her door when she got back. She pulled the light green envelope off and carried it into her flat with her.

Just a little thank you for the lovely party yesterday. Muriel

Bessie smiled as she tucked the slip of green paper into the front of one of her new books. It would work quite nicely as a bookmark. She was always using random things such as torn theatre tickets or unwanted business cards in the many books she read. They were just as effective as the things marketed as "bookmarks" and they were generally to hand.

She fixed herself a light lunch and then curled up with one of the books. The sound of a door slamming disturbed her a few minutes later. Someone knocked on her door. Bessie sighed and set her book down.

"Ah, Bertie, how nice to see you again," she said politely when she'd opened her door.

"I was just heading down for some Sunday lunch at the pub and I wondered if you'd like to join me," he said, giving Bessie a bright smile. "As a thank you, like, for yesterday."

"I just had lunch," Bessie told him with an apologetic smile. "Maybe another time."

"Next Sunday?" Bertie asked. "I'll collect you about this time, if that works for you."

Bessie felt a bit stuck. "Sure, that sounds great," she said reluctantly.

"Good, okay then." Bertie glanced down the corridor. "I suppose I should ask Muriel or Ruth to join me today," he said, sighing. "I hate eating alone."

Bessie gave him a sympathetic smile. "I've grown quite used to it over the years," she told the man. "I always take a book."

"I don't read much," Bertie said. He took a few steps down the hall and knocked lightly on Muriel's door.

Bessie stood and watched, curious as to what was going to happen next.

"Ah, Bertie, how are you?" Muriel asked. Bessie could see that the other woman looked slightly flustered, but delighted to see the man on her doorstep.

"I was just going down to the pub for lunch and I fancied a bit of company," Bertie replied. "Just friendly, like."

"Oh, I'd love that," Muriel gushed. "I was just wondering what to do for lunch." She disappeared back into the flat, presumably to get ready.

"Don't forget your money," Bertie called after her.

Bessie pressed her lips together so that she wouldn't laugh out loud as she turned and went back into her flat.

After that little bit of excitement, the rest of Bessie's Sunday was uneventful. Soup was her evening meal, and then she spent some time trying to come up with some sort of plan for the next week. She needed to see if Bahey was right about the post, she wanted to leave notes on Bahey's door to see if they disappeared, and she hoped to spend more time with Margaret Green. Bessie had a feeling that Nigel's mother knew everything that was going on in the building, but she had to find a way to communicate with the woman.

Up at her normal time, after breakfast on Monday morning, Bessie took a long walk. She dropped letters addressed to herself in three different post boxes along the promenade. Back at home, she stuck a note on Bahey's door and then let herself into her own flat. A moment later she walked back out, uncertain of what was different, but sure that something was.

There was a welcome mat in front of Bertie's door, Bessie realised. And it looked exactly like Bessie's own. Her own mat was still there; she would have noticed its absence immediately, but the new one had only barely registered in the back of her mind. She shrugged. There was no law against Bertie buying the same mat.

Now that she was living in Douglas, Bessie decided it was time to take advantage of all that the town had to offer. Accordingly, she spent the day at the Manx Museum, first taking a slow stroll around the exhibits she'd seen hundreds of times before and then tackling some research that she'd been meaning to do for weeks.

She'd never had a set routine for working in the museum library, instead coming and going as she pleased, but now that she was within easy walking distance of the place, she felt like maybe she should make some sort of formal arrangement.

"I think I'll try to come in on Mondays, Wednesdays and Fridays while I'm staying in Douglas," she told Marjorie, when her friend stopped at the table where she was working.

"It would be great to have you here that often," Marjorie replied. "We just received another box of papers from one of the parish churches and I haven't even opened it. I would love it if you could catalogue it for me."

Bessie beamed. That was exactly the sort of work she loved

best. Who knew what treasures might be hidden away in the piles of papers? "I can start now," she suggested to Marjorie.

"How about after lunch?" Marjorie countered. The pair had a quick lunch together in the small museum café, where Marjorie insisted that Bessie practice her Manx.

"Kys t'ou?" Marjorie asked.

"Oh, um, ta mee braew," Bessie replied awkwardly. "And I don't remember any food words, so please don't ask."

Marjorie shook her head. "You've taken my beginner's class what, three times? You should be able to have a simple conversation by now."

Bessie sighed. "I'm sorry," she said with genuine feeling. "I wish I could, but somehow, no matter how hard I try, none of it seems to stay in my brain."

Marjorie patted her hand. "You need to practice more," she suggested. "If you're going to be at the museum three times a week for a while, I'll try to stop by and chat with you whenever you're here."

Bessie forced herself to smile and thank her friend. Marjorie meant well and truly loved the difficult Celtic language. The least Bessie could do was try a little harder.

After lunch Bessie dug into the newly arrived box with enthusiasm. Each paper had to be read through and categorised and then listed on an index. Bessie only managed to get through a small portion of the box before it was time for the library to close for the day.

"I'm afraid I didn't get very far," she said apologetically to Marjorie as she passed the box back to her.

"I'd rather you took your time and did it correctly," Marjorie replied.

"I know, but so far I haven't found anything interesting, either," Bessie said. "I was hoping for a really detailed will or an eighteenth-century household inventory, but it's all been sheets from the parish register and letters from the bishop so far."

"I have a researcher who is always excited about new sheets from the parish registers," Marjorie said. "She's working on the demographic history of the island. I'll have to ring her and let her know about this box once you've finished with it."

"I'll be back on Wednesday," Bessie promised. "Or maybe even tomorrow if I'm bored."

Marjorie smiled. "Your move to Douglas could be very good news for the museum."

Bessie stopped at her postbox and found it empty. After exchanging quick greetings with Nigel, she headed up to her flat. There she found another note taped to her door.

Got your note. Hope you get this one.

Bessie chuckled. She recognised Bahey's handwriting, so it didn't matter that it was unsigned.

On Tuesday morning Bessie stuck another note on her friend's door before heading into town again to do a bit more shopping. Again, she posted several letters to herself in different postboxes. After a quick lunch at one of her favourite Douglas cafés, she found herself at a taxi rank with a burning desire to head for home.

The trip to Laxey seemed to take forever and Bessie found herself wishing she could drive, as the man behind the wheel of the taxi seemed to be in no particular hurry to get anywhere.

Bessie's cottage felt abandoned and unloved to her after she'd let herself in. She frowned as she walked from room to room, unable to stop herself from touching nearly every piece of furniture as if she hadn't seen them in years. After several minutes she gave herself a mental shake and took herself out for a walk on the beach she knew so well. By the time she got home, having had to dodge a dozen flying discs and what seemed like hundreds of small children, she felt ready to head back to Douglas. The sheer size of Douglas beach meant it never felt as crowded as Laxey beach did today.

She rang her regular service and her favourite driver picked her up only a few minutes later.

"I guess you won't be needing me on Friday," Dave said as he drove her back to Seaside Terrace.

"No, I did tell them to cancel my regularly scheduled pickup," Bessie told him.

"How's Douglas treating you?"

"It's okay," Bessie said thoughtfully. "There are things I like and things I don't. I suppose everywhere is like that."

Dave laughed. "I think you're right," he agreed.

Back at her building, Bessie checked her postbox. It was still empty.

"What time does the post come?" she checked with Nigel on her way to the lift.

"Oh, he came about an hour ago," the man replied. "But he comes at different times every day. You can never be sure."

"I was expecting something today, you see," Bessie told him.

"Post can take an extra day here," Nigel said. "Something about sorting out for the individual postboxes or something. It will probably arrive tomorrow."

"I don't suppose you could check the other boxes, just in case my friend put the wrong flat number on the letter?" she asked.

"I wish I could," Nigel told her. "Only the postman has the key to get into the back room to deliver the post, though. That's for everyone's security."

"I didn't realise that," Bessie said. "Interesting."

She headed up to her flat, wondering if she'd have another note from Bahey. She did.

Got today's note (Tuesday). We're going for dinner at six if you want to join us.

Bessie looked at her watch. It was half six, so she'd missed them. It was just as well; she still had some leftover party food that she should eat. Her phone rang at around eight o'clock. Bessie had brought her answering machine with her from her cottage this afternoon, but she answered the call anyway.

"Ah, Bessie, I just wanted to let you know that I received your lovely note today," Mary Quayle said. "We were so happy to have you, you didn't need to thank us."

"I won't argue about that," Bessie replied. "But I'm glad the note got there so quickly. I just posted it yesterday."

They chatted for a moment about the two parties before Mary said, "Are you free for tea one afternoon this week?"

"How about Friday?" Bessie suggested. "I'm going to be working at the museum on a project, but I'll definitely need breaks.

We could do tea or lunch, whichever suits you."

"Oh, let's do lunch," Mary said with a laugh. "Shall I meet you in the museum café at midday?"

"That sounds perfect," Bessie agreed before finishing the call.

While she had the phone in her hand, she made a quick call to Doona, as she'd promised.

"Just checking in," she told her friend.

"No news from there?" Doona asked.

"Nothing, what's happening in Laxey?"

Doona sighed deeply. "John's extended his holiday by another week," she told Bessie. "We get to keep Inspector Kelly until the end of the month."

"Oh, I am sorry," Bessie told her.

"Not half as sorry as I am," was Doona's reply before she rang off.

Bessie was certainly sleeping better in her new flat, but she still wasn't used to the sounds of doors opening and closing in the night. On Wednesday morning she headed out for her walk and stopped. The mirror was gone and her welcome mat had been turned around again. Apparently the prankster was back. She fixed her mat and walked quickly up and down the corridor. The mirror was nowhere to be seen.

She enjoyed her walk along the promenade, but her mind was racing. She thought about a spy novel she'd read recently. What she really needed was the sort of equipment the man in the book had had at his disposal. A tiny hidden camera that could record everything that happened in the corridor would quickly identify who was moving things around in the public spaces. Another one on the ground floor would let Bessie know who was using flat number five.

Back at home, she stuck a new note on Bahey's door, telling her about the mirror and the mat. On her way out to the museum, she took a detour down the ground floor corridor, but the mirror wasn't anywhere visible there, either.

Once she reached the museum, she put Seaside Terrace out of her mind and focussed on her job of indexing the box Marjorie had given her. Even though she only took a very short break for lunch, she wasn't even halfway through the box at the end of the day.

"I'll be back on Friday," she told Marjorie when she returned the box to her.

"I'll be getting spoiled," Marjorie replied.

Back at the building, Bessie checked her postbox. A flyer from the nearby Chinese restaurant addressed to "Occupant" was all she'd received. Bahey had left another note on her door.

"I haven't seen the mirror. My mat hasn't moved since it came back."

Bessie let herself into her flat and fixed herself some dinner. She poured herself a glass of wine and nibbled her way through a couple of the chocolates from her box. It suddenly occurred to her that she hadn't actually baked anything in her new flat. Back in Laxey, she baked regularly and almost always had homemade goodies available.

As such treats were primarily for the young visitors that used Bessie's cottage as a hideaway from parents who didn't seem to understand them, Bessie supposed she didn't need to worry about baking here. While she was an honourary auntie to most of the school-aged children of Laxey, she was more or less unknown to the children of Douglas.

That didn't mean that she didn't feel like a homemade treat, though. She dug through her cupboards, looking to see what ingredients she had available. There wasn't much, but she found what she needed for flapjack. Not much over an hour later, she settled into her chair with a book, a cup of tea, and a freshly baked flapjack.

It had begun to rain, a heavy soaking rain that had Bessie feeling grateful for her snug little flat. While it might not feel totally like home, she felt comfortable and settled. An hour later, she'd finished the book and was ready for bed. For the first time since she'd moved in, she didn't wake up in the night.

Thursday morning she walked to the nearest grocery store and did her weekly shop. Having filled her trolley, she took a taxi back to her flat. Perhaps she'd try the building's service one of these days, but there was something about food shopping that felt almost too personal to trust to a stranger. Once everything was put away, she decided to take a short stroll on the beach. Again, she posted letters to herself, and others, from several different boxes.

As she walked past one of the fish and chips shops along the promenade, Bessie impulsively bought herself some lunch. She sat on a bench, watching the families that were spread across the beach. Small children were building sandcastles and burying one another in the sand. Mothers were fussing and trying to feed their offspring, while fathers seemed to be mostly napping.

For a moment Bessie wondered how different her life might have been if she'd married and had children of her own. A small screaming boy with a dirty face quickly distracted her from her reverie. She laughed at herself as she got back up and headed towards her flat. She passed the postman as he was leaving.

When she opened her box, she was surprised to find letters inside. She tucked them into her bag and headed up to her flat. When she went through her post, she shook her head. All of the letters she'd received were the ones she'd posted on Wednesday. She still hadn't received the ones she'd posted on Monday or Tuesday.

Doona rang a short time later. "Just wanted to let you know that I got the note from you," Doona said. "It says Wednesday at the top."

"Thanks," Bessie replied. "You should get another one tomorrow, I think."

"I'll let you know," Doona promised.

They agreed to do something together on Saturday, but left making the final arrangements until later. After a light tea and some reading, Bessie headed to bed with the building's prankster on her mind. She dreamt of welcome mats that turned themselves around and around, the word welcome reflected back at her in a dozen mirrors. When six o'clock rolled around she still felt groggy and out of sorts.

A cup of tea did wonders for her disquieted nerves and she got ready for her walk with her usual enthusiasm. Outside her flat, nothing seemed to have changed from the day before. The day was already warm, but overcast, and Bessie wondered if they were due rain again. She felt as if it had been a rather wet summer, but since she enjoyed being outdoors so much, she nearly always noticed the rain more than the sun.

Back at her flat, she fixed herself some more tea and then packed up her notebooks and pencils, ready for another day at the museum. A knock on her door interrupted her.

"Bahey, what's wrong?" Bessie asked when she'd opened the door to her friend. Bahey was wearing a robe that appeared to have been pulled hastily over her pyjamas. Her hair hadn't been combed, and she gave Bessie a desperate look.

"It's Howard," she said. "He's missing."

CHAPTER FOURTEEN

"What do you mean 'missing'?" Bessie asked as she pulled her friend into her flat.

"He doesn't answer his door," Bahey replied, wringing her hands together.

"Maybe he's asleep or busy," Bessie suggested.

Bahey flushed. "I have a key," she told Bessie. "Just for emergencies, like. Anyway, I let myself in and he's not there."

"And he didn't tell you he was going anywhere?"

"No, I know he's been worried about his daughter, but he isn't meant to be visiting her until October."

"Maybe he changed his mind and headed across early?"

Bahey shrugged. "He would have left me a note," she said. "I don't want to ring his daughter to ask, because she'll get upset if he isn't there. She's in the middle of a very difficult pregnancy, you see, and she isn't meant to be upset."

"Did you try his mobile?"

"He doesn't have one," Bahey told her. "He isn't keen on modern gadgets like that."

"Is his car in the car park?"

Bahey nodded. "I went out and looked before I came here. But he wouldn't have taken it if he was going to the airport or the ferry terminal."

She sat down on Bessie's couch. "I don't know what to do,"

she said softly. "He's never disappeared before."

"Maybe you should ring the police?" Bessie suggested.

"Oh, no, I can't do that," Bahey replied. "He'd be ever so embarrassed if there's a simple explanation. He's a grown man besides, the police will likely say he can do as he chooses."

Bessie was inclined to agree with her friend. There were many possible explanations for Howard's disappearance and most of them were benign. "Were you suppose to get together this morning?" she asked.

"We didn't have formal plans," Bahey answered. "But I usually knock on his door when I get up and we have breakfast together."

"Maybe he woke up early and went for a walk or to do some shopping," Bessie suggested. "Did he take anything with him, like a suitcase or anything?"

Bahey shrugged. "I'm not about to start poking around in his bedroom to check," she said. "At least not yet."

Bessie nodded. That made sense as well. She couldn't imagine how awkward it would be for Bahey if she were going through his wardrobe and he walked in on her.

"Don't the police make you wait twenty-four hours before they'll investigate a missing person, anyway?" Bahey asked. "I guess that's what we should do. If he hasn't turned up or rung by tomorrow morning, I'll go to the police."

"Actually, I don't think you do have to wait," Bessie said. "But I'm sure the first thing the police would do is ring Howard's daughter. It might be better to wait until tomorrow for that, in case he is just at the shops or something."

"Yeah, okay," Bahey said. "I guess I'll go grab a shower and get dressed. I'm supposed to do my volunteer hours at Noble's today, but I'm not sure I want to leave my flat. What if Howard rings?"

"He knows your schedule, doesn't he? I'm sure, if he got called away suddenly, he'll ring later tonight," Bessie said reassuringly. "It's up to you, but I think you should go and do your volunteer work. There's no point in sitting around worrying, and they need you at Noble's."

"They do at that," Bahey agreed. "I help out in the maternity ward, cuddling babies so mums can rest. It's the best job I've ever had."

Bessie smiled. She'd never been overly fond of small babies, but as volunteer work went, it sounded quite nice.

"I'm off to the museum for the day," she told Bahey. "I'll be there if you need me. Otherwise, I'll come over when I get back this afternoon."

"Okay," Bahey said. She left, seemingly reluctantly, leaving Bessie to puzzle over Howard's unexplained absence.

If only he had a mobile phone, Bessie thought to herself, and then laughed. She'd lived very happily for nearly her entire life without a mobile, and now, after having had one for six months or so, she was annoyed with others for not keeping up with the newest conveniences.

Bessie took herself off to the museum, only slightly worried about Howard and Bahey. There she settled in with her box, working steadily until it was time to meet Mary for lunch.

Mary was already seated in the small café, perusing the menu when Bessie arrived.

"I'm sorry I'm late," Bessie said as she joined her.

"You aren't," Mary assured her. "I'm usually early, and today I was restless at home, so I was very early."

Bessie quickly looked over her menu and made her selection. As she ate at the café fairly regularly, it took only a moment for her to choose. The waiter knew her well and was very attentive. Bessie had her tea before she'd even had time to reply to Mary.

"I hope everything's okay," she said, letting her concern show in her tone.

"It's fine," Mary said with a sigh. "I'm just, well, things are just tense, that's all. George is working more and more hours and I'm simply not sure why."

"Have you asked him?"

Mary laughed flatly, "No, I haven't," she replied. "We don't seem to talk anymore. I'm starting to regret ever moving here."

Bessie patted her friend's hand. "I'm glad you're here," she said. "But I am sorry about George."

Mary shrugged. "One of these days I'm going to have words with Mr. Robertson about the hours George keeps."

"That sounds like a plan."

"I'm just a little bit afraid of Grant, that's all," Mary confessed. "He seems to have some sort of hold over George, and I find him quite intimidating."

"Oh, dear," Bessie exclaimed. "I didn't much like him when I met him. I can see where you might find him intimidating."

"Never mind," Mary said. "Let's talk about something pleasant."

Bessie filled the lunch with all of the most interesting details from the box she was indexing. While she hadn't found anything terribly exciting, she'd found a few documents that would add bits of knowledge to the island's fascinating history. By the time their sweets arrived, Mary was looking more relaxed.

"How are things in the new flat?" she asked Bessie as she dug into her sticky toffee pudding.

"They're fine, I suppose," Bessie replied. "Do you remember Howard? He's been dating Bahey."

"The very polite and handsome man who arrived with your friend? Yes, I remember him."

"Well, he seems to have disappeared, although I'm sure there's a logical explanation."

Mary frowned. "When did this happen?" she asked.

"I gather, from what Bahey said, that he was perfectly normal last night but gone this morning," Bessie replied.

"George got a phone call around midnight or even later last night," Mary told her. "I only heard his side of it, but I heard him mention 'Seaside Terrace' and something about 'sorting out that problem once and for all.' I don't know what it all meant, but it makes me worried for your friend."

Bessie sipped her tea, grateful that she'd finished her profiteroles before Mary had spoken. She felt as if she'd suddenly lost her appetite.

"It might be nothing," Mary said. "George went out for a short while after the call, but he was back this morning. He didn't seem upset or worried, well, not any more than normal."

Bessie patted her friend's hand. "I'm sure whatever George was dealing with had nothing to do with Howard, but I might just have a word with a friend, just in case."

"A friend like Inspector Rockwell," Mary guessed.

"Except he's not on the island at the moment," Bessie said. "I'll have to settle for the next best thing."

After lunch, Bessie reluctantly returned her box of documents to Marjorie and headed out of the museum. The nearest police station was only a short walk away. Once there, she asked for Inspector Corkill.

"He works out of the main station," the girl behind the counter explained. "Would you like to go to him or should I ask him to come to you?"

"As I don't have a car, I'd rather he came to me, if it isn't too much bother for him," Bessie replied.

"I'll ring him and ask."

It seemed only a few minutes later, just as Bessie was getting absorbed in the paperback she had tucked in her handbag, that the inspector appeared.

"Miss Cubbon, this is a pleasant surprise," he greeted Bessie, his ever-present frown in place in spite of his words.

"I just want a quick and informal word with you, if I may," Bessie replied.

The inspector showed her into a small room that was marked "Conference 1" on the door. An old and badly scratched wooden table sat in the middle of the room with five or six folding chairs arranged around it.

"Sorry, this is about as luxurious as we get around here," the inspector said, waving Bessie into a chair.

"It's fine," Bessie replied. "I hope I won't be here long."

"So what's on your mind?" the man asked after he'd settled himself across the table from her.

"Something strange has happened at Seaside Terrace. It may well be nothing, but I wanted to mention it to you in light of all of the other odd incidents."

Corkill frowned more deeply. "Go ahead."

"You remember meeting Howard Mayer, who lives in number

twelve?" she asked.

He nodded.

"Well, he seems to have disappeared."

"How long has he been missing?"

"I think I told you that he's been dating my friend Bahey? She went to his flat this morning for breakfast and he wasn't there."

Corkill glanced at his watch. "So about four or five hours?" he asked.

Bessie shrugged. "About that," she agreed. "But it's out of character for him."

"Have you tried ringing his mobile?"

"He doesn't have one," Bessie said with a sigh.

"Do you want to file a formal missing persons report?"

"No," Bessie said, shaking her head. "It's possible he was just out somewhere or even that he's gone across to see his daughter suddenly. Bahey doesn't want to ring her and worry her in case he isn't there."

"I can ring and have someone from the local force take a look, but I'd rather do that with an official report behind the request."

"Bahey wants to wait until tomorrow to do that," Bessie explained. "She doesn't want to embarrass Howard if there's nothing wrong."

Corkill shrugged. "I'm not sure what you want me to do, then," he said.

Bessie sighed. "I don't really want you to do anything," she said, frustration evident in her tone. "I had lunch with Mary Quayle, and she said George had a weird phone call in the night and she thought it was something to do with Seaside Terrace. I guess I'm just a little bit worried, that's all, and I wanted to talk to someone official, just in case."

To Bessie's surprise, the inspector leaned over and patted her arm. "I understand your concerns," he said. "And after everything that's happened lately, I suspect there might be something going on at Seaside Terrace that could concern the police, but I don't think your friend's disappearance is part of that. I suspect he had a late-night call from his daughter and rushed off to see her without giving Bahey a thought, or something like that.

I'll stop by your flat tomorrow afternoon, and if he's still missing, we can talk more."

"Thank you," Bessie said, feeling foolish for having bothered the man. "As you say, it's probably nothing."

On her walk home, though, she kept replaying his words about there being something happening at Seaside Terrace that might concern the police. Was he talking about the missing man or something else?

Bessie checked her postbox when she got back to her flat and was surprised to find all of the letters from Monday and Tuesday had finally arrived. She shook her head. She hadn't posted anything today, and now, with Howard's disappearance, she wasn't sure she cared very much about the delayed post.

She knocked on Bahey's door before she stopped at her own flat. One look at her friend's face told her what she wanted to know.

"You haven't heard from him," Bessie said flatly.

"No," Bahey replied sadly. "I went and did my volunteer hours, but it was hard. Now I guess I'll just sit here and worry."

"Maybe we should ring his daughter," Bessie said. "We just need to make up some excuse for doing so."

Bahey let Bessie in, and the pair sat down and discussed their options.

"Maybe you could ring and say you're trying to come up with ideas for presents for his birthday," Bessie suggested.

"The thing is," Bahey said slowly. "Carla and I don't really get along very well. That is, we haven't actually met or anything, but she doesn't like the idea of her father dating. I've only spoken to her twice, and both times she was openly hostile to me."

Bessie frowned. That rather complicated things. They tossed around a few other ideas, but nothing seemed appropriate. After a while, Bessie fixed them both some dinner, but neither woman had much appetite. Bessie finally headed for home at nine.

"Ring me or come over if you hear anything," she instructed her friend.

"I will," Bahey promised.

Bessie let herself into her flat, where her answering machine light was flashing.

"Bessie, it's Doona. I'm going to have to cancel for tomorrow. The regular weekend receptionist has one of those awful summer colds and just can't seem to get rid of it. I told her I'd take her shift tomorrow so she can sleep. Sorry."

There were a handful of other messages, including two from Alan Collins, asking if she'd made up her mind on the flat yet. Bessie deleted them all. It was too late to return Doona's call, so Bessie got ready for bed and curled up with one of her new books. Within minutes, she felt as if she couldn't keep her eyes open and gave up on reading.

At exactly six o'clock the next morning she woke up feeling rested and refreshed. As soon as her mind cleared, she immediately felt guilty. Poor Howard was missing and Bahey was a wreck; the least she should have done was sleep poorly.

After a shower and breakfast, Bessie headed out into a light rain for a short walk. The promenade was deserted and Bessie stuck to its paved surface, rather than struggle her way through the wet sand. That was one advantage to living in Douglas, she had to admit. There wasn't any pavement along the beach in Laxey.

Bahey was already dressed when Bessie knocked on her door just after eight.

"I don't know what to do," she said as a greeting. "I don't want to ring the police, but I'm worried about Howard."

"I saw Inspector Corkill yesterday," Bessie told her. "I told him about Howard, unofficially. He's going to stop by today to talk to us."

Bahey nodded. "Maybe Howard will ring before the inspector gets here," she said, hopefully.

"Do you want to come over and wait in my flat?" Bessie suggested. "That's where the inspector is planning to meet with us."

"Sure," Bahey shrugged. "Howard can leave a message on my machine if he rings," she said, sounding miserable. She followed Bessie to her flat and Bessie opened the door. The sound of another door opening caused them both to stop.

"Ah, good morning, ladies," Bertie beamed at them.

"Good morning," Bessie said.

"Bahey, you don't look very happy," Bertie said, putting an arm around her. "I do hope you aren't this sad just because Howard's gone away."

"How do you know Howard's gone away?" Bessie demanded.

"I saw him getting into a taxi with a suitcase," Bertie replied. "Why? Is it meant to be a big secret or something?"

Bessie shook her head. "Sorry, no, we just didn't know that everyone knew, that's all."

Bertie looked from one woman to the other and then shrugged. "Anyway, if you're lonely, I'd be happy to take you to dinner tonight," he suggested to Bahey. "I know we both like that little Italian restaurant on the corner."

Bahey shook her head. "Thanks, but I'm busy," she said, almost mechanically. She stomped into Bessie's flat, leaving Bessie to wind up the conversation with Bertie and then follow her.

"It sounds like Howard went willingly," she said to Bahey once she'd joined her.

"Yeah, without bothering to tell me," Bahey said miserably.

"Maybe it was an emergency," Bessie replied. "Why don't you wait and see what he says when he gets back?"

Bahey shrugged. "I don't know."

Bessie tried to start several conversations with her friend, but Bahey clearly didn't want to talk. After a while, Bessie handed Bahey a book and then curled up with the one she'd started the previous evening. When she began to feel drowsy again, she decided it was the book rather than her body that was at fault and switched to an old favourite instead.

By midday Bahey seemed in better spirits.

"I don't usually read much," she told Bessie. "But this is pretty good."

Bessie smiled at her. "Rex Stout is one of my favourite authors," she replied. "He wrote a great many books about Nero Wolfe. I can lend you dozens more."

Bessie fixed a light lunch for them both, and they were just sitting down to it when someone knocked on Bessie's door.

"Good afternoon," Inspector Corkill said formally when Bessie opened the door.

"Hello, inspector," Bessie replied. "Please come in. We were just having some lunch. Would you like something?"

"A cup of tea and a biscuit would do nicely," he told her. He sat down next to Bahey at the table while Bessie fixed his drink. She piled a dozen assorted biscuits on a plate and set that on the table when she rejoined the others.

"Have you anything to report from last night or today?" he asked Bessie after he'd finished a couple of biscuits.

"Bertie, who lives across the hall, told us that he saw Howard getting into a taxi the other night," Bessie said. "Apparently he had a suitcase with him as well."

The inspector raised an eyebrow. "That certainly suggests that he left voluntarily," he said. "It doesn't mean you can't file a report, but I question whether it's necessary."

"I don't want to file anything," Bahey said. "He's probably gone to see his daughter and just didn't bother to tell me."

"I'm sure he was just in a rush," Bessie said, soothingly.

"He hasn't rung since," Bahey pointed out.

The inspector looked at Bessie and then down at his cup. He finished his tea and grabbed a couple more biscuits as he stood up. "I guess you won't be needing me, then," he said. "I'll just go and have a little chat with the building manager before I leave."

Bessie showed him out. "I wonder what he was going to talk to Nigel about," she remarked to Bahey as she sat back down at the table.

Bahey shrugged. "Probably checking on Bertie's story," she said.

"Probably," Bessie agreed.

After lunch Bahey insisted on returning to her own flat, leaving Bessie with an empty afternoon. The museum closed at one on a Saturday, so that meant she couldn't get any further on her indexing today. After a few minutes of indecision, she headed for the nearest taxi rank.

The taxi ride into Ramsey was uneventful. Her driver was a Manx native and he filled the journey with complaints about all of the recent comeovers who were taking all the good jobs and driving up house prices. Bessie simply bit her lip and let him rant. The trip to Ramsey was far too short to change the man's mind about anything.

Bessie spent an hour in her favourite bookstore, buying a few new books and chatting with the helpful staff. She stopped at each of the charity shops in town, checking their second-hand book piles and just generally looking around. After a couple of hours, she was ready to head for home. She had a taxi take her to her cottage in Laxey, using Bahey's new interest in reading as her excuse.

An hour back in her own little home improved Bessie's mood considerably. She dug out a handful of Rex Stout novels for Bahey to borrow and found a few books she wanted to read as well. A short stroll on the beach reminded her of how much she loved her home and also why she was enjoying her time in Douglas. The beach was crowded with large and noisy families who seemed determined to enjoy their holiday in spite of the weather. Although a light rain was falling, children were building sandcastles and people were splashing in the sea. Bessie dried off in her cottage and then rang her usual service for a ride back to Douglas.

The driver was one she barely knew. They chatted about the weather and his favourite football team until they arrived at Seaside Terrace. Bessie checked her postbox on her way in, but it was empty.

"How are you, my dear?" Nigel asked as she walked past.

"I'm fine," Bessie replied shortly. She was in no way his 'dear.'

"I thought maybe you'd like to get a drink tonight," he said, smiling at her. "Maybe around seven?"

"Thank you, but no," Bessie said firmly.

"Oh, but why not?" Nigel demanded.

"I'm not much of a drinker," Bessie replied. "And I rarely go out on an evening." And I find you rather repellant, she added to herself.

Nigel opened his mouth to reply, but was interrupted. "Nigel?"

a voice shouted from the corridor behind the man. "Nigel? I need you."

The man rolled his eyes. "Mother's just awake from her nap," he explained to Bessie. He headed off down the hallway, leaving Bessie to wonder at how clearly she could understand the woman today.

The rest of the weekend passed slowly for Bessie. She spent much of Sunday watching the rain coming down heavily and reading the books she'd bought in Ramsey.

Monday felt like a fresh start to her and she was pleased to see the sun peeking out as she headed out of her flat for her walk. Her welcome mat hadn't moved and there was no sign of the mirror, which made her feel even better. She waited patiently for the lift, contemplating which direction she felt like walking today. The soft "ping" warned her just before the doors to the lift slid open. Bessie took a step forward and almost fell over Howard, who was just emerging.

"Oh, goodness, I wasn't expecting anyone to be on the lift," Bessie said, apologetically.

Howard laughed. "I wasn't expecting anyone to be waiting for it, either," he said. "And I'm rather very tired, so I not really paying attention to what I'm doing."

"Bahey and I have been very worried about you," Bessie said. "We nearly rang the police to report you missing."

"But I left Bahey a note," Howard protested. "I stuck it on her door before I went."

"Well, she never received it," Bessie told him. "Maybe the building prankster took it."

Howard shook his head. "I didn't even think about that as a possibility," he said. "I've never really taken the whole prankster matter seriously. Bahey must be terribly upset with me."

"I think she's more worried than upset," Bessie said. "But where were you?"

Howard smiled. "My daughter went into early labour," he explained. "They thought the baby was coming and I dropped everything to be there. Turns out it was just a false alarm, and the doctor reckons she's got another month or more to go. I'm only just back for a few days, though, and then I'm going to head back across. I want to be close in case she needs me."

Bessie nodded. "I can't imagine how exciting a grandchild would be."

"It's amazing," he said. "I wish Harriet was able to share the experience with us all."

"I'm sorry," Bessie said.

"She's been gone for quite some time now," he said. "I've grown pretty used to be on my own, and, of course, now I have Bahey." He hesitated. "Do you think, that is, what do think Bahey would say if I asked her to come across with me for a while? I'd like her to get to know my daughter and I'm sure she'd be a big help with the baby once he or she gets here."

"There's only one way to find out," Bessie said. "Ask her and see what she says."

Howard nodded and looked at his shoes. "I really care about Bahey. She's nothing like Harriet, but that's part of why I like her so much. I, well, I guess I'll have to ask her and see."

Bessie boarded the lift feeling relieved that Howard had turned up unharmed and happy that Bahey had found such a nice man. She walked slowly along the promenade, not really paying attention to her surroundings, her thoughts focussed instead on the strange happenings at Seaside Terrace.

CHAPTER FIFTEEN

When she got back to the building, Nigel was cleaning the glass panels in the front doors.

"Good morning, Miss Cubbon," he said cheerfully. "How are you this morning?"

"Oh, I'm fine, how are you?" Bessie replied absently, her mind still mulling over Howard's missing note.

"Just great," Nigel replied. He looked past Bessie and frowned. "Or I was, anyway," he muttered.

Bessie turned around and smiled at Inspector Corkill, who was walking towards them.

"Good morning," she said. "How are you this morning?"

"I'm fine," he said. "I'm just here to have a word with Mr. Green."

"With Nigel?" Bessie blurted out without thinking. "Oh, well, I'll just get out of your way, then." She took a couple of steps into the building and then turned back. "By the way, Howard's back," she told the inspector. "He was just visiting his daughter."

Corkill nodded. "That's good news."

Nigel looked like a rat caught in a trap as the inspector took his arm. Bessie was dying to stay and see what transpired, but she was clearly unwelcome. She headed back up to her flat and immediately rang Doona.

"I know you're going to say you can't tell me anything," she said to her friend, "but I had to ring anyway. What's Inspector Corkill doing here this morning?"

"I haven't the foggiest idea," Doona told her. "John's back this morning, but he's snowed under. I'll try to have a word with him when he takes a coffee break and see if I can find out anything from him that's not confidential."

"Thanks," Bessie said. "And tell John I'm glad he's back."

"We're all glad he's back," Doona said with a laugh.

Bessie tried to settle in with a book, but she couldn't concentrate. It could be anything, she told herself. Maybe Nigel has too many unpaid parking tickets or ran a stop sign. But that didn't bring out the CID, a little voice teased. After pacing around her flat for half an hour, Bessie decided to ring another source.

"Mary? It's Bessie. How are you today?"

"I'm fine," Mary Quayle replied. "Or mostly fine, anyway."

"What's wrong?"

"The police have been. They've been asking questions about Nigel Green, the manager at Seaside Terrace," Mary told her. "I was going to ring you later, when I knew more, but it seems like he's been doing something illegal there. George is at the office with Grant and the Chief Inspector."

"My goodness, it must be something serious if the Chief Inspector is involved," Bessie said.

"Yes, I suppose so," Mary answered. "I'll let you know when I learn more."

Bessie went back to her pacing. If she had to guess, she'd guess that this was something to do with the post. She knew it was against the law to tamper with post in any way, and she believed Nigel was doing just that. Perhaps he was taking everyone's post and then looking through it for money. Or maybe he was even opening people's post and then blackmailing them based on what he discovered in the letters.

She shook her head. It was no use letting her imagination run away with her. Forcing herself to sit down with a book, Bessie read the same two paragraphs for another hour or more. When someone knocked on her door, she was grateful for the interruption, no matter what the source.

Bahey gave Bessie a huge smile when Bessie opened the door. "I can't stay," she told Bessie when Bessie invited her in. "I have to start packing."

"Where are you off to?" Bessie asked, guessing her friend's conversation with Howard had gone well.

"I'm going across with Howard. The baby might be coming early, and when he told his daughter about how I do all that volunteer work at Noble's, helping out in maternity and even in the neonatal intensive care unit, she agreed that I might be a handy person to have around when the baby gets here."

Bessie gave her friend a hug. "I'm so happy for you," she told her. "And for Howard and his daughter."

"I feel bad leaving you here, though," Bahey said. "I mean you moved in here to help me and now I'm going across for a month or more. I'm really sorry."

"Don't be," Bessie said firmly. "I have a feeling all of the odd things that were happening here won't be happening anymore."

"What did I miss?" Bahey demanded.

"I'm not sure yet," Bessie answered. "But there's definitely something going on."

After she shut the door behind Bahey, Bessie did some more pointless pacing. I might as well just go for a walk, she decided after the twenty-third circuit of the small room. She grabbed her keys and headed for the door just as someone knocked on it.

Inspector Corkill looked startled when the door swung open before his hand had dropped.

"Inspector, this is a surprise," Bessie said. "Please come in."

The inspector glanced up and down the corridor and then followed Bessie into her flat. "I thought you were going to call me Pete," he said as he dropped into a comfortable chair.

"I keep forgetting," Bessie said, feeling as if his position in the police ought to accord him some respect, including being called by his title.

"There are a few things I'm going to tell you that you can't repeat," he said. "Although, knowing this island, they'll all be common knowledge in another hour anyway."

"Word does travel fast, doesn't it?" Bessie agreed.

"I've just arrested your building manager," the inspector told her.

"Can I ask why?" Bessie asked.

"We've had our eye on him for some time. There were a few things going on that triggered the investigation."

"Am I going to have to keep asking leading questions or are you just going to tell me everything?" Bessie asked, giving the man a smile to take any hostility from her words.

Corkill laughed. "I'll tell you the whole story, but please don't repeat it for now. I understand the Chief Constable is having a news conference at two. After that, I guess nothing will be confidential."

"Would you like a cuppa to go with your story?" Bessie offered.

The man hesitated and then nodded. "If you don't mind," he said.

Bessie made the tea and put a few biscuits on a plate as well. It was nearly time for lunch, but she was too eager to hear the story to offer to make lunch for the man.

Corkill took a sip of tea and then gave Bessie a smirk. "I suppose I've kept you in suspense long enough," he said. "The story starts some eight or nine months ago. We got a call from Linda Smith's daughter. She was concerned about Mr. Green's relationship with her mother. One of our investigators did a little bit of poking around, but Mrs. Smith passed away before he'd done much more than start. What he discovered, though, was enough to keep us digging."

He stopped and munched his way through a biscuit, leaving Bessie on the edge of her seat. The twinkle in his eyes told Bessie that he knew exactly what he doing, as well.

"To put it simply, the man was flirting with and dating the single female residents in the building in an effort to get them to buy him expensive presents and the like. We found three different women, over the last four years, who rewrote their wills in his favour as well."

Bessie sat back, angry. "What about the women's families?" she asked. "Surely they ought to have complained."

"These were elderly women, living on their own without family nearby," Corkill told her. "We're interviewing everyone now, but in one case at least, the woman's only child felt so guilty about never visiting her mum that she didn't feel she deserved anything anyway. None of them left vast fortunes, although that woman, at least, left more than the daughter realised. She's consulting a solicitor to see if she should sue."

"I hope she does," Bessie said. "That horrid man doesn't deserve the money."

"He did provide the women with companionship," Corkill said. "It's all a bit of a legal nightmare, and I'm happy to leave it to the solicitors and advocates to sort out."

"So that isn't why you arrested him?" Bessie asked.

"No, that was distasteful, but probably not illegal," Corkill replied. "What is illegal is tampering with the post and fraud."

"Nigel was tampering with the post?"

"Mostly, he was just collecting it all and taking his time going through it. From what we've managed to work out, he was going into the post room as soon as the postman left each day and collecting everything out of all the boxes. At night, he'd go through it all and then, early in the morning, he'd put back what he wasn't interested in."

"But sometimes he'd miss a day or two," Bessie said.

"Yeah, he wasn't terribly efficient at it," Corkill replied. "He'd been doing it for so long that he got sloppy."

"But what was he getting from the post?"

"Mostly he was intercepting letters for previous residents. That's where fraud comes in."

"Really?"

"When someone passed away or moved out, Nigel kept his mouth shut. Some of the residents moved here from across or even further afield and they were receiving pensions or other payments from elsewhere. If no one bothered to notify the correct authorities about the person's death, those cheques would simply keep coming. Nigel was quite happy to collect them all and keep the money."

"Hilary Montgomery," Bessie exclaimed.

"She passed away more than a year ago," Corkill said. "She didn't have any family left and named Nigel as her heir. He didn't bother to inform the company that was paying her pension about her death, so he's been collecting that money every month since."

"I knew I didn't like the man, but I never imagined that," Bessie said, shaking her head.

"He's trying to blame his mother at the moment. He said when she doesn't take her medication, she gets up to all sorts of trouble, wandering around the building. He said she's been stealing the post, although he can't explain how she managed to get all of the stolen money into his bank account."

Bessie sighed. "That poor woman. Who's going to look after her now?"

"She's been taken to Noble's for an evaluation, then we'll see what care she needs."

"But what about the missing man?" Bessie asked. "Who is he? Who beat him up and where has he gone?"

"We still don't know who he was," Corkill said. "But we've only just started questioning Nigel. At the moment, he's claiming he doesn't know who the man was or where he came from. Apparently Nigel was letting his mother use the empty flat, since the owners weren't using it. The folding bed was his."

"And one day he found the homeless man in there and beat him up?" Bessie guessed.

"Could be. To be honest, we have so many other things to charge Nigel with that we aren't all that interested in the missing man. As he isn't around to press charges, we haven't any case anyway."

Bessie nodded. "I still want to know who he is and what he was doing here," she said, thoughtfully.

"I do as well, but Nigel says he doesn't know, and Mr. Robertson and Mr. Quayle are already on record denying any knowledge of him."

"So they're going to have to find someone new to manage the building, aren't they?" Bessie asked.

"You'd have to talk to them about that," Corkill replied. "That isn't a police matter."

The pair talked through a few other aspects of the case before the inspector left to get back to work. After the inspector departed, Bessie made herself some lunch, then waited patiently until two o'clock. Once she was sure the news conference had started, she went and found Bahey.

"That horrible man," Bahey said once she'd heard the whole story. "Thank goodness I never succumbed to his questionable charms."

"You weren't his type," Bessie told her. "From what the inspector told me, he mostly went after women who were alone in the world. You have a sister right here on the island."

"So I guess that explains all of the weird things that were happening," Bahey said.

"It explains a lot of them," Bessie replied. "It seems Mr. Green wanted to keep my flat empty, either because of the fraudulent post he was getting to that address or so he could use it for something else. He was the one starting a fire in the lift every time there was a showing."

"And the moving mirror, the welcome mats, and the missing notes?" Bahey asked.

Bessie shrugged. "I think maybe there's a different explanation for those things, but I'm not sure yet."

Bahey and Howard headed off to his daughter's the next morning, leaving Bessie feeling somewhat alone in her tiny flat. She pottered around after seeing them off, reading and eating a light lunch. She was just thinking about an afternoon walk, when Mary Quayle knocked on her door.

"Do come in," she invited Mary.

"I do want to visit with you," Mary answered. "But first I'm going to have a chat with Margaret. I was wondering if you'd like to come along."

"Margaret Green? Is she back in her flat?" Bessie asked.

"She is, and I feel it's my duty to check in on her."

Bessie followed Mary down to the ground floor. Outside flat four Mary knocked and they waited for a reply.

"She's in a wheelchair," Bessie commented. "How will she even open the door?"

A moment later the door swung open and Bessie felt her jaw drop. The woman standing there was only barely recognisable as Margaret Green. Her hair had been washed and cut into a short bob. Her eyes were sharp and she looked at them suspiciously.

"What can I do for you ladies?" she asked.

"I'm Mary Quayle. My husband is part-owner of the building, and I wanted to check in on you and make sure you were okay."

"I'm fine, although I'm not sure what's happening now," the woman replied, her hostile look fading slightly. "I guess I need to find a new place to live. I suppose you'll be looking for a new building manager. No one is telling me anything, you see."

Mary nodded and then patted the woman's arm. "There's no rush for you to move," she assured her. "We'll work it all out in time. You must be very upset about your son's arrest and I'm sure that's causing you enough stress."

"Upset? More like delighted," the woman said with a derisive snort. "He kept me drugged up to my eyeballs, did my baby boy, and he spent every penny I had while I couldn't complain. Now he's gone to prison and I'm left with nothing."

"I'm sorry," Bessie interjected, "but I have to ask. Did you sometimes sneak around the building at night, moving things around and taking notes off doors?"

Margaret flushed. "When the drugs he gave me would start to wear off, I'd get restless," she said defensively. "Sometimes he'd be out, so I'd take a walk around the building, sure, why not? And if I stumbled over something on the ground, like a note, and I wasn't sure where it went, I might tuck it in my pocket, that's all."

"And the mirror and the welcome mats?" Bessie asked.

"Yeah, maybe," Margaret shrugged. "I didn't mean any harm, like. It was really the drugs doing the bad things."

Bessie wasn't going to force the issue. Clearly the woman wasn't going to accept responsibility for her actions, but at least she'd admitted to doing them. And finding out who was behind the pranks was what Bahey had wanted Bessie to move to Douglas to do. Now she could go home.

Mary assured Margaret that she wasn't going to have to leave the building any time soon and that someone would be checking in on her regularly. Margaret looked exhausted by the time the conversation finished.

"I think I'll just grab a nap," she muttered as she pushed the door to the flat shut.

"She's going to need a lot of looking after," Bessie remarked as she and Mary walked out of the building.

"I'll have someone assigned to check on her at least twice a day," Mary said with a shrug. "George and Grant can argue between themselves about who's going to pay for it. Grant is already paying for Nigel's expensive lawyer."

"Why?" Bessie asked.

Mary shrugged. "I have no idea. He said something about it being the least he could do, but I can't imagine why."

Bessie shook her head. "At least with Nigel behind bars, Margaret won't be overmedicated anymore," Bessie said. "Imagine having your own son treat you like that."

"I'd rather not," Mary said with a humourless chuckle. "I don't think my children would ever do such a thing, but I doubt Margaret was expecting it. I suppose you'll be moving back to Laxey now?"

Bessie hesitated and then nodded. "Bahey was worried about the strange things that were happening here," she explained. "I thought she was worried about nothing, so I agreed to poke around a little bit. I'm sorry I didn't tell you about it from the beginning."

"But with George being one of the owners, you had to be careful what you said," Mary suggested.

"Maybe that was part of it, but mostly I thought she was fussing over nothing," Bessie said. "But the thought of a month in Douglas really appealed. After the events after Tynwald Day, I really needed a change of scenery."

"I can understand that," Mary told her, giving her a hug.

"I am sorry about all your furniture, though. I suppose you'll have to have it all shipped back up to Jurby and I never even paid you for having it brought down here in the first place."

"Actually, I might not have it taken back right away," Mary replied thoughtfully. "I've been thinking that I need a little space to get away from things. Your little flat might be just what I need.

Perhaps I'll buy it and use it as my own little hideaway."

Bessie bit her tongue before the hundreds of questions she wanted to ask could pour out. "Let me know if you need to talk," she said instead.

"Thanks," Mary said, hugging her again. "I'll take you up on that soon."

Bessie watched as Mary climbed into her expensive car and drove away. The walk on the beach suddenly didn't appeal. She turned back around and headed into the building. Packing wouldn't take long and she could ring for a taxi if Doona was too busy to come and get her. Suddenly, she didn't want to waste another minute. Bessie was going home.

Glossary of Terms

Manx Language to English

fastyr mie	good afternoon
kys t'ou	How are you?
ta mee braew	I'm fine.

House Names – Manx to English

Thie yn Traie	Beach House
Treoghe Bwaaue	Widow's Cottage (Bessie's home)

English/Manx to American Terms

advocate	Manx title for a lawyer (solicitor)
aye	yes
bin	garbage can
biscuits	cookies
boot	trunk (of a car)
car park	parking lot
chippy	a fish and chips take-out restaurant
chips	french fries
comeover	a person who moved to the island from elsewhere
crisps	potato chips
cuddly toy	stuffed animal
cuppa	cup of tea (informal)
CV	résumé
diary	calendar or schedule
fizzy drinks	soda (pop)
flat	apartment

fortnight	two weeks
gaol	jail
holiday	vacation
homely	homey
jumper	sweater
lead	leash (for a dog)
lift	elevator
loo	restroom
midday	noon
pavement	sidewalk
pensioner	someone of the age to collect a pension (generally "retired" in the US)
petrol	gasoline
post	mail
pudding	dessert
queue	line
shopping trolley	shopping cart
skeet	gossip
starters	appetizers
telly	television
thick	stupid
till	check-out (in a grocery store, for example)
tin (of soup)	can
tip (children's game)	tag
trainers	sneakers

Other notes:

CID is the Criminal Investigation Department of the Isle of Man Constabulary (Police Force).

"Noble's" is Noble's Hospital, the main hospital on the Isle of Man. It is located in Douglas, the island's capital city.

When talking about time, the English say, for example, "half seven" to mean "seven-thirty."

In the UK, the ground level floor of a building is the "ground floor." The floor above that is the "first floor." In the US, we would call the ground floor the "first floor" and count up from there.

A charity shop is a store run by a charitable (non-profit) organisation that sells donated second-hand merchandise in order to raise funds for their particular cause. They are great places to find books, games and puzzles, as well as clothing, knick-knacks and furniture.

When island residents talk about someone being from "across," or moving "across," they mean somewhere in the United Kingdom (across the water).

The emergency number in the UK is 999, rather than 911, as used in the US.

If someone is trying to "chat someone up," they are flirting with them.

When someone is asked to "be mother," they are being asked to pour the tea (or serve the food).

Flapjack is a baked bar of rolled oats, butter, sugar and golden syrup, sometimes with raisins added in.

A Christmas cake is a cake made with dried fruits and nuts with alcohol that is often iced with marzipan. They are much nicer than what you might find in the US labeled "fruitcake."

Mince Pies are small pastries filled with "mincemeat," which is a mixture of dried fruits, suet and spices steeped in brandy or rum. Although they originally contained meat, they no longer do.

Someone who is "made redundant" is let go from his or her job. (Roughly equivalent to being "laid-off" in the US.)

As the Isle of Man is a country in its own right, it has its own laws related to employment. Anyone seeking work on the island (unless they are classed as an "Isle of Man Worker") is required to secure a work permit before taking up employment. The employer must apply for the permit and prove that there aren't any Isle of Man Workers available to fill the position.

Refrigerators on the island (and in the UK) tend to be small (what Americans would consider "dorm-sized," or slightly larger). Anything larger is considered "American-style" and, if you choose to purchase such an appliance, you shouldn't be surprised to find that it won't fit in your kitchen. (Ours lived in our utility room next to the washing machine.)

A "three-piece suite" consists of a sofa (couch) and two matching chairs.

The drinking age in the UK (and the island) is 18, but children from 16 can drink beer or wine with meals in public. When Hugh talks about Grace's younger brother not being into drinking yet, the young man is probably unusual in that. (My son is 16 and has stayed in touch with many of his friends on the island. Many of them seem to be drinking a great deal on a regular basis!)

In the UK they measure weight in pounds and stone, where one stone is equal to fourteen pounds.

Coming October 16, 2015

Aunt Bessie Goes
An Isle of Man Cozy Mystery
By Diana Xarissa

Aunt Bessie goes house hunting with her friend, John Rockwell.

CID Inspector John Rockwell asks Bessie Cubbon, a longtime resident of the village of Laxey to help him find the perfect house for him in the village. What they find in one of the bedrooms of the last house they visit isn't what either of them was expecting.

Aunt Bessie goes to look at furniture with John as well.

Again, they find the unexpected, this time in a furniture storage unit in Jurby. But are the two cases, separated by thirty years, connected?

Aunt Bessie goes to great lengths to try to figure out what's happening before anyone else goes missing or ends up dead.

Have you read all of the Aunt Bessie Cozy Mysteries?

Aunt Bessie Assumes
Aunt Bessie Believes
Aunt Bessie Considers
Aunt Bessie Decides
Aunt Bessie Enjoys
Aunt Bessie Finds
Aunt Bessie Goes (release date: October 16, 2015)

By the same author
The Isle of Man Romance Series
Island Escape
Island Inheritance
Island Heritage
Island Christmas (release date: December 1, 2015)

About the Author

Diana Xarissa lived on the Isle of Man for more than ten years before returning to the United States with her family. Now living near Buffalo, New York, she enjoys having the opportunity to write about the island that she loves so much. It truly is a special place.

Diana also writes mystery/thrillers set in the not-too-distant future under the pen name "Diana X. Dunn" and fantasy/adventure books for middle grade readers under the pen name "D.X. Dunn."

She would be delighted to know what you think of her work and can be contacted through snail mail at:
Diana Xarissa Dunn
PO Box 72
Clarence, NY 14031

Or find her on Facebook, Goodreads or on her website at www.dianaxarissa.com.

On the website, you can sign up for her monthly newsletter and be among the first to know about new releases, as well as find out about contests and giveaways and read the answers to the questions she gets asked the most.

Made in the USA
San Bernardino, CA
28 August 2016